D0481605

DONE
IN ONE

ALSO BY GRANT JERKINS

The Ninth Step

At the End of the Road

A Very Simple Crime

DONE IN ONE

GRANT JERKINS
AND JAN THOMAS

Thomas Dunne Books ⚏ New York

This is a work of fiction. All of the characters, organizations, and events portrayed in this novel are either products of the author's imagination or are used fictitiously.

THOMAS DUNNE BOOKS.
An imprint of St. Martin's Press.

Grateful acknowledgment is made for permission to reprint from the following: *Shane* excerpt used with permission of Paramount Pictures.

www.thomasdunnebooks.com
www.stmartins.com

Design by Omar Chapa

The Library of Congress Cataloging-in-Publication Data is available upon request.

ISBN 978-1-250-05486-9 (hardcover)
ISBN 978-1-4668-5784-1 (e-book)

St. Martin's Press books may be purchased for educational, business, or promotional use. For information on bulk purchases, please contact the Macmillan Corporate and Premium Sales Department at 1-800-221-7945, extension 5442, or write to specialmarkets@macmillan.com.

First Edition: January 2015

10 9 8 7 6 5 4 3 2 1

For Victor R. Daniel

and

For "Woodrow" Thomas
My half, my hope, my heart, my hero

There's no living with a killing. There's no goin' back from one. Right or wrong, it's a brand . . . a brand sticks. There's no goin' back.

— Shane

Screenplay by A. B. Guthrie Jr., additional dialogue by Jack Sher,
based on the novel by Jack Schaefer

DONE
IN ONE

White. Nothing but white. Stretching to the horizon in every direction, infinite and limitless and as full of potential as an unpainted canvas or a child's soul—pure, clean, unsoiled. But that will change.

The boy and the man, dark figures, break through the snow. It has a quarter-inch crust of ice on top, while the powder underneath yields to the energy of youth and the substance of maturity. It comes to the man's calves, just deep enough to be above the tops of his boots. The powder falls inside where it melts. But his icy sodden feet do not bother him. He is a hard man. He would think nothing of asking his wife to fetch his old flush-cut pliers from the toolbox to snip off a frostbitten toe. She has done this for him three times over the hard years of their marriage.

The snow reaches to the boy's thighs, and he finds it hard to break through the crust. But he does not walk behind the man, following a path that had been broken for him; he prefers to forge his own way, to walk beside his father, not behind him.

Because of the depth of the snow, the boy has to hold his rifle unnaturally. Sometimes he holds it high at his side, under his armpit, or slung over his shoulder, or even raised two handed above his head when he feels in peril of stumbling. It is a bolt action .22 caliber. Purchased used last spring for the boy's tenth birthday from the gunshop in town. "It's time," was what his father had said to him. It was a monumental thing. By far the most significant event of his short life. It was not the rifle itself— even though the rifle was the physical manifestation of it—that was so monumental. What was significant was that, although it was inferred, this was the only praise he had ever received from his father.

It's time.

The man had even paid extra for a small 3 X 9 scope to mount on it, and his father did not spend money on frivolities.

The boy obsessed over the rifle. He had it for three days before he ever discharged it. His bedroom was located in the oldest part of the house—the nucleus from which more modern additions grew. He spread a white towel over the wide gaps in the quarter-sawn white oak flooring laid down by his long-dead grandfather, bearers and joists visible underneath, and he took the weapon apart, amazed at how few parts it consisted of and how easy it was to put them back together. He wiped dirty black grease from the internal pieces and returned them to place with fresh light coats of 3-in-One Oil.

The stock was constructed from a solid piece of walnut, dark stained. The butt plate was of checkered black plastic and was held on by two pan screws. Stamped on the blued steel barrel were the words Revelation—Model 120 Western Auto Supply Co. CAL. .22 L.R. *His father noted that other than the brass dot front sight, it was the exact same rifle as the Marlin Model 60, but priced less and therefore a good deal. It was lovely. It was his. It was proof that his father believed in him.*

The .22 was not really appropriate for the objective of today. The .22 was for target shooting and small game hunting. It was for squirrels and rabbits and blue jays. But he had not shot any of those things. He had not killed any live thing. Not yet. Just cans and bottles and pictures torn out of a magazine. He was a good shot. Natural born. A few words of safety had been spoken, but his father had not yet instructed him in the art of shooting. The art of killing.

Still, while the cartridge chamber is empty, the brass inner magazine tube that rests flush to the barrel is full with fifteen rounds, each LR cartridge extracted from a compact red, white, and blue Mini Group CCI box, carefully fed in by the boy before they left the house. But the boy does not yet know that his father is going to instruct him to squeeze the trigger today. And the father does not yet know that he will tell his son to do so. Their minds and their intentions are as infinite and limitless as the snow. And as prone to corruption.

They come to a barbed wire fence, which because of the bright morning sun reflecting off the ice crust, is not visible until they are upon it. The man lays his Ruger on the frozen rind (it slides two feet across the gently sloping ice before it stops) and plunges his hand through the snow at the foot of the fence. His fingers find the bottom strand of the rusty wire and lift it up. He uses his other hand to sweep away the snow, creating a burrow for the boy to wiggle through. Once the boy is safely on the other side, the man raises his long legs and scissors himself across the top of the fence, both of their rifles held at his side.

The father's rig is a Ruger No. 1S Medium Sporter. The

checkered walnut stock is solid and substantial. While the bluing of the barrel is worn in places from regular care, there is not a hint of corruption. Many men (he knew because he had heard them say it) found the Medium Sporter—particularly with the addition of a scope—too heavy to carry comfortably for long distances, but he did not. The chamber held a single round. A .45-70 Government, Federal Fusion cartridge. Soft point with a fused lead core. It would just about knock down a building. Recoil was not an issue. And there was no magazine to the Ruger. A single shot was all you got. That was sufficient. It otherwise tempted prodigal ways. Sloppiness. Brutality. He was not a brutal man. He disliked suffering. Could not abide it. Animal or human, he just could not abide suffering.

The man did not say much to his son, did not offer him a great deal of fatherly instruction, but when he took the boy hunting he usually spoke aloud after he fired his weapon—never before. He prided himself (although he would never admit to that sin) on killing with a single shot. Done in one *is what he said after squeezing the trigger, but really he was saying it for the boy to hear. That was the instruction.* Done in one. *It was Godly.*

And it was always true.

Until today. Until this morning.

He wants to do better by the boy. Must be getting older and softer he reckons. But the boy is getting older, too. It's time. Time to be a better father. To teach his son the hard lessons. Because life was hard. It was goddamn hard. It was hard like the sheep blood and entrails he'd kicked snow over this morning. It *was hard like the anger he'd felt at losing another one. Had the anger altered his shot? Of course it had. He knew better than to shoot with emotion. Anger was the only emotion he indulged in. And he regretted it. Life was hard.*

Now on the other side of the barbed wire, the man and the boy take stock. The boy's eyes have become acclimated to the white glare. Before, they had been moving too fast, and the glare had been too great for him to see anything but white. Now he could see the tracks his father had been following all along. Shadows where the snow was disturbed. And the shadows conceal traces of something even darker. Something red.

He had never witnessed his father miss his target before. Yet of course he did not miss, he had hit what he was aiming at, but he had failed to kill with a single shot. And that was the same thing as missing. He knew his father was mad. Mad about missing and mad about losing yet another of his sheep. To the same predator. It was in the way he'd kicked the snow over the torn apart animal.

His father squats down beside him, and this disturbs the boy, because his father is not a man to hunker down with a child. But he does. And the boy looks off in the distance in the direction the man's thick, rough-hewn finger is pointing. He doesn't see anything. He tries and he wants to see, he so much wants to see, because he wants to be the good son. He wants to reward his father's lowering of himself to his level. To earn it. But he knows better than to try and fool the man. He knows not to nod or otherwise acknowledge what he does not really see or understand.

But then he sees. It comes into focus. He nods without looking at his father, and it is in the act of not looking at him that the father knows it's true. The boy sees.

Off in the distance, merging into the horizon, is the wolf.

The gray wolf.

It's time.

Dark figures, they pursue.

CHAPTER 1

In seven years or so, Deputy Maddox Brinkley would be known amongst his Cameron County Sheriff's Office peers as "Mad Dog" (shortened from "Mad Dog on the Brink" Brinkley), for the proclivity to violence this job would awaken in him. But that was in the future. Tonight the mad dog was just a puppy. It was only his third night of active duty, and he was as green as spring grass. A tall, skinny young man, the only fat on him was in his baby pink cheeks.

He was riding the night-darkened summer streets of Vista Canyon with his FTO—Field Training Officer—Donovan Carpenter. Vista Canyon was just east of Folsom and its fabled prison, and fell squarely into the jurisdiction of the Cameron County S.O.—the Sheriff's office.

FTO Carpenter was known as "The Builder" but other than playing off his surname, Brinkley didn't yet know why they called him that. Maybe it was because he was as big as a building. He really was. That big. Maybe he'd misheard and "Building" was what they called him. The man was a fat, doughnut-eating stereotype. And a smoker. Brinkley hated cigarette smoke. The first night, Carpenter had fired up a Winston 100 right in the patrol car, cracked his window wide enough to maybe slide a sheet of notebook paper through, and said, "Mind if I smoke?" Brinkley had not seen him without a lit cigarette dangling from his lips since then. The guy was a heart attack waiting to happen. Each night, thirty minutes before the end of their graveyard shift, Carpenter pulled the cruiser into a U Wash It and vacuumed up the pastry crumbs and shot three doses of a deodorizer called Ozium into the vehicle's interior. The stuff worked pretty good, because it completely obliterated the burned tobacco odor. Brinkley wished he could figure out how to get the odor out of his uniform without washing it every night.

The Builder or The Building, or whatever the fuck he was called, pulled into a Jiffy Kwik just off Green Valley Road. This was the third convenience store they had stopped at this shift. Maddox sighed. To himself. Not out loud. He still had a hell of a long way to go before he became a mad dog.

The vehicle rocked as Carpenter climbed out of the driver's seat and into the pool of illumination thrown by the store's lighting. There were no other cars in the parking lot. It was only 9:30, but Vista Canyon tended to roll up its sidewalks once the sun set. The asphalt lot was still radiating heat it had absorbed during the day.

Carpenter turned back to the patrol cruiser and asked, "Need anything?"

"Pack of smokes," Maddox said.

"Thought you didn't smoke."

"They're a gift. For you. Christmas in July."

Fucking punk, The Builder thought, as he navigated the bright aisles of the Jiffy Kwik. *Getting a mouth on him. "Christmas in July." Needs a lesson. Maybe take him to patrol the Sierra Nevadas. Out to Camptown, six-toe country, after dark, where they'd tell him, "You got a purty mouth." Teach him how to use it. Get all James Dickey on his ass. Fucking punk. Teach him to fuck with The Builder.*

When he thought of himself, which was often, The Builder thought of himself as *The Builder.* He liked it. He knew the punk was working up the nerve to ask him why they called him that. What he'd told all the other punks he'd broken in over the years—when they worked up the nerve to ask—was that he couldn't tell them the story behind his nickname until after they'd proven themselves. The truth was that he'd made it up himself and worked it into conversations to get it set in people's heads. "They know better than to fuck with The Builder," he'd say. And sooner or later someone else would repeat it. And Donovan "The Builder" Carpenter was thus born.

He felt like a burrito tonight. Something healthy. He knew all those doughnuts and Debbie Pies were making him fat. He was trying to do better. A burrito was just the thing. Lots of protein. Healthy.

They had some under a heat lamp next to some hot dog wieners going round and round in a rotisserie contraption like exhausted hamsters on an exercise wheel. But it all looked too old, too tired, so he pulled one from the freezer case, an Amy's Organic Beans & Rice Burrito—organic was very healthy—and tossed it in the microwave set up near the coffee. While it was being zapped, Carpenter scanned the store.

There was a monitor mounted above the sales counter, right over the cashier's head, that showed the closed-circuit security feed. It flashed different perspectives from the various cameras posted around the premises. Carpenter wholly endorsed such systems because they were not only a good deterrent to crime, but often proved essential in solving crimes later. He watched it beam an image of the deserted gas pumps outside, then the area behind the store, then an empty aisle inside the store, then it showed Carpenter himself standing in the hot-food area. He couldn't believe how fat he had let himself get. *This is no way for a Field Training Officer to carry himself. My God, I've let myself go,* he thought, and looked away from his image. Which was a pity. Because if Officer Carpenter hadn't looked away, he would have seen the live feed from the camera mounted directly above the cash register. And in that image he would have seen that something was very, very wrong in the Vista Canyon Jiffy Kwik. In fact, if Carpenter had not averted his eyes from the monitor, he almost certainly would have lived through this night. But he didn't. And the legend that was The Builder would be bleeding out on the Jiffy Kwik floor in just five minutes.

What he chose to look at rather than the monitor was the sales clerk. The cashier, a greasy, long-haired punk, was up front, behind the counter, ignoring Carpenter. It used to be that when an officer of the law came into an establishment, he was *waited on.* He was treated with *respect.* Owners and staff were grateful that the officer had chosen their establishment to patronize and thus make safer with his or her presence. Not anymore. Not these days. No sir. Not only was the cashier pointedly ignoring Carpenter, the greaseball was thumbing through a porno mag. A *Hustler.* Or maybe it was *High Society* or *Swank* or *Barely Legal.* It was all trash. The point was that even from back here, Carpenter could see pink. Full-on beaver shots. Not womanly mounds of dense pubic hair like back in the day (which admittedly was a little too wild and wooly even back then) but slick-shaved extreme close-ups that seemed more clinical than erotic. And with the Internet, who even paid for porn anymore? Couldn't you get it for free now?

The microwave beeped at him, and Carpenter pulled the burrito out, tossing it from hand to hand like a, well, like a hot burrito. He wrapped it in a napkin to insulate it. He poured himself a large cup of coffee, but it looked awfully black to be their light blend. He lifted the cup to his nose and took a whiff. It smelled burnt and sour.

He called up to the guy at the counter, "Hey, how old's this stuff?"

The greaseball did him the courtesy of looking up from his skin mag and said, " 'Bout an hour. It's still some good." Then his head dipped back down to the matter at hand.

Probably studying to be a gynecologist, Carpenter thought.

He could have poured it out and grabbed some of the blueberry or cinnamon or pumpkin spice or vanilla nut brew they had on tap, but Officer Carpenter considered himself to be something of a coffee purist. And even though there was no way this brew was just an hour old, he would still rather have regular joe, old and funky, than the flavored crap. Calling this swill an hour old was complete BS. But he wasn't going to push the point. He was ready to go. He needed a smoke. He figured he would have a Winston and sip his coffee while he drove. The cigarette would go a long way to masking the sour taste of the coffee. Then he would eat the burrito—the *organic burrito,* he reminded himself— then have another smoke, because he always liked to light up after a meal.

He dosed the coffee with real sugar—that artificial stuff could give you multiple sclerosis—and powdered creamer, put one of those little cardboard collars on the cup to keep it from burning his hand, and headed to the front to pay up.

He put his bounty on the counter right next to a photo layout of a young woman. A photographic study that he bet the young woman prayed her father would never see. It wasn't the pornography that Carpenter objected to—to each his own as far as he was concerned—it was the fact that the guy felt comfortable just paging through it like it was *Reader's Digest* or *The Christian Science Monitor.* Well, it wasn't. And he was going to say something about it.

In fact, Officer Carpenter decided he was going to get in the guy's face. Maybe scare him a little bit. He was going to lean right past the register and into his space. And if Carpenter had actually done that—leaned over the counter—he surely would have seen the girl on the floor behind the counter. The girl on the floor was the real cashier. And Carpenter would have seen the tears streaming from her bulging eyes. He would have seen the greaseball's boot planted square in the girl's stomach. And he would have seen the Glock 9mm that had been dangling from the greaseball's right hand the entire time his left hand had been thumbing through the skin magazine.

But Carpenter didn't see any of that. Even if he had, it wouldn't have saved his life. It was too late for that. In any case, he never leaned across the counter and got in the guy's face. Something caught his eye. Diverted his attention. It was a big glass water tower that set atop the sales counter. Bubbles gurgled up from the bottom, and a sign on the contraption invited customers to drop in quarters for a chance of landing one in the shot glass at the bottom to win a prize. It was all for charity, supposedly, but who knew for sure where the money really ended up?

Carpenter loved games of chance. Was a sucker for them. He and the missus loved to steal away to Vegas or South Lake Tahoe every now and again. Or hit up one of the half dozen or so Indian casinos in the greater Vista Canyon area and foothills. He considered himself a player. So he just couldn't resist giving this game a try. He dug into his uniform pocket, pulled out a quarter, and fed it into the slot on top.

Out in the patrol car, rookie Deputy Brinkley wondered just what in the hell was taking his FTO so goddamn long. He'd just about had it with the constant stream of convenience stores. How long did it take to grab a pastry and a cup of java? *For Christ's sake.* But for now, Brinkley would keep on keeping it to himself. It was a six-month evaluation period, and then a year's probation during which he could be terminated without reason. It was best not to make waves. After the evaluation, he would either be assigned a partner and an urban patrol zone, or he would become a single-man unit assigned to one of the vast, sparsely populated areas within the county. Six-toe-country. Camptown.

Through the plate glass window, Brinkley saw his FTO finally waddle up to the sales counter. What would Carpenter do if he had to chase down a suspect? Surely there were some kind of minimum physical fitness requirements officers had to continue to meet. Surely. Oh well, he didn't care. The training period was just six months. Then he would either be out on his own or partnered up with somebody long term. Someone of more modern habits he hoped. If he could just get through these six months. And was Carpenter *still* in there? How long did it take to pay for your shit and get out? Brinkley craned his neck to get a better look. Carpenter was doing something at the counter. It looked like he was putting coins into something. Was that a slot machine? *For fuck's sake.*

Carpenter watched his quarter zigzag lazily through the water, buffeted by the rising air bubbles. It missed the shot glass by a wide margin. He considered breaking a dollar to try again, but thought better of it. It was time to go.

Well, maybe just four more. He pushed a dollar bill down the counter over to the clerk. Before he fed the first one in, he glanced up again at the security monitor mounted above the counter. The clerk couldn't see it. It was strictly for customers to see. A deterrent. But Carpenter wondered if it was filming him putting quarters into this contraption. That wasn't necessarily a good thing.

He divided his attention between watching his quarter saw through the water, and looking up at the monitor to see if he was being recorded. He saw the area outside the bathrooms, the pumps, the deserted back of the store, the coffee counter. Then he saw the view from directly overhead: It showed the cash register, the clerk, a handgun held at the clerk's side, and, quite clearly, a girl lying on the floor at the clerk's feet.

What he saw registered in Carpenter's eyes. He knew that. He knew his eyes could have given him away. But what he didn't know was if the clerk was watching him at the time. If the grease-ball saw it register. Maybe, maybe not.

Carpenter sidled from the water tower back over to the register to indicate that he was ready to pay for his food. He grabbed a bag of Doritos from an impulse-purchase rack and added it to his bounty. Nonchalance personified.

"Quiet night?" he asked the guy. Easy breezy.

"Yeah. And I'm not complaining about it," the guy said, playing his part just fine. And that made Carpenter believe that he would very likely make it out of here without having to draw his service revolver.

"I don't blame you," Carpenter said. "Not one bit."

"Six-sixty-six," said the clerk, but the register said five-eighty-eight. Carpenter didn't call him on it, just pushed a ten-spot across the counter.

He gave some change back to Carpenter, who shoved it in his pocket without counting it because it probably wasn't the right change anyway, and he just wanted out of there so he could call for backup.

Carpenter didn't wait to be offered a bag. He took his coffee in one hand, Amy's Organic Burrito and Doritos in the other, and turned to the door. Easy breezy beautiful.

Behind him, the clerk leaned forward over the counter and peered up to see what the cop had been looking at. His timing was much better than Carpenter's. The monitor was displaying the clerk and the girl and the gun.

"Stop," he said to the cop. No emotion in his voice. Calm. Easy breezy, some would even say.

Carpenter pretended not to hear. He pushed at the glass door. He was trying to push the door open with his hands full of food and hot coffee, when the normal thing would have been to turn around and push it open with his ass. But if he turned around, he couldn't pretend not to hear the clerk.

"Goddamn it, I said stop." Nothing easy and/or breezy about his tone now.

Carpenter stopped. He turned around to face the clerk. The clerk had his pistol pointed straight at the cop. Those synthetic polymer Glocks were all over Cameron County. A plastic plague. They were the Anti-Visa: Everywhere you didn't want them to be.

"Christ," was what the cop said.

The gunman said, "You should've thought about Christ before." He pulled back and released the slide on the automatic. It was a single fluid yet crisp movement that put a live round in the chamber. It was a loud, attention-getting sound. Maybe not as attention-getting as a shotgun being racked, but it ranked right up there. It was a sound no cop ever wanted to hear.

"Do you know what it means to feel like God?"

Carpenter closed his eyes. He didn't really want to see it coming. And it was coming. He knew that much. The guy was one of the crazies. One of the violent crazies. *Do you know what it means to feel like God?* What the fuck was that? It was crazy talk. Probably from some rock song. Probably playing on a continuous loop in the guy's tweaked-out meth-burnt mind. Carpenter opened his eyes to face his fate, and there it was right on the guy's t-shirt. A dreadlocked zombie, and the words *do you know what it means to feel like God?*

It was over. Everything was over. And the last thought that went through FTO Donovan Carpenter's mind was that Jiffy Kwik didn't even sell skin mags. They were a Christian organization— beer, wine, cigarettes, condoms, rolling papers, and lottery tickets were all A-okay, but dirty pictures were anathema. So the crazy brought the magazine with him when he came to rob the store. He brought porn to a robbery.

Below the counter, the real clerk saw that the gunman's attention was with the cop and took a desperate chance. She lunged under the weight of his leg and managed to sit up enough to sink her teeth firmly into his calf. She bit down hard. Like she meant it. Like she was a cannibal and today was Thanksgiving.

The gunman screamed and kicked the girl viciously.

Carpenter saw that God had granted him a reprieve. And yes, it was true, he had let himself go to seed, gotten fat and lazy and stupid. All true. But in the end, he was a cop. He had a cop's instincts. A warrior gone to pot, but still a warrior in his heart. One of the good guys.

This was Carpenter's chance and he knew it. He didn't know why the gunman was startled and distracted, he just knew this was his chance to walk out of here a hero. Or at least alive.

Before his cup of coffee could hit the floor, Carpenter had hit the release on his holster and drawn his revolver while starting the trigger through its double-action cycle like he had done so many times before in training. When he got a sight picture, he completed the trigger pull and the weapon discharged. All of this in less than a second. He is a cop.

But he wasn't fast or accurate enough. The gunman fired at the same time as Carpenter. Carpenter's bullet went wild, as it usually did when he tried to shoot too fast, and the water tower exploded in a geyser of liquid and glass shards.

The gunman's bullet went wide, too, and the glass door behind Carpenter shattered.

Brinkley's head snapped up at the sound of gunfire. His mouth gaped. And all he could think was *ohmygod ohmygod ohmygod*.

In a very stupid move, Carpenter looked back at the shattered glass behind him. He was stunned. In all his years of police work, he'd managed to avoid being shot at. Until now.

He turned back to the gunman who was as much in shock as Carpenter. Bits of glass stuck out of the man's bleeding face, and to Carpenter it looked like porcupine quills or that guy from the horror movie with spikes all in his face. *Pinhead*.

The clerk's gun dangled at his side. His first chance squandered, Carpenter realized he now had another one. He raised his weapon and took a shooter's stance. Just as he was trained all those years and pounds and cigarettes ago.

He had the upper hand. Except that his foot slid out from under him in the spilled coffee on the floor. He was going down.

But before he did, the gunman raised his Glock and fired. The bullet pierced Carpenter's badge and slammed into his chest. It was like being hit with a sledgehammer. But his vest stopped the bullet from penetrating to his heart. The blow knocked the big man down, and he landed on his ass. Carpenter held on to his weapon and raised it to fire again, but before he could get off another shot, the shooter's next round found the Achilles' heel of his Kevlar vest. The bullet hit under Carpenter's raised right arm, went through his armpit, entered his thoracic cavity, and ripped through both lungs.

Black coffee and deep red pulmonary blood ran together on the floor.

Brinkley was out of the patrol car. He crouched behind the open door of the cruiser, his weapon drawn. He was screaming into the police radio, his voice cracking like a teenager's, "11-99! Shots fired! Officer Down! Officer Down! We need assistance!"

Thus did Officer Donovan Carpenter—connoisseur of convenience store coffee, devotee of the cigarette, defender of the doughnut, advocate of the organic food movement, hobby gambler, and tolerator of pornography—known far and wide as The

Builder—bleed out on the white tile floor of the Vista Canyon Jiffy Kwik in Cameron County, California.

Later, it would occur to Maddox Brinkley that he never got the chance to ask his partner why they called him The Builder. And even though he checked around later, he would never find out how Carpenter had earned that nickname, because no one else seemed to know either. Or so they claimed. Code of silence.

CHAPTER 2

Out in the humid night, an anonymous black van carrying the Cameron County Sheriff Department's Special Weapons and Tactics team rolled through the city streets. Fast. Insistent.

Inside, the eleven team members (ten men and one woman) were dressed in black tactical gear, and wearing balaclavas—black masks with eyeholes. They held on to overhead straps as the vehicle swayed. Fast. Insistent.

The team faced forward in the van, where a Dry Erase Board was mounted. Standing at the board was Lieutenant Joe Cowell, fifty-one, a tall, lean man who, unlike the fallen Officer Carpenter, hadn't let age or gravity or bad habits creep up on him. He faced the others, gesturing to the whiteboard.

The board showed a diagram of the Jiffy Kwik store, surrounding structures, and landscape. Several areas were marked in red, including an exterior spot marked SNIPERS DENTON/ SESAK.

Jacob Denton, whose designation was Primary Sniper, was,

at forty-five, the oldest actively serving member of the team. Jake was powerfully built with bowling-ball shoulders, a solid chest, and limbs thick with corded muscle. There was no hint of the athlete about him. Just brawn. As though he were carved from stone. In fact, he was built more like a doorkicker than a traditionally lean and lank sniper. When he saw himself in a mirror, he realized that he looked more and more like his father with each passing year. Solid, but rough hewn—an unfinished statue. His physical presence was, he knew, intimidating. Just like his father.

His partner was Kathryn Sesak, the only female in the van, a baby at twenty-four. Sesak was his spotter. Shorter than Jake, and certainly smaller, with a physical strength that fell more to the side of agility and grace.

Jake and Sesak studied the diagram. Jake stared at the red dot on the whiteboard that marked his position. And for a second the red on white blurred. It became fresh red blood spilt on crisp white snow. And he could hear the jagged heavy breathing of a boy struggling to break through the ice-crusted snow to keep up with his father.

Jake broke his gaze from the Dry Erase board to look at his partner. He and Sesak exchanged a curt nod of acknowledgment. They were ready.

Fast. Insistent. The SWAT van sliced through the intersection of Powell Inn and Green Valley Road and came to a stop just outside a convergence of cop cars and paramedics, their lights pulsing blue and red in the bruised blackness of the California night.

The rear doors of the van opened. The SWAT team deployed like parachute jumpers in two-man columns. They entered the madness of the scene, cool and collected, each knowing exactly where to go and what to do.

Lieutenant Cowell and another man moved toward the command post set up in the parking lot. From this vantage point, Cowell could see the supine body of the dead policeman. With his binoculars, the lieutenant could make out the gunman and the female clerk protected in an aisle of snack food. The hostage-taker held his gun pressed to the girl's temple.

Sergeant Ray Heidler, a burly, graying man, leaned over a diagram on the hood of a patrol car. Lieutenant Cowell clapped him on the back. Behind them Maddox Brinkley, the fallen officer's partner, paced back and forth, high color in his plump cheeks.

Cowell asked Heidler, "What've we got?"

"He graduated a year behind me, Joe."

Cowell glanced again at the body of the slain policeman lying at the front of the store. No time for emotion, reminiscence, or reflection. Not now.

"I'm sorry, Ray. Let's concentrate on getting the rest of us out of here alive. Current status?"

The distorted voice of a police negotiator on a bullhorn provided background noise.

"He's got the clerk in there with him. Young white female. He wants safe passage out, but he's been firing random shots every few minutes. Don't know how much ammo he's actually got."

"All right, Ray. We'll take it from here."

Cowell spotted the negotiator in the passenger seat of a

patrol car with the door open. His voice amplified to distortion by the bullhorn, the negotiator said, "We're gonna have to have time to locate a vehicle. You don't want to drive out of here in a cop car, do you? Let the girl go and I personally promise you safe passage out."

A gunshot from the store shattered the windshield of the patrol car. The negotiator dropped the bullhorn and ducked under the dashboard. The megaphone tumbled across the pavement.

Cowell wondered why someone hadn't found the store's phone number and established communication that way. The bullhorn and the yelling back and forth just put everybody's nerves even more on edge. Not to mention the media recording every syllable, and the onlookers with their smart phones capturing every last bit of it. Nothing in this world was real until it was captured digitally. It wasn't real until you rushed home and uploaded the experience to YouTube. Of course these days, Cowell realized with disdain, they didn't even have to rush home to get it online. They could upload it on the spot, ricocheted around the globe via satellite. What a world. A cop couldn't take a breath unless that cop was prepared for that breath to be recorded, broadcast, and analyzed.

From the floorboard of the patrol car, the negotiator was slamming his fist into the dashboard and yelling, "Son of a bitch! Son of a bitch! Son of a bitch!"

"I see you've still got the touch, Webster," Cowell called out to him.

He walked with deliberation across the parking lot and retrieved the dropped bullhorn, which was emitting a high-pitched whine of feedback. Cowell banged it against the heel of his hand to quiet it. Then he yelled into it.

"All right, now you listen to me, you fucking asshole. Fire one more shot and I personally promise that you will not leave here alive. Now wait for your fucking car!"

Cowell tossed the bullhorn to the pavement. Let them record that. Let them put that on their Googles and their Facebooks and their Twitters. Motherfuckers.

Webster, petulant like a child, said, "Cowell, that was totally and completely—"

But Cowell was walking away, speaking into his radio.

"Team Two, copy?"

From the rooftop of a single-story brick building across from the convenience store, Denton and Sesak had taken their positions.

Denton peered through his rifle scope and locked on target.

Sesak pulled out a pair of military-grade binoculars. (She had her Night Owls with her as well, but since the store remained well lighted, she had no need of night vision technology.) She adjusted the focus until the scene came into plain view. The suspect. The girl. The gun. The man's face was barely visible behind the girl's head. All that could be seen was the hostage's Christmas-ornament-sized earrings.

Sesak said, "Right rear of the store. Between the Twinkies and the potato chips."

"I've got him."

Jake peered through the scope. Kathryn cupped her hand to her ear, then keyed her mic.

"Team Two copies. Green light."

Then to Denton, "We've got the green."

Jacob heard the word *green*. His finger tensed around the trigger. Then the outside world faded as he focused every bit of his conscious self into his scope. He was down the rabbit hole. He was in what he thought of as *the perfect peace of the reticle*. All of his other senses seemed to fall away. Like snow mutes the sounds of nature. This was common in most snipers. It was why they worked in teams. It was why he had a spotter with him. Once he jumped down the rabbit hole, and the perfect peace of the reticle had made the outside world fade away, Kathryn Sesak was his eyes and ears. He had to trust her.

Through her binoculars, Sesak saw the gunman move.

"No shot. Target obscured."

Jacob's finger eased.

Although he and Sesak were working as a team, they were not equals. She was a spotter only. For now, she was a sniper-in-training, and she could never rise above that position without Jake's endorsement. Over the years, he'd had dozens of spotters, few of them lasting more than six months. The truth of it was that it was a brutal, regimented, and disciplined way of life. Not a career move, but a way of life. Those past partners had thought they wanted to be snipers, but they all seemed to wash out.

The gunman shifted his head from one side of the girl's head, then back to the other side again. With those huge dime-store earrings, it was just a guessing game. They were huge and spangled. Like mirror balls. Like something out of *Saturday Night Fever*. Who wore stuff like that anymore?

From the street, Cowell was looking through his own binoculars and speaking into his radio.

"We've got ten minutes. Confirming. You've got a green light."

Flat on her belly, from the rooftop, Kathryn watched.

"Still no shot. No shot."

There was simply no way to shoot. Only a sliver of the gunman's head was visible behind the girl. And those damnable earrings. *What was this, 1979?*

"He's not moving. No—"

A sharp crack erupted in the night.

Kathryn rolled away from Jacob, out of instinct. Fear. She stared at her partner.

Jacob, still locked in position, peered through the scope.

"Target down."

Kathryn rolled back to position, raised the binoculars again.

The suspect was slumped over the food rack. The girl stood over his body, screaming. Screaming her head off. A disco queen at a filming of *Soul Train* gone horribly, horribly wrong.

Kathryn keyed her mic.

"Target down."

She once again distanced herself from her partner. Rolled away. She watched him. Denton was still frozen, locked into position.

She waited.

Below she heard the rush of activity as SWAT team members burst into the Jiffy Kwik.

Jacob stood up and gathered his equipment. Kathryn had hoped he would speak first. But she couldn't keep waiting.

"But you didn't have a shot."

Jacob nodded toward the store. "Tell him that."

Kathryn stared below, mouth agape.

"And don't ever roll like that again. It draws attention. Get your gear. Let's move out."

Jacob left. Kathryn scrambled for her gear and hurried after him.

Uniformed deputies and EMTs streamed through the store like insects following chemical trails, each knowing their purpose. They stepped around the bodies, which would be there for many hours to come.

The female hostage stood with Sergeant Heidler. They'd already gotten her initial, adrenaline-fueled statement, and would get a more formal account once she'd calmed herself down.

"Ohmygod I've never been so scared in my entire life. Do you think this'll get me on a talk show or *Inside Edition* or anything?"

Behind her, a uniformed deputy raised his eyebrows at Sergeant Heidler. They had both seen this type of euphoria, this manic gushing, from victims who'd had close calls.

"This was un-fucking-believable! Did I tell you I bit the guy? I bit him. Bit him right on the leg. He kicked me in the stomach. What happened? How'd you shoot him? I don't know what happened but I almost peed my pants when he got shot! I had a gun to my head! I can't believe it!"

She raised her hands to the sides of her face. One of her earrings was missing.

"Oh shit. I lost an earring." She looked around, amid the blood and broken glass.

The uniformed officer ducked down the snack aisle. He spotted the earring wedged between two packages of Lays barbecue potato chips and plucked it out. He looked at it, then hid it behind his back as he emerged back up front.

"Did you see it? It was vintage."

He shook his head *no*.

She peered out the front window and squealed in excitement.

"Ohmygod! Is that Clark Avery from Channel Three? Oh my God. It is! Do you think he'll want to talk to me?"

Sergeant Heidler put a light hand to her elbow and steered her toward the door.

"I'm sure of it. Why don't you go on out while we finish up in here."

She ran her hands through her hair, down her clothes, straightening, fluffing and stuffing.

"How do I look?"

Sergeant Heidler gave her the OK sign.

The girl beamed and exited the store in search of fame.

The technophobic Lieutenant Cowell would have recognized the girl's need to seek out Clark Avery and mingle among the throng of gawkers, their handheld devices already poised to capture the human drama. She wanted to be recorded and broadcast and YouTubed and Facebooked. She wanted what had happened to her tonight to be documented. She wanted it to be made *real*.

Sergeant Heidler turned back to the officer.

"Let me see it."

The officer tossed the earring to Heidler. He looked at it, shook his head and tossed it back.

"Give it to Cowell. That's his department."

A few minutes later, Lieutenant Cowell approached the van, opened the back door, climbed inside, and shut it behind him.

The eleven team members were back in position. Cowell moved through them to the front of the van and knocked twice on the window to the driver's compartment.

And the anonymous black van carrying the Cameron County Sheriff's Department Special Weapons and Tactics team rolled through the city streets.

Fast. Insistent.

CHAPTER 3

The SWAT van pulled into the rear of the station and stopped. Cowell exited the van first, then turned to address his team.

"Debriefing in ten minutes."

Cowell turned and entered the station. The team members exited the van. They pulled gear from the van and removed their black masks. For some reason, they never removed their masks until they got back to the station house, as though they wanted to be ready for any eventuality while out on the streets. Jacob and Kathryn pulled their rifles out and slung them over their shoulders.

Cowell stuck his head back out through the doorway and yelled.

"Denton!"

Jacob looked up from his gear.

"Sir?"

"Inside."

Once Cowell ducked back inside, Kathryn said, "Shit. Wonder what we did wrong?"

The other team members looked at Kathryn, and she realized that she had made some sort of faux pas. Yet again. The
SWAT team was a world unto itself, and she was still struggling
to pick up on the ways of this secret society she had somehow
managed to breach. She was always conscious of being the FNG.
The fucking new girl.

Jacob patted her on the back.

"Have you tried decaf? It makes you less paranoid."

The rest of the team laughed, and somebody said,
"Fuckin'Denton"—run together into one word. Kathryn was
grateful to her partner for defusing the social blunder with a
joke. Everybody went back to stripping the outer shells of their
BDUs (battle dress uniforms—a leftover military term) and
gathering and stowing their gear. The gear was a big part of the
life—the ones who worked patrol kept most of their SWAT gear
(including BDUs of different colors for day, night, rural, urban)
in the trunks of their patrol cars, and if activated while out on
patrol, they geared up while driving to the scene or briefing site.
The meeting location could be anywhere—a lonely gas station,
a crowded mall parking lot, a little league ball field—where patrol
cars and private cars could converge, and the men could dress
down from street clothes and marked patrol uniforms to SWAT
BDUs. Sometimes they did it in the van (or at least they did before Kathryn broke the gender barrier), but it was essential they
be hot and ready to deploy when they hit the scene. It was a lot of
shit to keep up with. All the while maintaining the anonymity
they closely guarded.

And since they lived in such a huge county, some team members could be coming from farther away—off duty and not able to drive code three, using lights and sirens—but there were time constraints specific to each situation and the lieutenant might go in without the full team due to the intensity of the action. They were usually a twelve-man team but could deploy with ten or even eight, but that turned a sniper into a doorkicker sometimes.

Inside, the squad room was a large cavernous cube. Plain. With chairs and tables and clipboards hanging along a wall. Cowell stood at a chalkboard behind the desk at the front of the room drawing a diagram of the convenience store. Getting ready for the debriefing. Jacob bypassed the locker room, pulled out a chair near Cowell, and sat down. Cowell frowned at him.

"Maybe we better take this into my office, Jake."

Denton shrugged and got back up.

Once behind a closed door, Jacob waited for Cowell to speak first. Through the blinds, he could see the team members filtering into the squad room, sharing stories, stretching in their SWAT t-shirts, repacking gear bags, and wiping at the urban camo smeared around their eyes and necks. The black grease paint was needed to fill in any spots that the eyeholes didn't cover, or wouldn't cover if the balaclava shifted with motion.

It made Jacob conscious of the black greasepaint that still ringed his eyes and neck, and of the fact that he was separate from the rest of his team. But the sniper always was. A man apart.

"That was a hell of a shot."

"Thanks."

"How many is that now?"

Jacob shrugged. The Denton Shrug. It was practically patented. It conveyed exactly nothing.

"You telling me you don't know?"

To this question, Jacob gave a modified half shrug. Conveying, again, nothing.

"Come on. Don't bullshit me. You always try to bullshit me. For twenty years you've tried to bullshit me and it never works. How many?"

A three-quarters shrug with an almost imperceptible headshake thrown in to balance it out.

"Christ! We're getting too old for this, you know that?"

Although he had a nearly endless supply of shrug variations, Jacob took pity on his old friend and gave him something. "That's what Sesak keeps telling me."

Cowell took the ante and worked with it. "You two working out okay?"

"Well, she's a girl."

"No shit?"

"She's far from ready. Oh, she can shoot, but if she actually killed someone—I think it'd fuck her up." Jake genuinely thought she was a natural. Highly advanced in her accuracy. The kind that comes courtesy of DNA. But killing left a mark, and he didn't know if she could stand it.

Jake's comment made Cowell happy. Not what the words conveyed, but that Denton was talking. That was practically a speech. The Gettysburg fucking Address.

"She's killed in the line of duty. Doesn't seem like that fucked her up."

"This is different. On the street it's reflex. Kill or be killed. This is methodical. Cold blooded. There's not many men or women up to the task."

Jacob stretched and yawned. That did convey something. And it wasn't that he was tired.

"Listen, Jacob—"

Through the yawn he said, "Here we go."

"Now, goddamnit, you know this is part of my job. I have to ask you this."

"Shoot."

"Funny. You're a funny guy. Now look, although you claim not to know it, this is your seventeenth kill. Some people consider it quite strange that you've never accepted the free counseling after a call-out. So, for the record, I'm offering it again. Would you like to talk to somebody?"

"I'm saving my sessions up for Sesak. Trust me, she's going to need them."

"What makes you so damn sure you don't need them for yourself?"

Jacob leaned forward in his chair.

"You know, Lieutenant, what 'some people' don't understand is that I do talk to somebody after every case."

"I'm talking about professional help. Real help."

"So am I."

"Jill doesn't count."

"She'll be delighted to hear that."

"Don't be a dick. You know what I meant."

Jacob shrugged. A Denton classic.

The two men sat in an uncomfortable silence, each waiting for the other to speak again.

Cowell finally said, "You cut it a little close tonight, don't you think?"

"Well, let me see. There's a cop killer on his way to the morgue, and a very much alive young lady telling Channel Three what a damn fine job the Cameron County Sheriff's Department did of saving her life." Jacob threw in a demi-shrug and said, "My world is measured in thousandths of an inch, so no, I wouldn't say it was close at all."

Cowell pulled an object from his gear bag and dangled it in Jacob's face. The girl's disco ball earring with a perfect hole right through the center. It was a cheap glittery hollow plastic thing. If it had been made of a more rigid or brittle material, it would likely have been obliterated by the 7.62mm lead-core, copper-jacketed hollow point bullet. Or simply been pushed aside.

"Christ, Jacob! What if you had missed?"

"I didn't."

Lieutenant Cowell put the earring on his desktop.

"I never would have authorized that shot."

"Once you give me the green, you authorize whatever shot I take."

"That's not exactly the way it works. You work as a two-man unit out there. What the hell was Sesak doing? Her nails?"

"Don't blame her. She said I didn't have a shot."

"Then, why the hell—"

"From her vantage point it looked like I didn't. But from my vantage point I saw an opportunity and I took it."

Cowell picked the earring back up and dangled it from his fingers, like a lawyer holding up a piece of particularly damning evidence. He shook his head.

"I understand that dehumanizing the targets and the obstacles is part of the job. But that idea can go too far. It can breed callousness. I want you to see somebody. I want it in your file."

Jacob thought he understood what was going on here. In his world, a sniper's world, there was no such thing as too close. But the earring, the physical manifestation of that idea, was disturbing to Cowell. And there was an element of cover-your-ass at play here, too. Liability. If Jacob fucked up, or went 51–50, Cowell wanted to be able to say that he'd had Jacob checked out.

"It's not an option. It's an order. We have to know how these hits have affected you."

Jacob looked away, through the window, glancing at the men assembled in the squad room and said, "They haven't affected me." His first slipup. The looking away tipped his hand. It conveyed something.

"That attitude right there worries me more than anything else."

Back on track, Jacob shrugged.

"I just don't want to lose another good man. I'll make the appointment. With a private doc. No departmental politics in play. At least not until we get the results back. You have no choice in this."

Lieutenant Cowell got up from the desk. He walked past Jacob and gave him a pat on the shoulder on his way out of the room.

Jacob picked up the earring and stared at it. Then he shrugged.

CHAPTER 4

Jill and Jacob Denton lived in Maggie's Valley, just outside Morgan City. Once upon a time, Morgan City was known as Old Hang Town—with good reason, Jill Denton would tell you. There wasn't much to Maggie's Valley, just a mop-and-pop gas station, a bar, and Jill's old fire station. Once you left Morgan City, you could go one mile and be in the mountains. Switchback roads with steep canyons of death off to one side. Long, long stretches of acreage that may or may not be developed. And the road climbed steeply from there to the crest of the Sierra Nevada Mountains and then over into the South Lake Tahoe Basin. North of Morgan City, you went down, down, down a treacherous canyon gorge and then climbed an equally treacherous switchback on the other side—leading to the fabled "six-toe-country" where the more rugged and clannish Northern Californians lived—the kind of folks who would welcome the Timothy McVeighs of this world with safe harbor. And then maybe shoot them for being too liberal.

Maggie's Valley suited Jacob and Jill best. Their house, about ten miles southeast of Morgan City, was on a graveled cul-de-sac far back from the road, on a two-acre lot. It was given to them as a wedding gift by Jill's parents. Her father built the house himself. It was a simple, small house perfect for a newly married couple, and it was understood that Jacob and Jill would add on to it to accommodate the family they planned to have. But so far, there had been no children, so their home was quite modest at just over a thousand square feet: two bedrooms, one and a half bathrooms, with a freestanding workshop out back for Jacob. Rustic—landscaped by Jill with huge old wagon wheels on the exterior walls, weathered lumber saws, old farmers' seed machines—just western shit, she called it.

Tonight, the television set in the Denton house was tuned to Channel Three. Jill had muted the volume earlier, once she was certain her husband was safe, but now she turned it back up and listened as the giddy hostage gave a live on-the-scene interview to Clark Avery. The woman had the biggest smile Jill had ever seen, her eyes glassy like someone with a high fever. Jill knew that was just the remnant of adrenaline working its way out of the body's system. Jill smiled to herself, knowing the woman would almost certainly be horny later tonight. Another side effect of the hormones her body had released, but also because sex was life affirming, and after having almost lost her life tonight, life-affirming sex is what the woman would crave.

Jill Denton knew these things because she used to be a firefighter and an EMT. And she could still remember that feeling of living life on the edge, the close calls, the hairy rides through neighborhoods that were like combat zones—and when she got home from one of those shifts, she wanted a long hot shower. And then she wanted to screw. Not a pretty way to put it, but that was the word for what she wanted. Not to make love, but a good old-fashioned pounding.

"What are you smiling about?" Susan asked.

Jill looked at Susan and flushed. She switched the TV to Turner Classic Movies where some old black-and-white spook show was playing. Something with Bela Lugosi. She liked Turner Classics and usually left it playing all the time.

Jill tried to think up something to say to her writing student Susan Weaver, who was sprawled out on the floor near the coffee table. Kind of burrowing in there. Jill just shrugged.

"Happy your honey is okay?"

Jill nodded, still red faced about what she had been thinking.

The EMT gig had come to an end thanks to a moron playing his Metallica CD too loud who never heard the sirens of the emergency response vehicle. He slammed into the side of her unit. Jill's leg never healed quite right. She could get around just fine, but her first responder days were finished. She might have eked out a few more years as a medic, but her firefighting career was definitely over, and in the Cameron County Fire Department, you couldn't do one without the other. Nor did she want to.

During the long days of her recovery, she realized that she was losing whole chunks of her life in a hydrocodone hypnosis. But she needed the drugs to dull the pain of the external fixator— the steel rods that pierced her flesh and sat in the holes drilled in the bone around the fracture, or as she liked to think of it, that thing Stephen King had on his leg. She decided that she could either continue to stew in a Vicodin vapor while a never-ending stream of talk shows and infomercials played on the TV, or she could work through the pain and do something constructive.

So she weaned herself down to the bare minimum required for pain maintenance and did the one thing she had always wanted to do but swore to anybody who would listen that she just didn't have the time to do: She wrote a novel. She actually did it. Instead of fretting over the maddening itching her bones caused her as they mended, she wrote. And wrote and wrote and wrote. And she bought the latest edition of *Writer's Market.* And she queried agents. And she signed with one. And then the damnedest thing happened. The novel was published. By an actual publisher. An honest-to-God New York publisher. Her novel was called *Living Proof,* and it even racked up a few mainstream media reviews. Good reviews. Glowing reviews. But nobody much bought it. In fact, she never even earned out the extremely modest advance her publisher had paid for the book.

She didn't care. She wrote another one, *Drake's Valley,* for which she received an even lower advance that was equal to about three months of her EMT pay. The second book also got some decent critical notice, but, once again, nobody much bought it. And Jill's second book also failed to make back its paltry advance.

Undeterred, she wrote a third. Which the publisher turned down, citing how the downturn in the economy had lessened people's interest in literary fiction. Her agent had submitted the manuscript here and there, but she knew he was only going through the motions. It was a manuscript by a little-known writer that had been rejected by the little-known author's publisher. If the book, by some miracle, made it to the desk of an editor who was willing to overlook that rejection by the original publisher, a quick review of Jill's BookScan numbers would squash any nascent interest. She just didn't have the sales. So, in effect, her writing career was over—just under three years after it had begun.

But the two published books gave her the credentials to teach creative writing at Cosumnes Community College. And Jill found that she genuinely enjoyed teaching. That she was good at it. That her students' enthusiasm for writing—their naïve belief that writing careers were within their grasp—gave her back a little of that earnest self-belief. That foolish enthusiasm. She had even been thinking of slapping a pseudonym on her unsold manuscript and getting it back out there.

But there were bills to pay, too, and she was able to augment her teaching money by doing a little one-on-one tutoring on the side. Some of her students were more determined than others. They were willing to do whatever it took to get their manuscripts finished and polished. Each believed that they were capable of writing the Great American Novel. And who was she to disagree? She'd felt that way once herself. And was starting to feel it again. So if someone needed help and could afford to pay for her time, she would work for them, one on one.

Sometimes she regretted it, though. One male student seemed to develop a bit of a crush on her, so she had to tell him she was just too busy to see him outside of class. Susan was okay, though.

A little needy, but okay. She was maybe twenty years old, and still had a lot of maturing to do.

When Jacob was deployed tonight, she was glad she already had an evening session scheduled. She didn't want to be alone. She knew Jacob would be gone a minimum of three hours, and that could be a long time in an empty house when your husband was in harm's way. She used to spend those long hours on the phone with her mom or her sister, Megan, but things had gotten tense with them. They were getting fed up with the lifestyle Jill had married into. So, tonight there was Susan Weaver to fill the void.

She watched her now, on the floor, huddled over her laptop, tapping away at the keys. It struck Jill that Susan was a mousy little thing. Rodent-like. A little hamster or something. No, she looked kind of like a possum. Like a befuddled little nocturnal marsupial. A leftover character from *The Wind in the Willows*.

Without looking up from her computer, Susan said, "I think this is actually going to be worth a damn. I see now that it really can be a novel. Thank you."

"You're welcome. Even though I didn't really do anything but sit here and distract you with the TV."

Susan looked up at Jill. "I'm just glad your husband is okay. Guess he'll be home late tonight."

"Why?"

"They have to investigate the shooting? Make sure it was righteous."

Jill cocked an eyebrow and smiled. "Righteous?"

"You know. Clean—like they put him on leave while they investigate because it's an officer-involved shooting."

Still smiling, Jill said, "Like on the TV shows? No, this is different. A sniper wouldn't automatically be given time off with pay to investigate, because that's the entire point of his specialty. It's already been determined by calling SWAT that death is on the menu. A sniper shooting a bad guy just did his job."

"I had no idea. Scary."

"Yep, scary. But I'm sorry if it took away from our time together. Maybe we can get together on—"

"No, you don't owe me anything. I got what I wanted. I believe in my story now."

"You should. It's damn good."

That much was true. Jill really did like Susan's novel-in-progress. If she was being honest, Jill was actually a little jealous of the story Susan was building. It was about a little girl being raised by a single father who was a criminal. A hold-up man. Working his way up the crime ladder from knocking over convenience stores to armed robberies of liquor stores, to that "one big score" of robbing a bank. Sure, it was the clichéd stuff of genre fiction, but Susan had a knack for making it seem fresh. Something about the relationship between the girl and the father. The only real guidance that Jill had given tonight was to say that the father "was just a thug. Trash, really. Human trash." She was a cop's wife, and that's just the way she saw it. And the hurt she had seen in Susan's little possum eyes had been real. Her words had stung the girl. But that was just Jill's way. She was honest and blunt. And if the people around her didn't like it, well too fucking bad. Sorry, Charlie. Still, she was a good teacher, and her one rule in that regard was to follow up negative criticism with something positive. But the positive things had to be honest, too.

That hurt shining in her eyes, Susan was already opening her mouth to defend her work, her characters, but Jill held up a hand to stop her before she could speak.

"Wait. Wait a minute. The father is a thug whether you want to admit it or not. I'm sorry, but he is. I know he has his reasons for doing what he does, but all of them do. Listen. It's the little girl. Rose. It's Rose that redeems him. She's his soul. His conscience. Because of his love for her and her devotion to him, I find myself conflicted. You've stirred up emotions in me I didn't even know I had. Maternal feelings. What would a parent sacrifice for a child? What would a child forgive in a parent?"

The hurt and resentment faded from Susan's dark eyes. The flush faded from her cheeks. Jill had spoken the truth. And then Susan had curled over her laptop, clacking away, looking up only to catch glimpses of the real life drama unfolding on the television.

Now she saved the file and closed her laptop. "It won't take long at all to finish reworking these chapters. Do you think you could look them over and maybe give me feedback over coffee? My treat."

Jill was beginning to feel like she was spending too much time with Susan. Becoming a crutch for the girl. And she was about to say something to that effect, but Susan jumped in first, maybe even prefiguring what Jill was going to say.

"Of course I'll be paying for your time. It's worth every penny."

And damnit, why did it always come down to money? After years of bringing home a paycheck that was nearly equal to Jacob's, Jill still felt guilty about only being able to add just a little bit to their family income. It somehow made her feel *less than*. She wondered how Susan had so quickly zeroed in on her weak spot. It was probably obvious.

"Coffee sounds good," Jill said, and realized that she was making it sound more like a friendship than it really was. *Was she leading Susan on?*

Susan beamed and reached into her voluminous handbag— *her marsupial pouch,* Jill thought and smiled—and pulled out her date book.

"Is tomorrow too soon? I can finish the revisions tonight and e-mail them to you."

But Jill's attention was drawn by the sound of the key unlocking the front door. Jill snapped her own laptop shut and ran her fingers through her hair.

"Listen, Susan, it's getting late, but I'll see you in class, okay? We'll pick out a day for coffee."

That hurt look shone in Susan's eyes again, offended at her quick dismissal, because this wasn't how you ushered out a friend, it was the way you dismissed underlings in a business meeting. Jill couldn't stand that hurt look.

"Tomorrow. After class tomorrow is fine. E-mail me."

Now don't let the door hit you in the ass on your way out, Jill thought and immediately felt guilty. But at least the wounded look went away. Satisfaction glowed on Susan's face, but was soon replaced by awe and probably a touch of fear as Jacob Denton dragged himself into the room. He looked a bit haggard, spots of black face paint still ringing his eyes and nose. Jill wondered if he would be tired or horny later. Probably both, she decided.

She got up and hugged her husband tight. He hugged back.

When Jacob and Jill stood that close, their differences were striking. She only came up to chest level on him. Her eyes shone with curiosity and energy, where he projected a stoic demeanor.

"Hey handsome. I'm glad you're safe."

They parted, and Jacob took off his jacket and hung it on a nearby coat-tree. His duty belt with all of his police hardware was now visible.

"This is Susan Weaver, a student."

Jacob leaned down and offered his hand.

"Nice to meet you, Susan."

Susan stared at Jacob's huge, grimy hand, plainly afraid to put her own hand in his. Rather than offend, she shook his hand lightly, briefly.

"Sorry, I still need to clean up."

Susan scrambled from the floor, and scurried around Jacob. She seemed to be both fascinated and repulsed by the menagerie of cop hardware that he sported.

"No, I . . . I mean, you're fine, really. I just. I've gotta go, you know."

Once she had finally maneuvered herself around Jacob and was standing at the front door, she realized that she'd left her laptop back in the living room.

"Oh shit! I mean, crap. My, uh . . . My computer. If you could. You know what? I've gotta go. Jill, thanks again."

Jacob leaned down, retrieved the laptop, and took it to Susan. He held it out to her, and she seemed to be debating whether or not to accept it. She snatched it and said, "Thanks. Bye."

And with that Susan was out the door. Jill and Jacob stared at each other in complete silence.

"I take it you told her what it is I do for a living?"

Silence again.

Over the years, they had both seen this type of reaction too many times. A mixture of fear, curiosity, and repulsion. Some people freaked out if they met an undertaker. This was a similar phenomenon. It was irrational and ignorance-based, but the person couldn't help it. It was just a gut reaction.

On one memorable occasion, Jill and Jacob were at a New Year's Eve get-together with several other couples. At one point during the evening, it came up that in addition to being a deputy with the Sheriff's Department, Jacob was also the sniper on the department's SWAT team. Some of their friends knew this already, but some didn't. One couple, Jeff and Janice Stephens, did not know it. They were clearly distressed by the knowledge. Janice turned gray and looked like she was going to spew the bacon-wrapped cocktail weenies she'd been scarfing down all night. Jeff, with some half-assed look of moral superiority on his face, had said, "You kill people for a living?"

Jacob had nodded and said, "Yep, pretty much."

Jeff and Janice stuck around another five minutes or so, then mumbled an excuse, grabbed their coats, and hightailed it out of there.

They never saw the Stephens again. Ever.

Nowadays, when they socialized, it was with cops and cop wives. It was easier that way.

Jill nodded. "I told her."

Again, silence. Then she giggled. Jacob chuckled. Then they both burst out with laughter.

"It was on the news, what was I supposed to say? That I'm in love with Clark Avery?"

This sent Jill back into hiccups of laughter. Jacob moved into the kitchen and banged around in the cupboards, looking for something to snack on.

"I don't know. *Are* you in love with Clark Avery, the most dashing news correspondent since Anderson Cooper had his prematurely gray hair copyrighted?"

Jill got her laughter under control as it occurred to her that Jacob was the guy, the hero, who would take out a thug like the father in Susan's novel. She wondered if Susan had realized the same thing.

Jacob kept talking to her from the kitchen. "How was your day? Class went okay?"

"What can I say? They inspire me. I'm working on my own stuff, too."

"Ahh . . . a new novel, huh? Great."

Now there was another silence that was both comfortable and tinged with expectation. They still hadn't really talked about it yet. Not Jill's writing. But Jake's killing. Because that was the way they did it. They talked about it. It was kind of like a little magic trick they pulled off together. They made the abnormal seem normal. *Presto chango.*

"So what did Mr. Avery have to say?"

Jill sat down on the sofa and said, "Oh, the usual. Some SWAT guy got off a lucky shot."

The Bela Lugosi movie on TCM was still playing. Charles Laughton was in it, too. It was *Island of Lost Souls.* Laughton played a mad scientist trying to turn animals into people.

Jacob made his way back to the living room carrying a steaming cup of coffee and sat on the sofa next to Jill.

"I hope that's decaf."

Jacob took a careful sip and said, "It is."

On TV, Bela Lugosi was barely recognizable in his monster makeup. Half human, half beast.

"Why do you watch this old junk?"

"It's not junk. I just like old things. Like you."

Jacob grunted. At forty-five, he was ten years older than Jill.

"So . . . how are you?" *Let's make the abnormal normal.*

"I'm okay."

Jill ran her fingers through Jacob's hair.

"This was the seventeenth, right?"

Jacob shrugged. "Something like that."

"Dirt bag, or average Joe having a really shitty day?"

"A parolee who served time for rape, assault with intent, burglary." Jacob took a bigger sip of coffee. "Now a cop killer. Otherwise, a model citizen."

Jill's hand rested on Jacob's shoulder. He took her hand and noticed the nails had been beautifully manicured and painted—a healthy coral pink with white tips.

"And how much did these cost?"

"Cost to you: zero. I did it myself. It's called a French manicure."

"Nice."

"Did you know the suspect you shot?"

"No."

"Did you know Carpenter well?"

"No, just in passing. Cowell and Heidler knew him better, so it was harder for them, I'm sure."

"A brother is a brother is a brother. I'll send his family flowers. I'm very proud of you."

Jacob leaned his head onto Jill's head.

"Thanks. I think."

"You think? We'll have none of that. If you're starting to think too hard about what you do or why you do it, then it's time to get out of this line of work."

"You're rougher on me than my teammates."

"That's because they're all afraid of you, sweetheart, and I'm not."

Jacob raised up, kissed her forehead and smiled.

She held him at arm's length and asked, "Are we clear?"

It was a line from *A Few Good Men*. And they used it privately to make sure they were each okay. That whatever bump they had navigated around was safely behind them.

Jake gave the correct answer. He said, "Crystal."

"Good, because the rest of us need guys like you out there watching over us. I feel safer already."

Jill cuddled close to him again.

"You're very good at this."

"Can I show you something I'm even better at?"

"Sure, teacher. Give me a minute."

Jacob set the coffee cup on the table, and headed for the bedroom.

Jill grabbed the coffee for herself. She settled back into the couch and took a sip. She was pretty sure it was the regular caffeinated brew. She could tell. The decaf just didn't taste the same. Oh well. It didn't really matter. All that mattered was that the wand had been waved. *Presto chango. Alakazam.* The magic was done. The abnormal was now normal.

They were clear. Crystal.

She turned up the volume on the movie. She liked this part. Charles Laughton had just confessed that he was creating the beast men as evolutionary experiments, and he asked the young guy who was stranded on the island, "Do you know what it means to feel like God?" Rob Zombie had made a song using that line. Jill liked Rob Zombie. She liked this movie, too. But she did not know that Donovan "The Builder" Carpenter and a petty criminal whose meth-fouled mind had driven him to the worst crime of all, had both had this phrase in their heads earlier tonight.

In the bedroom, Jacob opened the door of the walk-in closet that he and Jill shared. He retrieved a small lockbox from a high shelf. It had been concealed under a stack of sweaters he seldom wore. The shelf was too high for Jill to be able to see what was on it, much less use. He supposed that if she wanted to she could stand on a chair to snoop around. To see if he kept anything up there besides seasonal clothes and boxes of ammunition. But Jill wasn't like that. And he supposed that if she found the lockbox in the midst of an uncharacteristic fit of spring cleaning, that it could intrigue her enough to ask him what was in it. But Jill wasn't like that. And he further supposed that if Jill somehow stumbled across the box, asked him about it, and wasn't satisfied with his answer, she could wait until he was asleep and locate the key on his key ring (he hadn't married a stupid woman—far from it) and unlock the box so that she could see for herself what it held. But Jill wasn't like that.

Jacob took the metal box with him into the master bathroom and locked the door.

He turned on the shower. He told himself it was to let the water get hot, but really he knew it was to mask his sounds in case Jill came into the bedroom.

He unlocked the box and pulled out the only thing it contained. A small nylon drawstring bag. It was an old jewelry pouch. But this bag did not contain jewelry. Well, of a sort, perhaps.

Jacob loosened the drawstring and dumped the contents onto the vanity, where the spent cartridge shells it contained tumbled and clattered. Even though there was no reason to do so, Jacob counted them. Of course he knew how many there were. There were sixteen of them. Jacob reached into his pants pocket and pulled out the shell from that night's kill. He studied it a moment as though the object might impart some hitherto unconsidered insight or wisdom. But it did not. He then tossed it on the counter where it dinged and danced before settling with the others. He considered his macabre collection for a moment, perhaps in the hope that if a single brass shell would not give up its secrets, then as a group, they might have something to say. But they did not.

He wasn't even sure why he saved them, what they represented to him. Maybe they were souls of the people he had killed. But souls should get lighter, not heavier. These were more like links in a chain. They were heavy, weighing him down, dragging him under. If he kept adding to it, the chain might eventually break him.

Then again, that could all just be a load of bullshit.

He scooped them up and returned them to the bag, and returned the bag to the box. He locked the box.

In the mirror, he watched his reflection as it was swallowed by the white steam from the shower.

The movie was over, and Jill had switched out the coffee for wine. She had a glass for each of them on the living room table. She took a sip from her glass and looked up to see Jacob framed in the bedroom doorway. Freshly scrubbed and wearing nothing except a towel wrapped around his middle.

Jill went to him and moved into his open arms. They kissed. She yanked off his towel and held it up to him.

"Lesson one. Lose the towel."

CHAPTER 5

The squad room was filled with regular duty officers pouring cups of morning coffee and taking seats for roll call. Those who also happened to serve on the SWAT team were here on little or no sleep. They had the option of taking the day off, but preferred to get the hours. Overtime was scarce.

Sergeant Heidler sat at the front desk writing on a clipboard. Cowell's diagram from last night's debriefing was still on the blackboard.

Jacob grabbed some coffee and pulled out a chair next to Kathryn, who looked up, quite bright-eyed and bushy-tailed.

"Hey partner. Short night, huh? Did you sleep? I couldn't sleep. I was still so pumped from last night."

"Are you always like this?"

"Like what?"

Jacob stared at Kathryn.

"Eager. Are you always this eager?"

"Hell yes. Thought that was why you picked me for your team."

"Eager is not a desirable trait for a sniper. Think about it."

At the front, Heidler said, "All right ladies and gentlemen, listen up."

The room fell silent. Kathryn leaned closer to Jacob and whispered, "So why'd you pick me?"

Jacob ignored her.

Heidler continued, "Let's get through these items quickly so you can all get right out onto the streets to maximize those taxpayer dollars."

There were a couple of chuckles and a few groans from the officers.

"First item. We've had another death threat on Captain Bryant."

Several officers raised their hands or nodded.

"That was me."

"Right here."

"I did it."

Heidler ignored them.

"This latest threat now includes his family."

This sobered them up. Violence and the possibility of a violent death was the day-to-day reality of these men and women. They accepted it. They made light of it. It was the life they had chosen. Families, though, were off limits.

"Let's step up those extra patrols around the captain's house. If you're not on a call, swing by."

Heidler flipped a page on his clipboard and continued.

"As most of you already know, our SWAT team had a call-out last night where they effectively neutralized one more menace to society, thereby making the world a safer place for all of us."

This earned some non-ironic hoots, whistles, and applause from everyone but the perpetually sour Deputy Billy Simon, a tall, gangly cop whose duty belt seemed to weigh more than he did. Simon had applied for SWAT three times, specifically as a spotter—a sniper in training—and had three times been turned down. Simon was a hell of a shot, an amazing shot, maybe even better than Jacob, but as Jacob had told Lieutenant Cowell, marksmanship was only half of it. Probably less than half.

The latest insult, for Simon, had been when Sesak was taken in from another jurisdiction, and brought on the team as a spotter. It truly was a slap in the face. Simon had taken to needling Jacob, both out of resentment at not being accepted to the team, and as proof to the others that he was not scared or intimidated by Jacob Denton.

"Hey, Fuckin'Denton, how many notches on the old gunstock is that anyway?"

Jacob ignored him. Everybody called him Fuckin'Denton, but Simon always gave it an extra little sneer the way he said it.

Deputy Hank Baker slid a piece of paper and a pen toward Kathryn and asked, "Can I have your autograph?"

Kathryn started to take the pen, but Jacob grabbed her hand. The officers erupted in laughter. Deputy Simon stood up.

"Now boys, this is no laughing matter. Suppose our friend Deputy Denton here should snap," Simon said, snapping his fingers to illustrate the point. "Like our last sniper did? It could get ugly."

Jacob's jaw tightened. Kathryn glanced from Jacob to Simon, and the look on her face made it clear she didn't know what Simon was talking about.

"You haven't heard this? You're kidding. That last sniper we had, what the hell was his name?"

"Lee Staley," Baker said. "Oz."

"Right. Oswald."

"Oswald?" Kathryn asked.

Simon said, "Lee Staley. Lee Harvey Oswald. Get it? As in crazy motherfucker with a gun."

Jacob glared at Simon. He was getting pissed. Oz was family as far as Jacob was concerned. And you don't fuck with a man's family.

Heidler, who gave his deputies a great deal of latitude during these roll calls, felt the atmosphere darken.

"Boys. Play nice."

Simon said, "Hey Sergeant, I think Sesak should hear this."

Baker agreed and said, "Sure she should. Nice and quick, eh, Sarge?"

Simon launched into it before Heidler could say one way or the other. "Oswald's on this routine call-out, right? Hostage situation, gun to some lady's head. He gets the green light, takes the shot, hits the suspect, but . . ."

"But what?"

Simon made a gun of his thumb and forefinger and placed it against Kathryn's temple.

"But the suspect's hand jerked when the bullet hit him and he pulled the trigger anyway."

Simon pulled the trigger on his pretend gun, his hand rocking in mock recoil hard enough to pivot Sesak's head.

"Blew her fucking brains all over her color-coordinated kitchen."

Kathryn looked to Jacob for confirmation. He shrugged. It was true.

The squad room was quiet now. Jacob tapped his right trigger finger on the table. It sounded like a metronome.

Jacob looked at Simon and said, "Feel better?"

Simon didn't answer, but he closed his hand and put it in his pocket. He'd fallen under Jacob's sniper glare. All that could be heard was the tapping of Jacob's trigger finger.

Baker said, "Hell, Denton, it happened. You can't deny Oswald lost his mind after that. They had to retire him."

Simon said, "Seems a hell of a lot more natural than someone who can kill like—"

Heidler had had enough and said, "Simon, will you shut the fuck up for Chrissakes?" He turned to Kathryn and said, "And that's why we call Billy here Simple Simon."

"Yeah, well, Simon says every last one of you can kiss my ass."

Heidler let it go and said, "All right, enough of this bullshit. Next item is serious. I'm sure everyone also knows that we lost an officer last night. His name was Donovan Carpenter. Patrolled Zone Four, graveyard. I knew him, and I'm sure some of you did, too. He was a good cop. I'm taking up the collection for his family."

Heidler held up an empty coffee can.

"I expect every one of you to give and give big."

Most all of the deputies unlimbered their wallets and formed a line in front of Heidler.

CHAPTER 6

Kathryn drove the patrol unit, and Jacob rode shotgun.

"How come you never told me?"

"We're scheduled for sniper training later today. Did you bring your gear?"

"Yeah, I brought my fucking gear. Did you hear what I said?"

"I heard you."

"Well?"

"It wasn't something you needed to know. Take a right at the next light."

"One of your partners goes 51–50, out on a psych retirement and you didn't think I needed to know?"

Not even a shrug.

"I don't get you at all. Fuckin'Denton."

"You wouldn't be the first."

When the unit stopped at a traffic light, Jacob turned to look at Kathryn.

"Do you realize that what you've decided to do with your life is kill people?"

"Yeah, bad guys."

"Killing's killing."

"Well, goddamn, Captain Sunshine, no wonder your partners flake out."

Jacob cracked a smile at that.

"Green light."

"What do you mean?"

"The light. It's green."

Kathryn looked ahead, then started forward but caught herself and turned right. She could have turned right on the red in California, but she had been focusing on Jake's words.

"If I was driving and you told me the light was green, I wouldn't have checked to be sure. That's the kind of relationship we need to have."

"I get you. And it's not like I want to kill people."

"You don't? That's what we do. You better want to do it. Turn left here."

Morgan City abruptly faded, and the environment shifted from city to country. No buffer. They were heading into Vista Canyon.

"Aren't we supposed to be patrolling Zone Six? We're going the wrong way."

"Extra patrol for Bryant or did you just not listen to briefing? Bad sign. Too much in your head at once?"

Now Kathryn went silent. Busted.

Jacob hated going into Vista Canyon on patrol. A lot of it had to do with Jill's tree. But the tree was just a symbol of what was wrong here. He found Vista Canyon to be a bizarre collection of strip malls and banks and rich-people mansions all in a country setting, but their owners failed to notice that those expensive houses were of generic cookie cutter designs and packed into the canyon merely a few feet apart. Tenements for the wealthy. Tract housing for the upper echelons of management.

This was where Sacramento County yielded to Cameron County, with Folsom a mile back, just over the county line. The canyon was a wedge of prime real estate where Sacramento people moved to feel rugged and rural, and Morgan City people moved to feel suburban and affluent. Folsomites were quite happy where they were.

For police management like Captain Bryant, who called Vista Canyon home, that address on the mailbox came with the knowledge that though they were still county employees, they had reached a new plateau.

Jacob genuinely hated it here. It was the rich people who always gave him the most trouble. They were the ones who complained about stuff that wasn't important and never failed to tell responding officers, "I pay your salary! You work for me! You tell those kids in that cul-de-sac to stop playing basketball!" Jacob would rather have dealt with the *Deliverance*-people in the high country than face rich-people condescension any day.

Most of the upper echelon moved to this suburb as they were promoted to ranks like detective sergeant, or lieutenant and on up—whether they could afford it or not. Vista Canyon was still technically within their jurisdiction, but it couldn't have been further away from its Gold Country roots.

Still, Captain Bryant lived here and Jacob would never forget a former SWAT team member, no matter what. He would have headed this way without the sergeant's order. They were like the military in that way. A brotherhood of the elite few.

"What I'm saying is I've got a skill that I want to put to good use. We're the good guys, they're the bad guys. You don't need a philosophy degree to figure it out. It's pretty cut and dried."

"Do you have any idea how many guys on the job can plug a dime at one hundred yards? That 'skill' is common as dirt. Except that they're shooting at targets. We're shooting at people. It's what's going on up here that matters. You shoot with your head, not your heart."

"That makes no sense. I shoot with my eye and my finger. What does my heart have to do with anything?"

"It means the second you start thinking about it, you overthink it. The guy in your sights, does he deserve to die? Does he have a family? What led to this? And what about the times the situation changes a split second before you fire? Because that can happen. What if the guy gives up just as you've started to squeeze the trigger? Another second and you would have ended his life. It can be that close. And you might spend your evening thinking about the other times you've put down a target, and you'll wonder, what if I'd waited just a second longer? He might've given up. But what if you'd waited that extra second, and the hostage died? The 'what-if's' will eat at you."

He could see Kathryn was at least considering what he was

saying. It wasn't really Jacob's nature to get mystical, Master Po and Grasshopper, but he'd had a variation of this conversation with every spotter he'd ever worked with.

"And thinking about the hostage can paralyze you completely. Once you're in your heart, you're done. Yes, sometimes you've got clear-cut bad guys. The true predators. The wolves. Then you've got the Average Joe just having a really shitty day. What about him? Are you okay with taking out somebody's jealous husband who's never been violent before? Are you gonna feel okay running a bullet through somebody's grandpa who's having a bad reaction to his antibiotics?"

"So it's not always cut and dried."

"It's not your job to decide. Some asshole pulls a gun on you, it's kill or be killed. Self-preservation. And still there are some guys who can't handle even that. There are some cops who shoot a suspect in the line of duty. A clean shot. And they never come back from it. This is the deliberate targeting of a human being and keeping him in your crosshairs anywhere from ten seconds to ten days. You never know when that green light is coming. You've got plenty of time to wonder if maybe you should've gotten that philosophy degree after all."

Ahead, at the curb of one of the slightly less pretentious homes, Jacob saw a yellow school bus pulling up to the figure of a man and two children. Captain Bryant seeing his kids off to school. Jacob indicated to Sesak that this was their destination.

The school bus pulled away. Bryant saw the patrol car and waited in his driveway.

Kathryn parked the unit. She approached Bryant first and shook his hand.

"Good morning, sir. I trust your morning has been uneventful."

Bryant took her hand warmly in two of his own.

"How could it be anything but, when I've got goddamn suck-up cops stopping at my house every three minutes?"

Bryant let Kathryn squirm for a second then erupted in laughter.

"Sorry, Sesak, I couldn't resist." He winked at Jacob over Kathryn's head. "The first female candidate on the sniper team? You gotta expect a hard time from the old boys like myself. Jacob, it's good to see you."

They shook hands.

"So, this is the greener grass I've heard so much about," Jacob said, as though he'd never been out to the canyon before. Where they were standing, everything was flat and green and new. A bit off in the distance, some older growth trees and brush fringed the ridges that surrounded the small valley.

"Yeah, and it cost me a hundred bucks a square foot for this fucking sod. Now I've got Folsom Prison in my backyard and assholes all around me. I'd go back up country if I could afford it."

Jacob said, "Yeah, Jill is still pissed about her tree." He walked a few feet away, pointed, and said, "In fact, I think it was right about there, wasn't it, Sesak?"

"Looks right to me," she said, even though she had no idea what he was talking about.

Bryant just shook his head. "She knows I couldn't control that. Doesn't she?"

Jill never failed to point it out each time they passed by. It had been visible from Highway 50. Up on a small rise overlooking Sacramento in a large golden meadow (the "Golden State" really meant dry, dead, combustible grass each fire season) had been an ancient Valley oak, perfectly shaped, nobly present, and with a stone fence marking a boundary from the distant past. It was a living remnant of an era of fortune hunting and staked claims. What remained from settlers making a go of it, panning for pay dirt, seeking their fortunes and guarding their turf and livestock with stone and lead, not wire and plot easements. It had been a beacon for her. A place she sought out to gather her thoughts and center her mind. To commune with the past.

Then one day she had seen the usual bulldozer-wide "fire line" made in all such areas after the green meadows turned gold each year. As a former firefighter, Jill thought the fire lines were ridiculous, because for the break to work, it needed to be one and a half times the height of the fuel. With dry grass several feet tall, as in this case, a fire line the width of a single dozer blade would never stop a fire from spreading. It was just a token effort. What had caught Jill's eye was the fact the bulldozer not only remained parked nearby, but it was between two other large, earth-moving machines.

It marked the beginning of the end for her. To her dismay, she watched as the ground was razed and stripped of any and all life—including her beloved Valley oak—in order to build yet another subdivision. Now Jill refused to come here and simply gave the area a double-barreled middle-finger salute whenever they drove by. She would not condone the insanity of ripping up perfectly aged trees only to plant new ones. She was holding a grudge on this one, and rightly so, Jacob reckoned.

But Jill, being Jill, made a joke of it, too. *Come to California,* she would say in the seductive tone of a tourist board commercial. *Come to California. If you see something you like, we'll cut it down, or blow it up.*

Come to California.

Sesak was enjoying the captain's discomfort and said, "I heard she's still pretty pissed. You're right on her tree!"

Bryant gave Sesak a look that told her she was close to overstepping her position. In fact, he was finished indulging both of them. He said, "Jacob, take a look at this," and pulled something from his pocket. He looked back over his shoulder as he handed it to Jacob.

"Found it in my mailbox. I haven't told Liz."

It was a small plastic bag. An evidence bag. Jacob took it to get a better look, but he had known immediately what the baggie contained. He ought to. It was a single cartridge. It could've been from his personal supply.

"That's a .308 caliber, Federal Match round," Sesak said.

She knew her shit, Jacob had to give her that. The Federal Match, right out of the box, was department standard for snipers. Officially, it was what Jacob fired from his Remington 700. It was what most snipers preferred—.308 with Federal Match casings and 168g Sierra Hollow Point Boat Tail bullets in them. A few holdouts still shot .223 caliber, which was great for short-range situations, but Jacob found their lack of stopping power and tendency to splinter on impact too great a liability.

For snipers, ammunition was a fetish, and Jacob was no exception. He studied and kept himself informed. He knew that the recent military engagements in Afghanistan and Iraq had encouraged a compromise between the .50 cal and a .308. The .50 caliber was a heavy and bulky rifle to carry, so the military had gone to a smaller round, a .338 Lapua, that while smaller, outdistanced and outperformed the larger .50 caliber in active combat duty.

He'd fired them all, but Jacob's purest sniper dream would be the .338 Lapua for its long-range performance, but his locale and demographics—his hunting ground—made it impractical for his normal SWAT duties. The department was worried enough about liability without added caliber and the potential for collateral damage.

Jacob handed it back.

"I'll drop it off at Science on my way in," Bryant said. Through the plastic, he held the brass cartridge upright between thumb and forefinger, studying it, as though he might be able to see any fingerprints with his naked eyes.

As he held the large .308 cartridge up to the lighted blue sky, Bryant's hand exploded in a red mist. At least that's what it looked like.

Any other observer would have thought the live round had simply exploded in Bryant's hand, but Jacob had heard the crack of a rifle report that directly followed it—a bullet moving faster than the speed of sound had struck the cartridge in the captain's grasp. He knew they were being fired upon. Instinct took over, and he dove for cover. The patrol car was closest. Sesak scrambled as well, huddling against the lee of the car.

Bryant remained standing. It was the goddamndest thing Jacob had ever seen in his life. And Jacob Denton had seen some crazy shit. Bryant was standing stock-still, holding what was left of his hand out in front of him, staring at the bright red blood pulsing from the stubs of his missing thumb and first two fingers.

"Sir! Take cover!"

Kathryn had climbed into the floorboard of the cruiser and was yelling into the radio, "11-99! Shots fired! Officer down!"

No, he's not quite down, Jacob thought as he drew his .45 automatic and craned his head over and around the patrol car, scanning the wooded ridges, trying to determine the origin of the shot, aware that Bryant was still standing there, dumbfounded, staring at his hand.

"Sir! Captain Bryant, Sir! Take cover! Ben! Take cover!"

Bryant still wasn't responding. Jacob put one foot forward, readying himself to spring out from behind the car and take Bryant down and drag him to safety. But just as soon as he put that foot forward, a bullet tore up the ground at his boot. Jacob recoiled.

Another shot and Bryant's left ear came off as cleanly as a surgeon's slice. Blood poured down the side of his face. But the man still wasn't moving. Against all reason, he remained standing. He was in shock. Jacob scanned the hillside, the pockets of vegetation, estimated the distance, and thought of the calculations that would go into making a shot like that at that distance. The wind today was intermittent. Not easy to prefigure. Jacob knew that. He was always aware of the current wind speeds, the direction. That was part of his life. The temperature. Humidity. They all factored in. The intimacy with your rifle. Knowing it. The difference between a cold barrel shot and a hot barrel shot. All of this went through his mind in less than a second. As he considered his enemy. For there was an enemy out there. They were under attack. By either an amazingly good or amazingly lucky sniper. The shooter wasn't missing his killshot. He was picking Bryant apart. And the groundshot had been a warning to Jacob. Stay back.

He was about to attempt another lunge at Bryant, but another crack of rifle thunder rolled through the canyon. Jacob could not see where it struck the man, but the bullet spun him around and brought him to his knees. Then he saw. The lower half of Bryant's jaw was gone. Jacob could see his upper teeth and his exposed tongue working back and forth. The upper teeth must have been dentures, because they fell out of his ruined mouth and landed softly in the plush carpet of Bermuda grass that Bryant kept watered and green.

Behind him, Jacob heard Sesak let out a sound that was not quite a scream.

The next bullet grazed Bryant's scalp, splitting it like the skin of a late summer muscadine. A huge flap of scalp—gray hair clinging to it—drooped down like loathsome bunting, obscuring Bryant's horror-show face. The last shot took off the top of the captain's skull, cracking and peeling it back like the shell of a perfectly boiled egg, with most of his brain going with it.

Ending everything.

The man was angry at losing another sheep. But he was more angry at having let his emotion affect his shooting. He had stemmed the anger the way a tourniquet stems the flow of blood. But a little still seeped through. He was getting old. He would teach the boy before he was too old to be any good to anybody.

They trudged forward. Breaking snow.

The animal was losing a lot of blood. The father's shot had not been perfect, it had not been Godly, but it had wounded the Gray Wolf, almost certainly gravely. There was too much red blood on the white snow. The animal could not survive. It was looking for a place to die.

On another day, if he had been alone, the man would have let the animal be. He would have turned back to the warmth of his home and his wife's coffee. The animal was dead. It just didn't know it yet. He could have gone back home without guilt. Only regret for not killing the wolf cleanly.

But the boy could learn.

Ahead, they could see the animal. The wolf had stopped. It was resting. The man moved forward with caution. He knew that no matter how close to death the animal might be, it would use any last vestige of life left in it to turn and attack.

He hunkered down next to the boy and pointed. He watched

and nodded his approval at the boy's stance as he raised the weapon, the comb to his cheek, the butt snug to his shoulder, so that the telescopic sight fell in line with his eye.

The .22 was just a toy, really. Against a Gray Wolf, it was just a toy. But the animal was wounded, damn near dead. The .22 would suffice. The boy had to learn.

"Aim with your head, not with your heart."

"I don't understand that." The boy had learned to always be honest with his father. It was better.

"You will. Remember, when you're ready, half breath out and hold."

The boy nodded minutely. His eyes took on a haunted, depth-less look. The father knew that the boy had gone down the rabbit hole.

"You're ready." An echo from the outside world. Green light.

He squeezed the trigger. The barrel recoiled up and to the right.

The report was tiny but still shocking and lonely in the mountains. Out of place somehow.

The wolf jumped several feet in the air, and then was gone, as though it had never been there. Except for the red snow.

Father and son took off in pursuit, their breath ragged in the frigid morning air.

They came upon the place where the wolf had been. The blood patch.

"I'm sorry. I missed."

"You didn't."

The man pointed up ahead, and the boy saw that there were

now two parallel blood trails. Close together, but distinct. He'd hit it after all. The wolf was twice wounded.

Father and son kept after the animal.

The man was amazed that the wolf could still move. That much blood, he thought. He had already respected the wolf. Had felt anger toward it. Now he felt another, less common emotion.

They pursued.

CHAPTER 7

The ridge overlooking Captain Bryant's Vista Canyon neighborhood was clotted with dense pockets of red-barked manzanita, sharp-bladed tall grass, and live oaks—providing ample cover for his killer. Jacob knew it was the kind of terrain firefighters hated. The tall grass could get as high as three feet, and it only stayed green for about three weeks. Then it was golden brown. Just ready for a spark. Manzanita burned longer and hotter than other shrubbery, stubbornly refusing to succumb to the water. And yet it provided perfect cover for anyone who could crawl under and into the heart of it. Once there, the manzanita itself provided a canopy of concealment.

On the ridge, two deputies strung crime scene tape around trees in an area Jacob and Kathryn had scouted out, marking it as the secondary crime scene. Technicians from Science Division were en route, as were homicide detectives. The news vans wouldn't be far behind.

Jacob and Lieutenant Cowell hunkered to the ground to peer

down the hillside toward Bryant's house. Kathryn stood behind them.

"The shooter could have ended it in one shot," Jacob said. "But he shot the cartridge in Bryant's hand first. That was purposeful. The shot in the ground was to warn me back. All the rest of it was just torture by bullet."

Cowell asked, "Why?"

The two men looked at each other. Jacob shrugged.

Kathryn said, "Maybe he was showing off?"

Cowell grunted. Noncommittal. He thought more about it, then said, "For Jacob?"

The two men exchanged another look. She was right on the money.

"Our counter-snipers are anonymous. Nobody knows who they are. It's unlikely the shooter would know Denton was anything but another officer checking on the captain. And why would the shooter want to show off?"

"To make me think he's better than I am," Jacob said. He already believed Kathryn was right. It had been a show.

Jacob lay on his stomach, facing down the hill, over the ridge. Below, he could see detectives, a CSI van, gloved men in suits, and police tape at the primary crime scene.

"Based on the trajectory, I'd say he shot from up here somewhere."

Jacob slid over a few feet.

"If it were me, I'd shoot from right here."

Jacob held his arms out in front of him as if holding his own weapon. He looked to his right.

"Here we go."

Jacob got up, took a pen from his pocket and inserted it into the end of a shell casing on the ground. Once he had it, he rotated the pen in his hand, examining the casing from different angles.

"Looks to be the same ammo we use, L.T., Federal Match casing, and probably a Sierra Boat Tail bullet. When we recover one of the bullets on the scene, I'll know for sure."

"Why Sierras?"

"Because that's what all the cool kids shoot."

Off in the distance, they could hear the low, almost tribal sound of rotor blades beating the air. News choppers.

"Just the one casing? He fired, what, six rounds?"

"Six, yes sir." Jacob looked around. "I only see the one. I'm sure Science will bring metal detectors. But I doubt they'll find any more. The single casing was probably left on purpose. The shooter is far too disciplined to be messy."

Kathryn pulled an evidence bag from her pocket, and Jacob dropped the casing inside. Cowell reached for the bag and said, "We should keep this to ourselves. Just for a bit."

"Why?" Kathryn asked.

"It's one of our own."

"Hold on. That's a hell of a jump. All I said was it's the same ammo. Any hunter can buy it."

"It's one of us."

"How, L.T.?"

"The marksmanship, the ballistics, the target, the note."

"Note?"

"Earlier today. Said Bryant should never have given the

green light. That he should have known what would happen. The term 'green light' was specifically used."

"You have someone in mind?" Jacob asked, but of course he knew the answer. He'd been thinking the same thing, long before it occurred to Cowell. Maybe ever since the second bullet went in the ground at his feet, warning him off.

"I do."

"You're wrong."

"Why is it his name came to your mind, too?"

"Not Lee Staley. No."

"It got pretty ugly at the end. It might be you next."

"That's not going to happen."

"The man has a grudge. And you took his job."

"Oz didn't do this."

Kathryn's radio crackled to life in the background. She spoke into her shoulder mic and had to raise her voice to be heard above the helicopters now overhead. She turned to Jacob.

"SWAT activation."

The homicide detectives would be handling this case from here on out, so even though he wanted to, Jacob had no real reason to stay. He realized this was going to be one hell of a long day.

CHAPTER 8

Wallace Biggsby was a good man. All of his life, he had been a good man. He prayed to God. He was true to his wife. He was an attentive, involved father to his children. He worked hard at his job. He was a manager at McDonald's. Not a shift manager, but a restaurant manager. And he had every expectation that within three years he would be promoted to district manager, with fourteen restaurants under him. This was not the kind of career path people went on Facebook and posted about so all their high school friends could see. But Wallace Biggsby didn't care. Wallace Biggsby did not have a Facebook account.

But soon, the Internet would be buzzing about Wallace. Social pages would be updated with breathless posts of *I was in grade school with that guy, he used to pick his nose and wipe boogers on his Toughskins.* Wallace would be summed up in 140 characters or less: *Dude, that guy is my boss. Total dick. Always knew he would snap.* In fact, in just a few hours, Wallace Biggsby would be trending on Twitter.

She said she was going to leave him. That she was taking the kids and going. She wanted more from life. That they weren't right for each other. They'd grown apart.

She didn't come right out and say it, but he knew the grease smell bothered her, too. No matter how often he bathed, Wallace always smelled vaguely of deep fryer oil and the reconstituted onions used on the hamburgers and Big Macs. They used to joke about it. It was cute. But she never kidded him about it anymore. He knew that she had grown to hate the way he smelled. It was a symbol to her. It was everything that was wrong in their lives.

She said he didn't love her anymore. He was distant.

Distant? Well of course he was distant. He was working his fucking—*forgive me, Lord*—ass off to support her and the children. He was away working himself to death dealing with acne-faced teenagers who had zero respect for anything in this world. So yes, he was distant.

He was not going to let her take his children and leave him. He was not going to let another man step into his life and be a husband to his wife and a father to his children. A man who in all likelihood would not smell of grease and onions. A man with ambitions. Wallace could not abide that.

Working fast food didn't mean you weren't ambitious. A lot of famous people have worked at McDonald's. It's true. Jeff Bezos. Jay Leno. Sharon Stone. James Franco had worked the drive-thru, and Star Jones had gone from fry cook to cashier. It didn't have to be a dead-end job. Wallace knew he would likely never get his own talk show or found a Web-based multinational company. But he could be a district manager. He knew he had that in him.

Ellen said he'd changed. That he was a different person now. Well, didn't she think she'd changed, too?

He had images of pushing Ellen's head into a vat of boiling oil. See if she still wanted to leave him then. And that violent thought had made him feel good. He was a good man having bad thoughts. He thought of the gun hidden in his closet in a box marked *TAX DOCUMENTS*. He retrieved the gun. The gun made him feel powerful. In control.

He walked down the hall of his red brick ranch-style house, holding the gun at his side. It was a .38. He'd bought it for protection.

He opened the door to Christopher's bedroom. It was empty. Stripped of everything. Carly's bedroom was the same. Barren. And his and Ellen's room. Empty. She'd robbed him. He had nothing. They were gone. Ellen had taken the children and left him.

He wanted to die. Was ready to die. Fuck it. Fuck it all. Fuck the grease, fuck the teenagers, fuck the district manager position, fuck Ellen, fuck living. And fuck God. That's right. Fuck every last motherfucking motherfucker in the motherfucking world. Fuck it. Just fuck it.

He was going to shoot himself. A bullet right through his brain. That's what he told the 911 dispatcher. He just needed a little help.

He was a good man.

#wallacebiggsby was trending.

•   •   •

They were in position. Belly down on a hilltop amongst a patch of prickly yellow star thistle. The sun beat down on them, baking them in their brown and tan desert BDUs. They watched the modest brick ranch house below. It looked just like the other houses in the neighborhood, except there were several patrol cars parked in front of it.

"Okay. We've got this guy contained with the perimeter team. He's armed, but has no hostages. Our job here is to provide high cover while the negotiators try to talk him out of the house."

"Well, at least it gets us out of training in this heat."

"Training isn't a chore. It's what keeps you alive. This will probably be over in about fifteen minutes."

Jacob's mind was consumed with the shooting death of Captain Bryant. And he couldn't help but believe that the showmanship aspect of it had been intended for him alone. The sniper could have taken Bryant out with a single shot—*done in one*—while he waited for the school bus with his children. Or likely a thousand other times before that moment. Jacob knew. A sniper did not just climb a hill and pop off a shot thirty minutes later. That's not the way it worked. A sniper located his target or the place that target was likely to appear. Then the sniper staked out a position above his target, in this case the crest overlooking Bryant's house in Vista Canyon. He would probably assume a position on his belly, setting the bipod on his weapon. The bipod was collapsible so it folded flat against the gun while in transit, and was then flipped out to hold the barrel up while the back end, the stock, was on the ground, or nestled into the sniper's shoulder. Without the bipod extended, the barrel was always lower than the target, and thus below the point of aim a little.

Once in this position you could see a sniper settle and melt into his weapon. They became one. Breathing changed, everything.

But there was work that went into making a shot before the rifle was even taken out of its case or sheath. In larger jurisdictions with heavy gang, drug, prostitution, fugitive hunts, etc., law enforcement sharpshooters were always absorbing information. Up until the point they jumped down the rabbit hole, they were diagramming houses and buildings, sketching the geography and physical layout of the property. How many ways in and out were there? What does the target person drive? Which vehicles never move? What's his routine? What was the collateral risk? Who comes and goes? The variables were endless. Human behavior, the way your target held his body, the way he walked, swung his arms, the rhythm of his gait. There were facial recognition points, in case someone grew a beard or shaved one off, cut their hair, or had extensions put in, or simply put on big sunglasses and a floppy hat.

Collateral concerns. Were there kids in the house? Is the target guy actually there or did he just leave? Is it safer to stop him on the road or wait until he comes back to the house? It all evolves and changes as the sniper hunts and stalks. It was better with an observer, a spotter. The observer just keeps eyes on everything. But it felt unlikely Bryant's shooter had a partner. And of course the sniper has to be invisible, too. Ghillie suits were good for that. For invisibility.

Assigned to guard a witness, Jacob had once built a hollow metal air-conditioning unit on the roof of a building across the street from the store of the man he'd been charged with protecting. He sat in the metal box for three days and kept eyes on a high traffic area where the stakes were much higher for civilian interaction. He never pulled the trigger, and no one ever knew he had even been there.

"How do you know this'll be over in fifteen minutes?"

"He's the one who called 911."

Kathryn cupped her hand over her ear.

"Copy. Suspect to exit by the front door. Team Two ready and in position."

Jacob looked at Kathryn and raised an eyebrow. Then returned to the rifle scope and lost himself.

Kathryn said, "So? Even a stopped clock is right twice a day."

Her tone changed to all-business. "Front door opening. He's coming out."

The front door swung wide. The man had one hand behind his back.

"Gun," Kathryn said.

"I see it."

Kathryn thumbed her mic.

"Suspect has a gun in his right hand. Handgun. In suspect's right hand."

Below them, Wallace Biggsby strolled out onto the front walk. He stopped about halfway and closed his eyes. Clinched. Like he was gathering courage. He brought the weapon out from behind his back and put the barrel in his mouth. He pulled back the hammer. And held that pose, shaking.

Kathryn and Jacob could hear the shouts from below, the clearest being Billy Simon, "Drop the weapon and put your hands in the air!"

Wallace opened his eyes. He uncocked the gun and pulled it out of his mouth, trailing stringers of saliva. Tears smearing his cheeks, he gestured with the gun—toward the police on the street, in his front lawn. The blue line ebbed back.

"He's brought the gun out."

"I can see that."

"You've got the green. Men are in danger."

Jacob simply stared through the scope, finger on the trigger.

Biggsby now held the gun down, at his side. He stared at the police presence the way an animal will look at humans that are watching it in a zoo—with mild curiosity.

Now Baker's voice was prominent. "Drop the gun and put your hands in the air. Do it now!"

Jacob had the man in his sights. Caught in his reticle. His finger resting lightly on the trigger. It would be an easy shot. Cold barrel. No wind. No obstructions. No known collateral.

The man wiped his tears with his left hand. He looked around, curiosity morphing into bewilderment. *How did it come to this?*

Below, Baker repeated, "Drop the gun now! Drop it!"

It was often better to stick to one clear message. In the end, all any of them wanted was for the man to drop the gun. Anything else could wait for later.

Wallace Biggsby's hand began to shake and tremble. He

brought the gun up, tilted the barrel, but overall, it was still pointed downward. If it discharged, the bullet would go in the ground.

Kathryn said, "Jesus, Jacob. What the hell are you waiting for?"

Now Simon's voice floated up, "I need to see your hands! Now drop the gun, damnit! Don't make us do this."

The man raised the gun ever so slightly more.

Baker moved out from behind his squad car door.

Simon, off script, said to Baker, "The fuck you doing?"

"Relax, it's okay."

Kathryn said, "Jacob . . ."

"Easy, partner."

Jacob's finger tensed on the trigger. He was prepared to end this in a heartbeat. He knew that Baker putting himself forward like that was a vote of confidence. That he trusted Jacob to protect him. Baker wanted to stay alive as much as the next guy. He wasn't stupid.

Baker, hands open, said, "C'mon man, you don't want to do this. Just drop it now." Baker quieted his voice in the same way he'd physically opened up his body.

Biggsby lifted the gun higher and Jacob's finger began a slow deliberated squeeze.

Baker said, "You agreed to come out and give up the gun. Let's end this. Drop it."

Biggsby's hand steadied for a brief second, then it came up so that it was pointing straight at Baker. In that same motion, Biggsby relaxed his hand, and the gun fell to earth. He sank to his knees and began sobbing into his hands.

Uniformed officers and SWAT members rushed to him, kicked the weapon out of the way and put him facedown on the lawn, then cuffed him.

Jacob relaxed his hand.

"Why the hell didn't you take the shot?" Kathryn was genuinely stunned. She would have put the man down. "He could have killed one of us."

"He didn't."

Jacob inspected his rifle, thumbed back the bolt, ejected the unused .308 cartridge, and snatched it out of the air. He studied it a moment and then pocketed it.

"Listen closely, because I will never say this again. When I am in the reticle, I am gone. I'm not here or there. I'm in a kind of middleground. And when I'm in the middleground, you are my eyes and ears. I depend on you for that. But you were badgering me while I was in the middleground. Stick to your job. I will train you. I will tell you why I did A or B, but don't ever tell me when to pull the trigger. Understand?"

Sesak looked wounded. Jacob was putting up a wall, marking boundaries, defining their roles.

"Never tell the primary when to discharge his weapon. I am the primary. Are we clear?"

"Yes, sir."

"Okay. Now ask your questions."

"He was a threat to the officers. I thought we were providing them cover. Keeping them safe."

"We did."

"Why didn't you shoot?"

"Because he wasn't a threat to anyone. He didn't take hostages. He hadn't harmed anyone. He just wanted to die. But he didn't have the guts to take his own life, so he tried the next best thing. Suicide by cop."

Jacob realized that he had become quite talkative of late. Chatty. A shrug would have made a far better answer to Sesak's question.

From below, Simon caught Jacob's eye. Simon pointed his finger like a gun and fired it at Jacob. His smile was filled with contempt.

Jacob said, "Looks like Simon sees it your way."

"Because the man could have fired upon our officers. He held that gun a long fucking time."

"I could have killed him faster than he could have ever shot Baker. That knowledge gives me leeway, because I know that a precisely placed shot will stop all motor function instantly. There's no way the gunman could have shot and hit any of the officers."

Jacob slung his rifle over his shoulder.

"Besides, he never would have fired it."

"You can't know that."

"I saw it in his eyes." Jacob debated whether or not to say what it was he saw in Wallace Biggsby's eyes. But he realized that he had come to the point in his life that his own father had once come to in his.

He was ready to give instruction. Godly instruction.

"He wasn't a wolf."

And there it was. The truth. He had spoken the truth.

CHAPTER 9

Cameron County was seven thousand square miles. Massive by most standards. It had vast expanses of unspoiled rural beauty that still echoed with the promises of the gold rush. Morgan City was the county seat, a business center with congested streets and tall buildings that gave way to suburban sprawl and clusters of pastel houses on treeless lawns plunked down amongst TAN/NAIL/LIQUOR strip malls. Vista Canyon was the newly developed upscale community for the upwardly mobile.

And there was Hangtown, an urban center similar to Sacramento. It was here that the affluent (who had not yet fled to Vista Canyon) and the abject poor gathered. The middle class stuck to the suburbs.

Like most cities, Hangtown had its red brick rows of public housing, the neighborhoods where the gas station convenience stores posted signs that they accept food stamps—CalFresh EBT cards.

This was where Lee Staley lived. Lee "Harvey Oswald"

Staley they had called him, once upon a time. "Oswald." Sometimes just "Oz." It was still how he thought of himself. And truly, that was where he was now, the land of Oz. With his retirement pension and disability compensation, he could have set himself up in a pale green split-level in the suburbs, but Hangtown was where he had been drawn.

He had let himself go. He knew that much. The truth was, he wasn't entirely sure how it had all come to this. He lived in Warter Estates, amongst the dopers and the deviants. The disabled and chronically unemployed. The single mothers who turned afternoon tricks to make ends meet. The woman upstairs who performed homegrown plastic surgery on teenage girls—injecting them with silicone purchased from Home Depot. The misfits. The relegated.

The forgotten.

The cops had a name for it when one of their own checked out, turned his back on the regular world and the people who populated it. The ones who couldn't hack it anymore. The ones who grew overwhelmed with seeing just how deep our society had eroded, and had to divorce themselves from it. No cop was ever going to tell you his partner took early retirement due to an overwhelming spiritual angst—your garden variety existential crisis. No, they had a truer name for it. It was a poetic term. Oz liked it. He liked the poetry of it. They would say, *That guy? Oh, he burned out. Now he's a blue recluse.*

Maybe, in the end, that was all he really wanted. To be a blue recluse. To forget and to be forgotten.

But why? Why go gentle into that good night? Why be forgotten? Why fade away?

The booze was certainly helping him get there, though. He was forgetting himself. Erasing his mind one drink at a time. He'd grown fond of Old Crow. They called it bourbon, but they might as well have labeled it amnesia in a bottle. It made you forget. And when you weren't drunk enough to forget, the paralytic hangovers made you too sick to care.

It was a good balance. Too drunk to remember. Or too sick to care. Life was good that way.

But there was the middleground. That in-between time. The middleground could be a nuisance. The time when your stomach sourly revolted at the thought of the day's first shot of Old Crow. When you had to put food in your belly, but what you really craved was alcohol. It was the time when your existence crept into that shadow world called sobriety. That was a bitch. A real motherfucker. The state of sobriety was a motherfucking bitch. Luckily, it wasn't a state Oswald had to enter very often. He preferred the country of the forgotten. He would go drunk into that good night.

But what was it he wanted to forget? Nothing. There was nothing to forget. The shooting. Of course the shooting. That was what everybody thought had happened to him. (At least those who thought of him at all. Here in the dim nation of the forgotten, where the light had died long ago, invisibility was issued along with your passport.) But Oswald knew it wasn't the shooting. He knew that. He had made peace with that long ago. He was good. It's all good.

Sometimes when he found himself in that in-between place, that middleground, and the thoughts were flowing whether he wanted them to or not, Oswald thought about Julius Edenfield.

Julius Edenfield was a good cop. Nobody ever said otherwise. And he had his head on straight. He was solid. As solid as they come.

Edenfield was involved in a fatal shooting while on patrol. Nothing to do with SWAT or the kind of calculated killing Oswald had saturated himself with.

A guy pulled a gun on his partner, and Edenfield shot him.

He was never the same afterward. And no, he didn't become a stumbling drunk or even a blue recluse. He was just. Never. Quite. The same.

It was a clean shooting. A good shooting. Everyone said so. Even Edenfield himself. But he was different. And the thing is, no cop ever knows how he's going to react after a shooting. After taking another human being's life. Even if it's self-defense. And the risk of change remains whether it's the officer's first suspect killed in the line of duty, or the fifth. No one ever knows just how it affects the guy. Just exactly what thoughts a killing will set loose in someone's head. No cop thinks it will be him or her who gets the bad reaction. They think, *I would never feel bad or guilty or uncertain if I took a life in self-defense or to protect the safety of the innocent. That's my calling. That's why I'm here. That's why I'm wearing this uniform.* The idea that doing what they were born to do could somehow fuck them up was an idea of utter lunacy.

But nobody ever really knows until they pull the trigger and end a life. It's a fucking crapshoot.

Edenfield never made a decent decision after the shooting. It completely changed him. He tried to act like the same guy, but everyone saw the difference. He'd been married four times since that shooting, moved on to private work, had been employed by three different security agencies, and was now retired after he injured his back wrestling with a stuck floor-to-ceiling steel security gate at a mall jewelry store.

Because his shooting happened while on patrol, the media printed his name, and of course the guy he shot had local family who insisted that their father, though drunk and pointing a shotgun at two cops, "never intended to hurt anyone." So there were letters to the editor and a lot of Monday morning quarterbacking for the whole world to see. That was what changed him. He knew it had been a good shooting, but it was the aftermath that did him in.

Edenfield had learned what Oswald had now learned. Sometimes it is far better to go gentle into that good night.

You just never knew. A crapshoot.

And Oswald remembered looking down on Edenfield. As weak. As a man who should never have been a cop in the first place. He disdained Edenfield. Disdain wasn't a cop word, but it was what he felt. Because Edenfield had succumbed. He had failed to rage against the dying of the light.

And even now, a full-blown alcoholic and the most reclusive of the blue recluses, Oswald did not believe it was the unfortunate event with the hostage that had brought him to this point in his life. No, Oswald simply believed he was a man smart enough to take early retirement when the department offered it to him. He was living the good life. He was retired and he was going to by-God enjoy it. Maybe he drank too much sometimes, but everybody did after they retired. That was the whole point.

The gunman's hand had jerked when Oswald shot him. It had been a perfectly aimed, perfectly delivered bullet. Oswald had done nothing wrong. In fact, he'd done everything right. No one would ever dispute that. Oswald himself did not dispute it.

The gunman's hand had contracted when Oswald's bullet entered his left eye. It was an involuntary muscle spasm. Not possible to prefigure or foretell. The gunman squeezed the trigger, and the woman ended up with a bullet in her brain, too.

There was no way it could have been avoided. It was an outcome that could not be calculated.

Of course, if Oswald were a pessimist—which he wasn't—he could potentially play with the thought that if he had never fired, the woman might still be alive. He'd had the green light, but he didn't have to take the shot. It was at his discretion. He could have used that discretion to give the negotiator more time to reach the guy. If he was being very pessimistic—down on himself even—Oswald might play with the thought that he'd taken the shot prematurely. That he wanted to walk away the hero, yet again. Because that felt good. Putting the bad guy down and walking away the hero felt pretty fucking good. So was it within the realm of possibility that he took the shot sooner than he really absolutely had to?

But Oswald didn't have thoughts like that. He was no Julius Edenfield. He was not weak. He was just retired. Living the good life.

But on the few occasions he actually had indulged in such thoughts—and it was seldom, so seldom it was hardly worth mentioning—on those few occasions, the times he reflected on the past and came close to feeling sorry for himself, sometimes the self-pity gave way to resentment. Because, in the end, Oswald had been given the green light. Fire at will. He had been told that the situation warranted mortal measures. His was not to wonder why, his was to jump down the rabbit hole, to deliver the bullet to the intended target. And he had held up his end of that bargain. So, if a mistake had been made, it was made by the person who authorized the shot. The rabbit hole is like a black hole. Light can't escape. Thoughts can't escape. Morality doesn't enter it. You trust those outside the hole to make those calls. To decide if the negotiations were moving forward or not. The negotiator's job was to talk the bad guys out of it, and to stay as long as it took if the suspect hadn't hurt anyone yet or fired on law enforcement. And even if he had fired on them, they may still hold the perimeter, hunker down and keep trying. Shooting is the last resort.

But that day, had Bryant given the green light prematurely? Had he? And by the time Oswald got to the point of asking himself that particular question, resentment had given way to anger. To rage. Because, when you got right down to it, the green light should never have been given.

Rage, rage against the giving of the green light. Ha-ha.

So, sure, sometimes he indulged in self-pity. And that occasionally morphed into resentment. Anger even. Happened to everybody, though. That was normal. A guy gets a few drinks in him, he gets sentimental. Pulls out his photo albums, maybe. Or his mementos. His souvenirs collected over the course of a career. That was normal. Souvenirs and mementos. Trinkets and the like. That was normal. Taking a stroll down memory lane. That's what they called it. Memories. Of the way we were.

And so thoughts of the past played through Oswald's mind as he ate the Maple & Brown Sugar Quaker Instant Oatmeal that morning. What little he had eaten had settled his stomach. Taken the edge off his hangover. He felt much better now. No need to think about these things. In fact, Oswald glanced at his watch and reckoned it might not be too early to have a little shot of the Crow. Take wing, so to speak. Just to get his motor running. Get afloat. Airborne. Maybe watch some *Judge Judy* and catch a light buzz. He was retired and deserved to take it easy. Plus he wanted to celebrate—for once again having successfully navigated the treacherous waters of In-Between. The Middleground. He'd started in the Land of the Sick, and now he was ready to get his passport punched in the Country of the Forgotten.

He might just stay awhile.

Judge Judy was a rerun, so Oswald did a little channel surfing. He had his sea legs now, so a little surfing suited him just fine. He settled on *The View* on the local ABC affiliate. He thought that Rosie O'Donnell was funny, but Whoopi Goldberg pretty much pissed him off. There was just something about her. Was she a lesbian now? That girl from the Roseanne Barr show was gay now. She was on some talk show, too. It was kinda like *The View,* but *The View* was better. A better dynamic between the women. They were always arguing about something. Whoopi would usually say something, some little throwaway line about nothing at all, and the rest of the women would just start fighting over it. Then Whoopi would just kind of sit back and watch the women tear each other's throats out, then when it just about reached critical mass, Whoopi would swoop in, make some grand all-encompassing moral statement that shut everybody else up, and then they would go to commercial.

But still, it was entertaining, and then a special news bulletin flashed on the screen and Clark Avery was sitting at the anchor desk saying an unidentified gunman had shot and killed Sheriff's Captain Benjamin Bryant. They cut to some aerial footage of Vista Canyon and Bryant's house. Then Avery started using the word *sniper* and throwing around terms like *may not be isolated, city in danger* and *under attack* and *threat could come from anywhere.* Then he cut to a satellite hookup interview with a former marine sniper. Nathaniel DePoe. Avery introduced him by his unofficial title, "The Deadliest Sniper Alive." Oswald knew the guy. Deadliest Jackass Alive, maybe. DePoe had served five deployments to Iraq, and totaled 170 certified kills in the course of his career. Wrote a book about it. Oh, and look, he's got a second book coming out. Wasn't that a lucky break, to be on TV right when he's got a new book coming out? The guy was a complete jagoff. A phony. He'd been featured on the covers of several magazines. Oswald was getting mad. He helped himself to another shot of Old Crow and chased it with a sip from a can of flat Dr. Pepper. This was pissing him off. This guy was their expert? Fuck him.

Oswald listened to DePoe spout off arcane terms like Black Ops, STTU, false flag operations—none of which had even the most remote relevance to what had happened in Vista Canyon; he was just reciting his résumé—and wrap it all up by saying there were perhaps half a dozen men alive who were capable of that kind of shooting, one of them being DePoe himself, and the other five were not in-country.

Really? Half a dozen? Really? Oswald was fuming. There were many problems with guys like DePoe; the first of those problems was that they couldn't see past the military world. Secret Service, FBI, Special Forces, Black Ops guys. But that was it. They completely overlooked the Law Enforcement Sharp-shooter. During his career, Oswald's title was Deputy Staley. That was it. Deputy Lee Staley. Other than his closest peers, nobody ever knew he was a sniper (or more accurately, a counter-sniper). He was anonymous. All of the law enforcement sharpshooters were unknown, and they protected their identities for the sake of their families and careers.

The regular world never knew that the nice sergeant that lived down the street, the deputy who went to their church, or the patrol officer right next door could be a sniper. Most news reports simply said, "The suspect was shot by a SWAT Sharp-shooter." They always protected his identity. Some of that ano-nymity was naturally controlled by the perimeter that officers established initially, and then SWAT tweaked when they arrived, making it bigger or smaller. And many times, nobody even saw the sniper team come and go—which was the ideal objective. They appeared out of nowhere, handled their business, and faded into the shadows. And they bloody well liked it that way. The rest of the SWAT team understood and respected it and would step in front of a camera to protect a sniper's identity.

What guys like DePoe never understood was that they were actually the minority. Snipers were among us every day, everywhere, and no one knew it. They just weren't angling for photo ops and cover shoots and remote interviews and publishing deals. They were serving in silence.

Secondly, here you've got a guy who's called The Deadliest Sniper Alive (probably came up with that title himself), which basically meant he'd killed a lot of people. Now you go back to the Vietnam era and the legendary Carlos Hathcock, and he was out there alone, hanging by his ass, swamp-crawling in and out, and Hathcock, arguably the greatest sniper who ever lived, only got credit for a kill if someone else saw it. You had to have independent *eyes on* to get credit for a kill. Someone else had to see the body. Much of Carlos's career was in enemy territory when he was alone. And then, he still had to crawl the hell out of Dodge. The man had once shot—at five hundred yards, the length of five football fields—an NVA enemy sniper, with the round *going through* the enemy sniper's rifle scope and into his eye. Hathcock ended his amazing career with 93 confirmed kills—far shy of DePoe's supposed 170.

Plus, today's snipers have advanced technology. Determining distance and depth is one of the hardest skills to master. Eyewitnesses are notoriously incorrect when they tell the story from their vantage point. Simply because it's hard to gauge distance, especially at night.

So now you've got someone like Oswald himself who'd pulled the trigger for thirty years in various capacities and organizations, *semper fi,* and you've got this famous sniper, this Edgar Allen Fucking DePoe or whatever his name was, who did it thirty months. Did that make him a better or truer sniper than Hathcock? Or even someone like Oswald? Because his kill count was so high? Or could those kills be attributed to the fact that DePoe was working in a target-rich environment where he was taking out any and all bad guys as opposed to a single leader? And after he shoots, they just helicopter on over and count the bodies and he gets credit for all of the deaths. Well wasn't that special?

Today's snipers have the technology that gauges distance for them. A rangefinder sends out a beam that says 1250 METERS, the sniper dials his scope in and basically pushes a button. Today's guys had no clue what it meant to be a true sniper in its purest form. It was a dying art.

Many current snipers didn't even carry a dope book on them. That book contained the sniper's hard-won information gleaned from years of training and documenting what *his* gun would do under any and all conditions. Distance, weather, wind, population, material, all of that was sweated out from hours and hours inside the reticle. Down the rabbit hole. It was the only way. You recorded every result of how your weapon fired under every condition (not to mention your own condition—tired, sick, hungover, hungry, dehydrated, whatever). You would know your rifle and your physical response to it.

Few took the time or had the energy to do the work. Oswald

was an old-school sniper, and sadly, they were falling by the wayside. So guys like DePoe tended to piss him off.

Oswald had just clicked off the TV, thinking to himself, Fuck Bryant and Fuck DePoe. His rifle was on the coffee table in front of him. It was an imposing instrument. Model 70 Winchester .308. Checkered wood stock—Oswald didn't go in for that fiberglass shit—and worn leather sling. The Redfield scope was 3 x 9, fixed, with a police special heavy barrel. Imposing. Old school.

He'd done some shooting early this morning. Fired off more than a few rounds. Hungover and on an empty stomach. You had to know how your body would perform under different conditions the same way you had to know how your rifle would perform under strenuous circumstances. Sometimes you had to go to extremes. It was called hormesis. The booze hadn't affected his marksmanship. Not yet, anyway. He stayed on top of it. Practiced regularly. Still kept up his dope book. Notated his targets and filed them away. You had to be prepared.

He grabbed the cleaning kit from an end table. He needed something to calm his nerves. He leaned forward and opened the rifle's bolt. Then he opened a bottle of Hoppe's bore cleaner. He picked up a patch, wet it with the Hoppe's and began cleaning the bolt.

The loud knock at the door startled him. He stared at the door, willing himself to move, but just couldn't. Then the knock repeated. And, really, when cops knocked on a door, it somehow carried their authority. This was a cop knock. No doubt about it.

Oswald glanced at the coffee table and the kitchen counter.

He should have started cleaning up the second he saw the news story. He should have known he'd be getting a visit. Stupid. He'd neglected to clean up his mementos and trinkets and doodads from his last little trip down memory lane. Those misty water-colored memories could get you in trouble.

He yelled, "Just a second" at the door, then took the rifle, cleaning kit, and everything else to the bathroom, where he threw it all in the tub and pulled the vinyl curtain.

When he opened the front door, he found two detectives and one uniformed deputy on the other side. He knew one of the detectives from the old days. Cortez. Alejandro Cortez. Those watercolored memories just kept popping up.

"Oh! Hey, guys. What's up? Do you want to come in?"

He couldn't believe how idiotic he sounded. *Oh! Hey, guys? What the fuck was that?*

"Sorry, Oz. It's a business call. We need you to come downtown with us. Answer a few questions."

"Yeah, just saw it on the news. I thought you might look me up. Give me a second."

He left the door open and disappeared into a bedroom. Palucci, the uniformed deputy, followed him into the room, and Oswald held up his hand.

"Whoa, hold on there, Romeo. You haven't even kissed me yet."

Cortez said, "Palucci, just wait with us."

Once Oswald was in his bedroom, Sayeed Hasan, the second detective, whispered, "I smell Hoppe's. He's been cleaning a gun."

Cortez said, "Bullshit. How do you know it's Hoppe's?"

"My dick's getting hard."

"You're a funny guy," Cortez said, then called out toward the bedroom, "Yo, Oz, I gotta hit the head."

Ever since he had turned forty, Cortez was pretty much married to the bathroom. Enlarged prostate. Without waiting for permission, he crossed the living room and pulled the bathroom door shut behind him.

Hasan, a short man with dark, Indian features, picked up an open poetry book from the coffee table and thumbed through it. It was called *There Are Men Too Gentle to Live Among Wolves*, by James Kavanaugh.

Oswald reappeared carrying a light nylon jacket which he shrugged into.

"So, you're a poetry fan?" Hasan asked.

"I guess."

"'Because I could not stop for death, he kindly stopped for me.' You know that one?"

"Emily Dickinson."

"Sure. You'd do good on *Jeopardy!*"

"Sure I would. I can just imagine it: 'Today on *Jeopardy!* We welcome Lee 'Harvey Oswald' Staley, a retired police sniper from Hangtown, California, currently sought for questioning in the shooting death of his ex-supervisor.'"

They heard the muffled chug of the toilet flushing. Cortez stepped out and said, "So, Oswald, you're taking baths with your rifle now? Kinky."

Oz shrugged.

"Hey, Cortez, look. Poetry," Hasan said, holding up the book.

"Well, I'll be damned. A poet?" Cortez said, dropping his voice into the mocking lilt of a British schoolmaster. "The laddie reckons himself a poet?"

"That's from Pink Floyd's *The Wall,* right?" Oz said, playing along.

"You've totally got *Jeopardy!* written all over you," Hasan said.

"Let's go," Cortez said. "We gotta lot to talk about."

They all stepped out into the hallway, which smelled vaguely of piss and collard greens. Oswald locked his door, then put his hands behind his back and angled himself toward Deputy Palucci.

Cortez intervened and said, "Jesus, Oz. We're not going to cuff you."

"Two detectives and one deputy to escort little old me? You were clearly expecting trouble."

"We just want to interview you."

"You mean like for a job? I need a job."

"No, we're talent scouts for Alex Trebek."

"Funny."

CHAPTER 10

Jill had been dreading having coffee with Susan. It felt more like a chore than a treat. But why? This morning she'd had an insight. She now realized where those misgivings about the girl came from. It wasn't that Susan was clingy, it wasn't that she was buying Jill's friendship, and it wasn't that she looked like a possum.

It was, simply put, that Susan was a better writer than Jill. And that stung. That stung like a bitch. The terrible truth was that this manuscript about the little girl Rose with the criminal father was far more complex and far more evocative than anything Jill had ever written. It would be published. Make no mistake, it would be snapped up, published, and maybe even be a bestseller. Hell, it *deserved* to be a bestseller. It was that good. Literary and compelling, and heartbreaking.

She would pull off what Jill had tried to do and failed.

But, still, Jill had to be honest. It was her nature.

Without preamble, she said, "I love it. I absolutely love it."

Susan smiled as big as a jack-o-lantern. "I've been so worried what you would think. You know I love your books. Your opinion means everything to me."

"Well, it's good. Brilliant, even. If I'm being totally honest, it's probably better than my stuff. I can see this being a crossover hit. I mean, the violence is so over the top, but the way you pull it off, it feels more like poetry. It feels like something out of Cormac McCarthy or James Dickey. The literary community will love your use of language, the art you employ to get across the desolation of Rose's girlhood, the love she and her father share. Never cloying, never sentimental. In fact, their love and need for one another comes through in the things you don't say."

"I loved my own father like that. So it was easy. Not much art involved in it."

"You underestimate yourself. And I can tell you this much, he would be proud."

Susan smiled into her coffee, but didn't say anything else. It was too personal. All the really good writing is, Jill thought.

Keeping with her policy of complete honesty, Jill had to share her one lingering criticism of Susan's novel.

"There's one thing that bothered me, though. And I'm probably the only person in the world who is gonna feel this way, but I have to say it."

"I want you to say it. This is valuable to me."

But Jill wondered if that was true.

"It's the end. The climax. The bank heist at the end. To me, that made the father the bad guy. I didn't care what life circumstances brought him to that point. I was fine with the robberies to feed his family. I was fine believing that he had gotten so off track that he was willing to do that to get a better life for his family. It was wrong, but understandable. He was in a cycle he couldn't break. But when he took the hostages in the bank. And an innocent person lost their life. At that point, I wasn't rooting for him anymore. I wanted the police to take him. He deserved it. And I don't think that's what you were going for."

The disappointment in Susan's face was unmistakable.

"I'm just being honest. And like I say, I'm absolutely certain that I'm in the minority. Very few people would feel the way I do. We live in a culture where Hannibal Lecter has evolved into a hero of sorts."

"Well, he makes those choices because he's forced to. I hardly think Rose's father is on par with Hannibal the Cannibal."

"No, of course not. You're right. It's an amazing novel. It really is. Hell, I'm jealous of what you've accomplished here. And I'm telling you that from the heart. But I'm the wrong audience for this book. You've got to remember who I'm married to. My husband is the guy they call in to eliminate people like the father. For me, Jacob is always going to be the hero. He doesn't get a chance to ask these people if life has been hard on them. If they were abused as children. If their Pop-Tart was stale that morning. He just saves lives."

Susan's phone beeped at her, she glanced at it and started stuffing her things into her marsupial handbag.

"I've gotta go. Sorry."

Every other time they had been together, Susan ignored her phone the few times it rang. Jill understood the woman was hurt.

She understood, as a writer, that authors fell in love with their characters. It was part of the process. The hallmark of the really good ones.

Susan flopped two limp twenties on the table and scurried away with a mumbled "bye."

The tab would be less than half that. Jill wondered if the extra twenty was for the waitress or for her. It felt a little demeaning.

And then she wondered if in actuality she was the one who had demeaned Susan. Just how jealous was she of what Susan had accomplished with her fiction? She wondered how much it bothered her that the student had bested the teacher. Did it bother her enough that maybe she took some small degree of pleasure in delivering that last bit of criticism? And could it be that Susan picked up on that pleasure? Had Susan picked up on that schadenfreude? Had she felt demeaned? Was Jill just being a jealous bitch?

No.

No, Jill had just been honest. Maybe she could have been more tactful. But tact didn't make people better writers, did it? And if she had hurt the woman's feelings, well that was just too fucking bad, wasn't it? People like Jacob were the heroes, not the bad guys.

She stared at the two twenties for a long time, then she opened her purse and added another twenty.

At least it would be a good day for the waitress.

CHAPTER 11

But she couldn't let it go. Not like this. It felt wrong. In several different ways, it felt wrong.

After she added her twenty to the pile, Jill gathered her stuff and hurried out the door of the Morgan City Café. She saw Susan on the sidewalk up ahead. She called after her, but Susan turned into the shadows of the parking deck. Jill ran. She wouldn't be able to sleep tonight if she didn't at least make her part in this right.

She saw Susan making her way down a curving concrete ramp, and that image of a burrowing rodent returned to her. And that wasn't fair either. Why did she insist on thinking of the girl in those terms? Demeaning. It was demeaning. She would do better.

Susan heard her name called, turned and waited.

"I'm sorry," Jill said. "I was too rough."

"Did you ever stop and think that you're actually married to a professional killer? Kinda makes the father in my book seem pretty harmless when you think about it."

So she'd been right. Susan was hurt and angry. Jill decided

she wouldn't return those emotions. Besides, she'd heard this line of reasoning before. From her mother. Sister. Concerned friends. And other idiots.

"Maybe," Jill said. It was all she could think to say. But she refused to spit the venom back. There had to be a way to resolve this.

"How can you live with someone like that?"

"Like what?"

"You heard me. A killer. Not make believe. Not a story. A cold-blooded killer."

As much as she wanted to resolve this on good terms, Jill felt her blood rising. *Don't fuck with my husband. My hero.*

And then inspiration hit. She put her hands on Susan's shoulders, a gesture of friendship, and said, "Close your eyes."

"What?" Suspicious.

"Just do this for me. Close your eyes."

"I'm not going—"

"Please. Author to author. Friend to friend. Close your eyes."

It was the *friend to friend* that did it. Susan was hungry for friends. Real ones, not the imaginary kind. She closed her eyes.

With her hands still on Susan's shoulders, Jill took a deep breath. With cars rolling past them, and warm tangy exhaust fumes tickling their throats, Jill began to speak.

"Okay, you're in the bank one day. You need to make a withdrawal because you left your ATM card at home, so you stand in line to see a teller. It's almost your turn when the guy in front of you starts rummaging around in his jacket. Only it's summer and why would he be wearing a jacket? He keeps fidgeting. You see a flash of metal. And you're a smart girl. You know what it means. This is a robbery."

"A bank was robbed in Sacramento last month."

"It happens all the time, Susan. All the time. Keep your eyes closed. Imagine, suddenly there's a gun in the guy's hand. Looks like a freaking howitzer. He pops off a few rounds, the first one takes out the security guard. Then the cameras. You're in shock. You can't take your eyes off the security guard twitching in a pool of his own blood on the marble tile floor. You had noticed the guard when you first walked in, because he's about your age. Handsome. Strong, athletic type. He probably won't survive the gunshot, but if he does his days of being strong and athletic are behind him now. It's wheelchair city from here on out. Pressure sores and a catheter bag strapped to his ankle.

"You've never seen a person shot before. In the movies maybe. Described in books. But this is different. This is real. The blood is real. You can smell it. It smells like dirty pennies soaked in saliva. You're going to pass out. How can this be real?

"But you don't pass out. This is not a movie. This is not the news. This is you. This is your life."

Jill had her eyes closed too. Living this right along with Susan.

"This is *your* bank and *you're* in there with the gunman. He's just killed someone in front of thirty witnesses. He's already been captured on the security system whether he shot the cameras or not. The data is stored off-site. He has nothing left to lose. And now you're all side by side, facedown on the floor. This is real. This is happening. You are fucked.

"And then you hear it. Sirens. In the distance. Growing

louder. A silent alarm was tripped maybe, or someone heard the shots and called it in. All that matters is that help is on the way. You allow yourself a glimmer of hope. Maybe you'll live through this. The police arrive, but your gunman friend grabs the woman next to you, hoists her to her feet and drags her to the door. A police negotiator tries to initiate conversation, but your friend isn't listening. Instead, he shoots the woman in the head and pitches her out into the street."

Susan's breathing had gotten quicker. Jill could hear it. Felt warm little puffs of it on her face.

"He returns, only this time he pulls *you* up, holds *you* in front of him and presses the gun to *your* temple. The bore is still hot. It burns your skin."

Jill opened her eyes and saw that Susan's were open as well. She seemed to be holding her breath now. Jill kept talking, staring directly into Susan's brown eyes.

"You won't be seeing it played out on the news this time around because this time, you are the news. You are a human shield for an inhuman sociopathic animal. And both of you are completely unaware that somewhere, out in the quiet and the shadows, in a place you'll never see, doing things you'd never dream of, a man waits. All he does is handle situations like this. In all this hell you've been through, only he can make it right. Only he can remove this maniac from your life. And he does it. With one shot. One perfectly placed shot and you're free."

Susan let out a deep breath.

"Now you tell me . . . do you still think he's a professional killer?"

Susan broke her gaze and stared at the oil-stained surface of the ramp they were standing on.

"Jill. I am so sorry. I didn't mean . . . I never meant to imply . . ."

"Don't worry about it. Most people have no idea what the job is about. To some, maybe he is a killer. But to others, he's a hero. I choose to love the hero."

"What a job."

The tension between them was gone now. Peace had been made.

Jill smiled and said, "In fact, it really is just a job. Just like any other. You get a short in your wiring, you call an electrician. Leaky pipes? You call a plumber. A cranked-up psychopath takes you hostage? You call a police sharpshooter. You call a sniper."

Susan returned the smile and said, "Maybe I should be taking notes. Maybe there's room for another hero in my book."

CHAPTER 12

The Cameron County Range, the proving ground, was where Jacob and his partner were required to qualify on a monthly basis. The shooting range was a large rectangle, about the size and shape of a football field with markers at 7, 15, 20, 25, 50, and 100 yards. Targets were up at the far end of the range. Jacob was examining his used targets, making notations about environmental conditions directly on them and making notes in his dope book as well. He turned when he heard his partner approaching behind him.

Sesak had changed out of her training gear and into a ghillie suit. A large camouflage outfit with strange little tendrils sprouting from it, a ghillie suit blended with the environment and broke up a sniper's outline so it wasn't quite as man-shaped. These were not off-the-rack uniforms, or even special order gear. Snipers made their own. Typically, the sniper would start with an olive drab poncho and canvas field hat, add jute and burlap and even hunks of grandma's Christmas wreath if appropriate. The suit was usually finished off with scraps and cuttings of foliage from the immediate vegetation so that the blending effect was perfected not only in shape and color, but so that the suit would respond to the wind or the rain or the snow exactly as the surrounding environment. It was the ultimate expression of *trompe l'oeil*—deceive the eye.

Kathryn even had similar colors painted on her face. She could have been a tree if she had more arms. She peered out at Jacob.

"What are we doing again?"

Jacob indicated the grassy meadow that sprawled out from the maintained shooting range. It was several hundred yards long and about a hundred yards wide. The meadow was an undisturbed expanse of trees and tall golden grass—a plot of the past that seemed to have arrived on this spot as though delivered by a time machine. Jacob was pretty sure one of the trees, a beautifully gnarled live oak, was an Indian trail tree that predated the first white settlers to this end of the country. The Indians purposely bent and deformed certain trees to permanently point the way to water or food or safety. The massive trunk of the live oak in this meadow came straight out of the earth, then bent at a near ninety degree angle about five feet up so that the trunk was actually parallel to the ground, then bent again and continued straight up. The horizontal plane it created pointed to the freshwater stream at the bottom of the meadow. (Jacob was ashamed to realize that he didn't even know what tribes were aboriginal to Northern California, but he recognized the oak for what it was the instant he first saw it. His father had taught him about Indian trail trees.) Now the oak seemed to point in accusation. That so many other trees had been bulldozed so that the land could be developed. Maybe he and Jill were both haunted by trees.

For Jacob, it was a stark reminder of the substance of the past that always surrounded him, pulling at him. The settlers, pioneers, forty-niners, and the cowboys migrated across the country in search of good land, homes, gold, wide open space—a place where they would be free to live by their own codes. They found all those things when they got here. Only problem was that there was nothing past California. The dream came to fruition and then ended here. Jacob and his kind were the last vestiges of that western spirit. The Sheriff's posse now rode in patrol units and SWAT vans. But they were still trying to bring order and justice to the Wild West. They still believed the American dream was worth protecting. For a while anyway. Until the bad guys and the system that seemed to support those bad guys wore them down. Wore their resistance to nothing. Everything simultaneously culminated and ended in California. And now even the good guys were fleeing this apogee of America.

The Land of Milk and Honey, where the homesteaders came to be free of oppressive government and live by their own personal code, now had more legislation per capita than anyone, anywhere. Yes, they had codes to live by. Thousands of them. Cops and firefighters put in their twenty, then fled the state at the earliest opportunity. Maybe that was what the Indian trail tree was pointing to. The way out.

•   •   •

"We'll be stalking each other through this meadow. I'll start at the other end. We'll have radio contact." Jacob began putting on his ghillie suit too, smearing his hands and brow with a handful of dirt, snapping off strands of grass and vine and attaching them to his suit. "The objective is to spot me before I get close enough for a hand-to-hand kill. You, of course, will be trying to stalk me as well. When you think you've seen me, indicate the location on the radio, and I'll let you know if you're right. I'll do the same."

Sesak smiled and said, "And you won't be pissed if I win?"

Jacob shrugged. "I hope you do. Remember, patience is the key. You have to move in tiny, minute increments to avoid detection. Be conscious of everything you're wearing and everything around you. What could cause a glare or reflection. A sound not consistent with the environment. Things like that. Okay?"

"Fine. Let's get started. I'm burning up in here."

"You'd be in one of these things for *days* if you were waiting to take out a strategic military target. Not only that, an enemy sniper would be hunting you. That's the point of the exercise."

"We're not military snipers."

"No shit. But we can still learn from them." Jacob paused, then said, "Make your weapon safe."

Kathryn opened the bolt to reveal an empty chamber and showed it to Jacob.

Jacob nodded, satisfied. "I'll signal you when I'm in position at the other side."

"Got it."

In his ghillie suit, Jacob moved into the tall grass, knelt down, and then virtually disappeared. *Trompe l'oeil.* Kathryn scanned back and forth trying to spot movement. All she could see was the gentle breeze ruffling the seeded tips of the switchgrass in the meadow.

"I'm working with a ghost."

CHAPTER 13

Oswald sat on one side of a small table in an interrogation room at the Cameron County Sheriff's Department. The two detectives sat in chairs opposite him. The laminate-topped table between them was spotted with brown blooms of cigarette burns from the olden days when everybody smoked. To Oswald, the burns looked like melanomas. One concession to modern times was that the two-way mirror had been drywalled over, and a reflective dome that concealed a closed circuit camera was mounted to the ceiling. Lieutenant Cowell and Sergeant Heidler watched the feed from the monitor room.

Cortez asked, "Any particular reason you would be cleaning a sniper rifle when you are no longer employed in that capacity?"

"I always keep it clean. Just the way I was taught. No matter what."

Detective Hasan asked, "Not because you shot it earlier today?"

"You know, I didn't give you guys permission to search my place."

"Nobody searched anything," Cortez said. "I was just taking a piss. I could smell the Hoppe's."

"Which prompted you to look and see if I let soap scum build up on my shower tile?"

"Some people do. It's hard not to think less of them once you find out."

"Did you have time to rifle through the medicine cabinet, too?"

Hasan jumped in. "That's a good pun."

"What the hell are you talking about?"

"Rifle. You used the word 'rifle' as a verb meaning 'to ransack' when the real focus of our conversation is the Winchester rifle you tried to conceal from us by hiding it in your bathtub."

"You have a great mastery of the English language. Preparing for the citizenship test?"

"I was born here, just like you."

"And actually, Hay-Seed—"

"It's Sayeed. Sayeed Hasan. Detective."

"Fine. But I didn't use rifle as a verb. I used the infinitive. As an adjective. Time to rifle. That's what I said."

Cortez said, "Are you two fucking kidding me?"

"I'm just trying to help your partner become a full-fledged American citizen."

"Kiss my full-fledged ass, Lee Harvey."

Cortez said, "Oz, maybe you could just tell us why you felt compelled to grease up and wipe down your scope-mounted sniper rifle on the same morning Captain Bryant was shot up like Sam Peckinpah was directing his life."

"You're full of film references. But you know there's more to our culture than movies. There are books. Novels. Music. Painting. Poetry."

"And TV. TV is a cultural force. So why did you clean your gun this morning?"

"Rifle."

"How's that?"

"Rifle. Not gun."

Cortez frowned. "So we're back to rifle. It's an infinitive, right?"

"No, my weapon is a rifle, not a gun. 'This is my rifle, this is my gun. This is for fighting, this is for fun.'"

"*Full Metal Jacket.*"

"Right."

"Oz, for the last time, why did you clean your rifle this morning?"

"Because I wanted to."

"Oz. C'mon."

"Look, all I'm saying is that I'm allowed to own and maintain firearms. That's one right I still have."

Hasan said, "Which begs the question: Why conceal it from us? Why go to the trouble to hide something that's perfectly legal? Why are you acting guilty?"

"Whoa, slow down there, chief. You're rifling these questions at me pretty fast. See what I did there? Transitive verb."

"Okay, okay, okay. Enough. Oz, you up for a powder residue test? That would put this to rest."

"Residue test? What would that prove? I could've worn gloves. I mean, you know, if I was the shooter."

"Seems to me, if I recall correctly, and I think I do, that you were kind of well known for your, oh let's say, disdain, of gloves. That they were impure. An unnecessary barrier between the sniper and his tool. That sound about right?"

"Yeah, I was like Brooke Shields in that regard. Nothing came between me and my Winchester."

Cortez said, "How about you let us run a ballistics match on your rifle against the .308s recovered from the murder scene?"

"Yeah, I could do that. But like I said, nothing comes between me and my Model 70. So I reckon I'll decline that offer. I don't trust you boys with my baby. Sorry."

"Well Oz, you're here right now. Let's run the residue test then. You're in, you're out."

"Look Cortez, I fire more days than I don't. What else have I got to do with my time? You'd find residue on my hands, arms, clothes, hair."

"So where were you between eight and ten this morning?"

Oswald said, "I was in bed. Asleep. Class dismissed."

This was a lie. One of several he'd told. But Oz was through with these two. He was here as a courtesy only. Fuck 'em.

He looked up at the ceiling and spoke directly to the dark reflective dome that concealed the closed circuit camera. He figured Heidler and maybe Cowell were in the monitor room, watching. "You want my weapon? You want the residue off my body? Get a warrant. Otherwise, you're wasting my time."

CHAPTER 14

Kathryn had advanced about fifty yards into the meadow, snaking her way through dense clumps of deer grass, its long-legged seed stalks waving in the light breeze. She was sweating more than she thought she had ever sweated in her life. The full-on sunlight and the suffocating ghillie suit combined in a sauna effect. Using no extraneous movement, she pulled her canteen from her utility belt and took a gulp, conscious of the sound the water made as it flowed through the neck of the canteen, and the sound her throat and esophagus made squeezing the water down into her stomach.

There was a light hiss of radio static through her earbud, then Jacob's voice. "Easy on the water, we could be here awhile."

With no apparent need to worry about the sound, she threaded the cap back on the canteen and clipped it to her utility belt. Then she continued, crawling deeper into the brush.

In her ear, like the voice of her own conscience, Jacob said, "Hot, isn't it?"

Kathryn scurried through the grass hoping to avoid Jacob's gaze. She now realized that avoiding detection while simultaneously detecting the presence of another cancelled out the efficacy of each. She keyed her mic.

"Do you see me now?"

"Nope. But I know something you don't."

"What's that?"

"That I can find you whenever I want to. I think you forgot something."

Kathryn looked around her immediate environment, knowing Fuckin'Denton was probably fucking with her head. Still, her hands flew around her clothing, checking pockets and her utility belt for items that might be missing. She keyed her mic.

"Nice try, old man. You're just messing with my head. I've got everything I'm supposed to have."

His voice in her head: "You've definitely got all that you need. More than enough."

She spoke into the air. It was like having a conversation with God. "Just watch your back. I'm coming for you. Hope you wore your Depends."

Kathryn continued to crawl forward through the deer grass, the tufted blades of bunchgrass grabbing at her. Then, out of nowhere, her utility belt erupted in electronic noise so out of place out in the field. BEEP BEEP BEEP. Her phone letting her know she had a new text message.

Jacob stood up in the grass. A mythical god pronouncing himself real. He was only ten feet away from Kathryn.

Kathryn rose up, shoulders sagged in defeat. Jacob held his cell phone and pointed it at Kathryn like a gun.

Kathryn just shook her head. She ripped off the hat of her ghillie suit and took a long pull from her canteen. Then she up-ended the canteen and poured the rest of the water over her head. Jacob smiled and walked right by her back to the shooting range.

"That's cheating," she said over her shoulder. But of course it wasn't. Her phone gave off a single beep to remind her she had an unviewed text message. She looked. It said, *BANG BANG, SHOOT SHOOT*.

Kathryn went to get more water, then followed Jacob.

The Cameron County shooting range was deserted except for Sesak and Denton. As leader of the SWAT's sniper team, Jacob was accustomed to training either alone or with his spotter. The entry team—the doorkickers—still had to qualify as shooters, and Jacob and Kathryn would have to pass basic tests and per-form at some level with every weapon and every specialty in case a team member went down. But the sniper team and entry team often trained separately, because doorkickers sometimes didn't mix well with sharpshooters. They also trained together, obviously, because any man or woman assigned to SWAT would sacrifice for a brother or sister. Still, the star-bellied Sneetches often did not train with those Sneetches who lacked a green star.

Jacob and Kathryn laid at the hundred-yard mark, bellies down, gripping their sniper weapons.

Jacob carried a Model 700 Remington .308 with a Brown Precision Fiberglass stock and a U.S. Optics Fixed 10X scope. He had camo'd the stock himself with paint and leaves native to this area of Northern California. In an urban environment, like a city street or rooftop, he simply used black netting to conceal his weapon.

Kathryn's newly issued rifle was also a Model 700, with a 4.5 X 14 Leupold Scope. The fiberglass stock on her rifle was done up in forest green camo straight from the factory.

They both wore ear plugs and safety glasses. Kathryn discharged her rifle. Jacob looked through his scope and pulled out one earplug. Kathryn did the same.

"Aim point?" Jacob asked.

"Left eye."

"Your hit?"

"It's low. Left cheek."

"I guess she won't be singing for Destiny's Child anymore."

"Uh, Lisa 'Left Eye' Lopes sang for TLC, not Destiny's Child. And besides that, she's dead now."

"Yeah, I know. You just killed her."

"Cute. Maybe you should stick to Beatles references."

"Fair enough. Okay, refocus on your breathing. Half breath out, and hold."

"Wait."

Kathryn rolled over to her sniper case. Identical to Jacob's, it was a Pelican-Hardigg hard-shell resin composite case capable of holding two M16s with or without grenade launchers. Inside, each case was unique in that the air-compressed foam conformed to each individual sniper weapon. Meaning, no two cases held the exact same weaponry or paraphernalia.

The Pelican case also had a pressurized O-ring seal with a pressure release valve in case there was a need for air travel. There was a humidity indicator. And the case was weatherproof and the foam eliminated any vibration to the rifle while it was being transported. It was virtually indestructible. It could take a direct hit from a mortar round.

In addition to her rifle, Kathryn's case held what Jacob referred to as *wazoo gadgets*. Modern tactical technology. *Gizmos.*

She now extracted a rangefinder and affixed it to her weapon. Jacob didn't comment. He didn't approve, but he didn't comment. He knew what it was. What it would do. It was an instrument that sent out a laser beam and then told the user the distance. He knew they were currently one hundred yards out, the length of a football field—the distance at which most trainees start to balk—but of course Kathryn was not yet familiar enough with this range to know that. But he also knew that the hardest thing for anyone—sniper or not—to judge was range. Distance. And the size of the objects in your line of view and how they changed your impression of distance.

Jacob knew that it was critical she be able to plug these targets dead on at one hundred yards. Anything beyond that was less critical, because on call-outs, the sniper team was almost always able to get to one hundred yards or less. The more populated the area, the more accurate your shot needed to be. Especially if there were houses next door, across the street, etc.

He considered what Kathryn was doing with the rangefinder to be cheating. But he also didn't want to be thought of as a Luddite. So he made no comment. Not yet. But it rankled. Sharpshooting was a skill that was earned, not accomplished with the flip of a switch. It took real shooters to do it correctly. Guys who'd grown up hunting and bringing meat home for dinner. Guys, if he was being honest, like himself.

Kathryn resumed her belly-down position next to him. She flipped on the rangefinder and put her eye to the scope. Then she lifted her head, looked at Jacob, embarrassed.

"What? Does it pull the trigger for you, too?"

"Battery's dead. No beam, no ping. I've got a backup."

She started to roll back to her case, but Jacob grabbed her by the wrist and stopped her.

"Are you on fire or what? Stop with the rolling thing. It draws attention. A sniper never gives away his location. And why isn't all your gear right here next to you?"

Using elbows and toes, Kathryn slithered low to the ground to retrieve her gear, but once again, Jacob stopped her.

"No. Uh-uh. You're on a mission. Call-out simulation. You *can't* change your batteries. Those few seconds mean someone's life. You've got the green light. You've got to take your shot. What we do is not a video game. It doesn't run on batteries."

Kathryn nodded.

"Don't think about the crutch you don't have. Just remember your breathing. Half breath out, and hold it."

They replaced their ear plugs. Kathryn sank into her scope,

breath out halfway. The sharp report was a muffled crack to them, but it rolled across the range like a dire warning. Kathryn looked through her scope and smiled.

"Left eye."

"Well done. Okay. Make your weapon safe. I'm going down-range and put up a new target."

Kathryn thumbed back the metal bolt and cleared her weapon.

"Clear to go downrange."

Jacob rose, opened his bulky camo bag, and pulled out a new target and a staple gun. Once downrange, he stapled the new target right on top of the one Kathryn had just shot. The target was the size of a sheet of paper—8½ by 11. There were two black-and-white heads copied on it. The bad guy was wearing a ski mask and was only half visible behind Lieutenant Cowell's face. The overlap was several inches.

Jacob walked back to his bag, replaced the staple gun, and lowered himself back down between his bag and Kathryn.

"Okay. On my command. Ears on."

They both replaced their ear plugs.

"Okay. Target acquisition."

Kathryn looked through her scope and the face of her lieutenant came into sharp focus. Jacob was fucking with her head. But the margin of safety was comfortable. Plenty of room. Let him fuck with her.

She said, "On it," meaning that she had picked where she was going to place the shot—be it the bad guy's cheek, forehead, eyehole, whatever, it was her decision.

"Green light."

A loud crack as Kathryn discharged her weapon.

Jacob said, "Don't look at your hit."

Kathryn averted her gaze from the scope.

"I'm going back downrange and retrieve the target."

Kathryn thumbed back her bolt again, clearing it.

"Clear to go downrange."

Kathryn tapped her fingers on the side of her weapon, watching Jacob make his way to the target and then back to her. A hundred yards took some time to cover round-trip on foot.

"How do you think you did?"

"I really don't know. I think I shot the bad guy. It was a tight shot, but not that tight. I've had slimmer margins for error. You know that. It wasn't a hard shot. You know what I'm capable of."

"Then why aren't you sure? Why do I hear hesitation?"

"Probably because you're acting all Zen Master on me all of a sudden. And it's freaking me out."

He showed Kathryn her target. She had shot Lieutenant Cowell. Barely, but she shot him.

"Shit."

"What happened? Like you said, you're capable of much tighter shots than this."

"I'm not sure. My aim point was right in line."

"With . . ."

"The bad guy's left eye."

"And you hit . . ."

"Higher and to the right. I hit the hostage."

"Lieutenant Cowell. You shot Lieutenant Cowell."

"Yeah, I know who the hostage was. What's your point?"

"My point is that you knew who the hostage was. And that affected your shooting. You hesitated. You doubted. You know Lieutenant Cowell. You like Lieutenant Cowell. He hired you. Your hesitancy and uncertainty made you—"

"Pull my shot. High and right."

"Just so you know, every sniper has trouble shooting at someone they know. Even in effigy. The first few times you can expect this. It's human nature."

Kathryn nodded.

"You have to learn to look past them. Make them obstacles, block them mentally, do whatever you need to do in your head to negate that familiarity. If you can't do that, bad things happen."

"Like Oswald?"

Jacob stared at her. Then said, "What happened with Oz was different. But it underscores the mental aspect to all of this. Doubt. Hesitation. Guilt. These things can destroy you. After the shot is taken. Doubt. Hesitation. Guilt. These things can destroy the hostage. Before the shot is taken."

Jacob was amazed at his little speech. He really was getting all Zen Master and shit. Over his career, he had trained many spotters. Only a few had gone on to become primary snipers in other jurisdictions. The only way for anybody to take Jake's job in this jurisdiction was to outshoot him or kill him. He figured Kathryn might be considering both of those options. But the odds were that Kathryn would wash out as well. That was just the reality of it. But he was treating her differently. Training her differently. He was giving her of himself. Not just the technical training, but what he had learned. And it wasn't because she was different. It was because Jacob himself was different. He had reached a point in his life where he felt a need to pass on the real things to another human being. He had no child, no son, to give this to, so he was giving it to Kathryn. And maybe the fact that she was a woman did make a difference. Maybe that was why he was able, for the first time in his life, not to just teach, but to give of himself, to reveal.

"If we keep shooting regularly and you keep practicing your dry firing, it'll become automatic."

"I was taught never to dry fire my weapon."

"Well, the department only buys us so much ammo, so it's not like you can just blow a thousand rounds through your new rifle. It gets expensive to buy your own. And we're not allowed to reload spent shells. So sometimes dry firing is the only way to learn your trigger pull and how it feels. If it bothers you, get a snap cap. A dummy round."

Kathryn nodded her understanding.

Jacob looked at his own completed target. He said, "And remember, 99.9 percent of the time our shots are cold barrel shots. So the closer you can get your three-round group to your cold barrel shot the better. Ideally, you'd want them all in one hole."

Kathryn rolled her eyes in an *as-if* gesture, and he showed her his target. His three rounds were all in the same hole. *Fuckin' Denton.* She sighed, nodded, then collapsed the legs of the bipod on her weapon. She rose and carried the weapon to its case and put it away.

Jacob laid back down and peered through his scope.

Kathryn looked skyward. The sun, like a bullet, unforgiving.

"So are we done?"

"You seem to be." His voice had a far-away quality. He was already down the rabbit hole. Seeking his perfect peace.

"But you're not?"

"Nope." Remote. Far away.

"Well, let's recap this day. We watched our captain gunned down like a dog in the street, put all of the officers we were supposed to be protecting in mortal danger by not taking out an armed maniac, played hide-and-seek in full ghillies at a hundred degrees. I just killed my lieutenant. Well, hell, the day's young. Let's practice for a few more hours."

Jacob kept his attention in the scope, downrange.

Kathryn kicked at a clump of bunchgrass. "What?"

Jacob didn't look up. But he spoke.

"Do you know how your weapon shoots at dusk? Do you know how changes in barometric pressure affect your ballistics? Have you ever shot when you're as tired as you seem to be right now? Are you just going to walk away on a call-out when it's been a long hot day? If so, keep walking. I can't use you."

Kathryn unpacked her gear and settled belly down in the dust next to her partner.

"Look, Jacob. Obviously I have a lot to learn. And no, I would not walk away on a call-out. I assumed you knew that or I wouldn't be here. Mentally, I'm still stuck on your previous partner losing his mind and Captain Bryant losing his life."

Jacob pulled himself from the scope.

"Fair enough. I know I'm pushing you but you'll never complete Phase One until you know the answers to those questions. I'm not a total asshole, I recognize it can be too much at once. You just need to know your limitations. Go home, get a good night's sleep, and we'll train tomorrow afternoon and maybe after dark."

She nodded and lifted herself from the dirt. She'd shown herself willing and that seemed to be enough for him. For today.

"Yes, sir. I'll be there."

"Don't call me sir. And don't expect me to stop pushing."

Once he heard Kathryn's car pull away, Jacob broke down his weapon. He'd had enough for one day as well. He wasn't as young as he once was. He'd just wanted to make a point. He collapsed his bipod and started gathering his gear.

The slanting sun swept the earthen parking deck that rested on a steep rise just above the training grounds. Jacob loaded the last of his targets and gear into the Ford Expedition, and paused a minute beside his vehicle to appreciate the view of the sun setting behind the hills that surrounded him. The embankment rose several hundred feet above the training grounds and served dual purpose as a firebreak. The sloping hill had nothing green growing on it and was striated with ridges and ditches to control soil erosion.

Jacob got behind the wheel and shifted the Expedition into reverse. It was a good solid vehicle with plenty of power. It was a DAS vehicle—Dope Asset Seizure. Unofficially, it now belonged to the SWAT team, and even more unofficially, it was the sniper's unit used for training and call-outs. All jurisdictions were different. Here, they would not spend the money for a dedicated sniper vehicle, but the Expedition just never seemed to make it to the seized assets auction, held quarterly. In these budget-tightening times, the only way to acquire a vehicle of choice was dope raids. Assets were seized and you grabbed the ATV or the bad-ass Dodge All-Wheel Drive as yours. Otherwise, you were at the mercy of a bean counter who thought he knew what suited your needs best. Jacob's daily patrol stretched west from Folsom Prison to Cameron City, and then all the way to South Lake Tahoe and Camptown—the high country where they pretty much had their own laws, and where most deputies would not patrol alone.

He needed a vehicle that could handle just about any terrain and any weather conditions Northern California could throw at it. From mudslides to brush fires, to snowstorms and black ice. With a push bar and winch on the front, studded snow tires in the winter, and mud and snow tires in the summer, the Ford Expedition fit the bill. It was a big-ass SUV, and Jacob could have had it tricked out, converting it into a marked unit with stars, badges, bells, whistles, everything. Even a P.A. to say "Pull your fucking car over NOW!" And if they didn't, he could give them an attention-getting tap with a little push-bar nudge. But he did none of those things. The sniper's code was anonymity. He had a bubble light inside in case he needed to suddenly drive code three. And that was it.

Even though he knew he was alone, out of habit he checked his rearview as he backed out of the space. A spark of light caught his eye. In the mirror, he saw a pinpoint flash in the brushy hillside. He dove down onto the floor. The sniper's bullet slammed through the back window and shattered the rearview mirror. The battered mirror frame bounced around and fell on Jacob's shoulder. He picked up the twisted remnant, looked at it, and tossed it away.

That's when he remembered he was moving. The car was rolling backward. He had not yet turned the steering wheel to angle out of the parking space, so the Expedition was rolling straight back. Straight toward the unvegetated slope of the parking deck. It was easily a three-hundred-foot embankment. He couldn't simply sit up and press the brake without exposing himself to more sniper fire. And his body was angled across the floorboard so that his boots were too tangled in the well to do him any good. So he shifted his body position, working to bring his head and shoulders to the driver's seat and press the brake pedal with his hand. But he didn't move fast enough. He felt the gentle *thlump* of the rear tires sinking over the paved lip of the deck. The vehicle picked up sudden speed. He had his hand to the brake pedal when the rear tires went into the first erosion ditch. The jarring movement slammed his whole body into the console and back into the footwell. The vehicle rocked as the tires rolled through one ditch after another. Jacob was wedged into the footwell, but still getting banged around pretty good. Near the bottom of the hill, the soil in one of the ridges gave way and caused the vehicle to shift so that it turned horizontally along the hillside. Jacob had righted himself once again and had his hand on the brake pedal when he felt the two passenger-side wheels slip over a ridge. The sandy soil gave way with a stomach-dropping finality. The Expedition rolled. Just one revolution, then it was at the bottom of the embankment. Resting on its four wheels like a child had picked it up and set it back down there. The roll bar had done its job. The vehicle was dusty and a little dented but fine. As was Jacob.

Before the shock absorbers had even finished swaying, Jacob imagined himself opening the car door and rolling out while drawing his .45 automatic. But it would leave him exposed. He was actually safer in the vehicle.

Crouched low on the floorboard, he retrieved his cell phone and dialed.

The lieutenant answered simply, "Cowell."

"So, Joe, what's the latest on that whole sniper/murder thing?"

"Cortez and Hasan brought Lee Staley in for questioning. Noncooperative. Kicked him loose."

"It's not Oz."

"You can't know that."

"Someone just took a shot at me, and I rolled the Expedition. I'm at the training range. Bottom of the parking embankment. Waiting to see if there's more fire coming."

"What?"

"Someone just took a shot at me, and—"

"Are you hurt?"

"No. Look, I watched this guy in action with Bryant, so I'm guessing that I'd probably be dead right about now if that's what he wanted."

"Sonofabitch. I'm sending units. Stay in your vehicle. Stay low."

"No kidding."

CHAPTER 15

Once he'd given his account and the medics had cleared him (he'd bruised a rib, but that was it), Cowell had called again and ordered Jacob off the scene. Told him to go home. He reminded Jacob that he could use the rest because he had the psych eval next week. Jacob told Cowell that he'd rather be shot at, but complied. One of the deputies took him back to the S.O. so he could get his personal vehicle.

On the way home, he debated the pros and cons of telling Jill what had happened. That somebody had taken a shot at him. Thank God he'd been in the Expedition. He didn't know how he'd explain the missing back window to Jill if he'd been in his own truck. It would be hard enough hiding his tender rib. She rarely missed anything. If she sensed him holding back, or lying, it could be ugly. Things rarely got ugly between them because they were always truthful with one another.

Here he was, having been shot at, but not hit, for the second time today. This was a deliberate action by the shooter, just as it had been at Captain Bryant's house. He made a mental note to review the interrogation room sign-out logs tomorrow. Just to see for himself if Oswald had still been in for questioning when the sniper had been setting up his shot. Even though he didn't believe his friend was behind this, he needed to know if it was possible.

He knew Jill needed to know for safety reasons. Death threats often came with the job, and he'd always passed on information of recently paroled felons or shown Jill pictures of people to watch for while she was out and about. The worst case scenario was someone showing up at their home. Jill was armed and prepared. She had guns all over the house and almost always carried concealed. But in this case, he could scarcely wrap his head around what this shooter was doing tailing him, and making a fucking game of it. This was the first time Jacob had been specifically targeted. These were uncharted waters he struggled in, and before he knew it he was turning into their driveway.

He sat in his truck a moment longer, still unsure. He decided he needed more information from Cowell and the officers at the range to compare what had happened there with what had happened at Bryant's house. He didn't want to spook Jill with only part of the story. He would wait until he got the latest intelligence from the investigators still working the range site. He finally decided he wouldn't tell her. He sighed and got out of the truck.

He had only ever had one secret from her in all the years of their marriage and that was his collection of spent shells. He hid that from her. But it was just a private thing. Jake himself didn't understand the significance of those shells. But he held on to them. Ghoulish mementos, he supposed. Watercolored memories, his old mentor, Lee Staley might have said. Of the way we were. Of the way *they* were. The seventeen people those brass casings stood for. They used to be alive. Now they were dead. Because of Jacob Denton.

He would make the shooting range incident secret number two. It would be wrong to place a burden of stress and fear on Jill's shoulders. He didn't want to do that to her. She was his center, but she had not been the same—mentally or physically— since the accident that had ended her medic/firefighter career. That career was how she had defined herself. They'd met on the job. They'd seen each other through a rain-spattered ambulance window. Just a glance. Then four years passed before they saw each other again, but they both remembered. And they fell in love. And now, these years later, although they still had no children, they were as close as a man and woman could be.

It occurred to him that if it were not for Jill, he would have lived his life as a loner. He would fit a profile. He existed on the far side of a spectrum that included folks like Timothy McVeigh and Ted Kaczynski. Even though he was one of the good guys, when he looked at McVeigh or Kaczynski—the urge to be apart from society, the inability to comprehend that society—he saw that he had things in common with them. Not a pleasant thought. But Jill brought him out of himself. He cared about her. And through that he saw that he cared about the world, too. Still wanted to be a part of it.

●　　　●　　　●

Jill was bustling in the kitchen with dinner under way. Jake dropped his big camouflage bag on the floor near the kitchen counter. With a dish in one hand, a spoon in the other, and her foot propping open the refrigerator door, Jill leaned toward Jake. He met her halfway and they kissed quickly.

"Hi, honey," she said and closed the refrigerator with her foot.

"Hello, beautiful, nice moves. Kitchen ballet," Jacob said as he went about his routine. He pulled his .45 from his holster and laid it on the countertop. Then he unzipped the bag and pulled out a thick stack of targets. He put them on the counter just as Jill said, "Did you shoot today?" She was stirring red sauce on the stove. It smelled nice and garlicky.

"Yes, ma'am," Jake said and moved to the refrigerator and took out a Corona.

Jill clicked the spoon on the pot, closed the lid and wiped her hands on a towel. She went to the counter and said, "Well then, let's have a look." She started thumbing through his used targets. "So . . . how are you?" she asked without looking up. "By the way, I had to defend your honor today. Again. Susan? That student of mine? She asked me how I could live with a professional killer."

"Wow. Harsh. What did you tell her?"

"I told her if she saw you naked she'd know how."

"How what?"

"How I could live with a professional killer. If she saw you naked, she'd know. Get it? Are you with me? I don't think you're here with me tonight."

Jake realized that he was thinking about his day, not paying attention to Jill.

"I'm here," he said. "That was a good comeback. You writers call it a quip, right?" He moved to the stove and peeked in the steaming pot. Spaghetti sauce bubbled.

"Right, a quip. That's assuming, of course, that she hasn't seen you naked."

"Not this week," he said.

She lifted her head from the targets and he winked at her. She held up one of the targets. It was a sheet of $8\frac{1}{2}$ by 11 paper with concentric circles and in the center, a black bull's-eye no bigger than a quarter.

"Ten rounds, 200 yards?" The center was almost completely shot out and no rounds had escaped that boundary. "Not bad," she said as if there were plenty of room for improvement.

Jake sat at the bar while Jill reviewed his targets. He was just starting to feel comfortable settling into their normal routine, when out of nowhere he heard, "So you don't have anything to tell me?" She lifted her eyes and stared right at him. "Nothing? At all?"

He started to open his mouth and stopped.

Jill tapped the targets into a stack and spoke, not necessarily to him, but at him. "You know, I'd like to think after all these years you would trust me enough to know you can tell me anything. Anything. I was a firefighter and a medic, remember? Before I got hurt? I can take bad news. It only makes it worse when I have to hear it from someone else."

"I didn't want you to worry," he said.

"Don't bother. I already heard about it from Jeannie Cowell."

Cowell must have told his wife, and Jeannie must have called Jill. Cowell was usually far more discreet than that. Jacob felt betrayed.

"Look at me," she said quietly. He looked up. She walked over to him. "You know with my background I'm not some timid little mouse who has to be coddled. I know there's ugly, evil shit out there. I've seen it often enough myself. But the only way to handle this stuff is the way we've always done it. Together."

He nodded. She lifted her hands to his face, held his head in her hands and said, "I just want to say this and then we don't even have to talk about it if you don't want to. I am so sorry about Captain Bryant. I know how close you two were when he was still on SWAT. I'm sorry you've lost your friend."

She pulled her head away and looked up at him. "Okay? So are we clear?"

He nodded again, and said, "Crystal." He'd been so far inside his own head, he had forgotten to tell her about Captain Bryant. He felt bad for not telling her right away—as he normally would have done—and for withholding the incident at the shooting range.

Jill walked back over to look at his targets, and he got up to taste the spaghetti sauce. He took the spoon, dipped it into the pot, brought it to his lips and said, "Hmmm." He knew for Jill, it was over. She never held a grudge, and once something was discussed and behind them, that's where it stayed.

Jill kept going through his targets. It was part of their ritual. He'd killed no one today, but the process of making the abnormal seem normal was a continuous one. The next target had a dime-sized bull's-eye.

One slightly misshapen hole was in the center.

"Three rounds, hundred yards?"

Jacob nodded, smiled, and took a drink. The next target was a woman's face with a man's face half visible behind the woman.

Jill held the page at eye level. The man's eye had a single shot through it. Jill put it down and moved on to the next one.

"Uh-oh. Lawsuit."

Jill held out a target.

"What do you mean 'lawsuit'? That's a great shot."

Two full faces on this one, a man and a woman. A third face, the bad guy, was visible behind and between the two hostage faces. The hostage-taker was visible through only about a quarter-sized space. Five rounds had been shot through it.

"Show me the lawsuit."

"Look. Right here."

Jill pointed to a tiny spot where one of the rounds touched the outline of the woman hostage's cheek.

"Hmmm."

"Well? What have you got to say for yourself?"

Jacob took another drink and shrugged.

"She flinched. I can't control everything."

"Be that as it may, she'd still own our house."

Jill restacked the targets, tapping them neatly on the countertop.

"A little sloppy," she said. "But if it were me, I'd still want you to take the shot, I guess."

"Thanks a lot."

Jill moved to the refrigerator and took out a Tupperware container of salad and set it on the counter.

"No matter how it ended up, I'd still love you."

"That's a relief."

"Even if it meant I'd be deaf in one ear and have to eat through a straw for the rest of my life."

She should have been smiling at her own joke, but a frown creased her lips and touched her eyes.

"I didn't see Sesak's targets. She kept hers?"

Jill moved back to the stove and Jake pirouetted to the countertop where she'd just been. Kitchen ballet.

"She left early, before I could grab them," he said.

The frown deepened.

"She left you? Her whole job is to watch your back while you're on target and she left?"

Jake could hear the irritation, indignation, and a touch of fear in her voice. It was only now that he considered what would have happened if Kathryn had stayed. He knew that the bullet was meant for him, not her. And only as a message for him. This person had waited for Kathryn to leave. Thinking about it made him reevaluate the wisdom of not telling Jill what had happened. Her voice brought him out of his own head again.

"Jake? She left you there?"

"Not in the way you think. And it really was a shitty day."

She cocked her head like a dog waiting to hear a word it recognized. "Of course it was," she said, "but it was shitty for everybody. That doesn't mean she gets to just quit! She'll never complete Phase One that way. She'll wash right out." Her arms were now crossed in front of her.

Jake could hear the weakness of his words in his own voice. "Well, I cut her a little slack because she's new."

"I've never seen you cut the guys any slack. Ever."

Jesus Christ. Would this day never end? Now he was defensive. On edge.

"Meaning?"

"Meaning you're treating her differently because she's a female."

Jake could feel his mouth trying to move while his brain raced. *Was* he treating her differently? Maybe. Jill was worried. He'd never worked with a female partner before. And she knew the reality of that scenario. They both knew from their careers that things happen. Kathryn was his new partner. And a partnership in this line of work was a marriage of sorts. You spent at least as much time with your partner as your spouse. You did an intense job together, and in the aftermath, exhaustion set in and professional barriers were relaxed. They had both seen it happen.

Yes, he was treating Kathryn differently. Any other spotter he would have ridden into the dirt. Pushed him to his limits. But his feelings for Kathryn weren't romantic or lustful. Far from it. What he felt for her was closer to what a father would feel for his daughter. He knew he could tell Jill this and her jealousy would end, because she would see the truth in it. But he couldn't say that to her. It would cause an even deeper pain. Because it would remind Jill that she had failed to give him a child of his own to raise and love and teach.

There was no winning this one. No way out.

He finally said, "It's not that. It's not because she's a female. It's what she could process as an individual and today was too much. Emotionally, I guess. At least for her."

Jill considered this and saw the logic in his point. And just like that it was over.

"Well then," she said, "she'd better learn to pull on her big girl panties or she won't last."

Jake chuckled and said, "I think she will."

Jill moved back to the refrigerator and Jake decided now was the time to escape. Tonight, after this day from hell, all he wanted was a shower, some food, and to hold Jill in his arms.

"Time for a quick shower before dinner?" he asked as he passed the refrigerator.

"Sure," she said, and he ran his hand across her butt on the way out. "Hey now, I'm working here!" she said in her normal, cheerful voice.

CHAPTER 16

In the kitchen, Jill sat on one of the barstools overlooking the stove area. She studied her hands on the counter in front of her. Her eyes went to her wedding ring and her right hand twisted it around her finger.

He'd become defensive and testy when she brought up Sesak. *Kathryn.* An attractive, younger, female cop. Jill knew what it was like to be a female in a male-dominated profession, so she felt a kinship with Kathryn. Women like them just kept their mouths shut and did their job and eventually the respect came. Jill knew how hard it was and she empathized. You had to work twice as hard to be thought half as good, and you really needed to have the physical strength for the job. Jill had caught a genetic break by growing tall and strong enough to do the work (even though she still seemed small next to Jake). She took special pride in having been hired before there were minority quotas. She kicked ass on her two-day mental and physical strength tests and won her job. So Jill was already in Kathryn's corner whether Kathryn knew it or not. But not if it meant a threat to everything she and Jake had been through and built together.

As much as she loved and trusted Jake, and as much as she understood and identified with the obstacles Kathryn faced, Jill also knew the reality of men and women working together in these public safety professions. You do an intense job and in the aftermath—while you're loading dry hose back on the engine, restocking your ambulance, cleaning it out, whatever—there was a bizarre sexual chemistry that came out as your exhaustion set in and you lowered your normal professional barriers by saying out loud what you'd been thinking for years, which might well be, "I'm hot for your body."

That's why you would see doctors and nurses become couples (especially emergency room ones), surgeons and surgical technicians, cops and firefighters. All of those adrenaline-junkie jobs ignited a post-call-out atmosphere of flirting and sexual tension. You'd just saved someone's life together and maybe even did it when the person was clinically dead when you got there. Or you might be so physically exhausted you could hardly speak, but what came out of your mouth was what you *really* thought about your partner.

Barriers dropped. And sometimes pants did, too.

Frankly, Jake had been an arrogant asshole about females in these professions. He railed about the ones who were hired "because they had to be" to fill quotas, and griped that they just weren't physically big enough to do the job. Or they were lesbians. Not that it mattered. Jill was often mistaken for one herself.

Add the short haircut—for safety reasons—and people just assumed you were gay.

After Jill and Jake met—at a murder scene no less—he said he remembered seeing her through an ambulance window years before. She remembered it, too. She had thought about him. But meeting him face to face, talking to him, she recognized his prejudice and silently went about her life showing him what a female could do. She was proud that she'd forced Jake to rethink his knee-jerk reaction about all females in male jobs. He saw she could not only do it, she excelled at it. She knew she had won his respect and his heart the day he put a license plate frame (that she had bought for him as a joke) on his personal vehicle. It said MY HEART BELONGS TO A FIREFIGHTER. It sealed their fate and they were soon married and both working exciting, adrenaline-junkie jobs.

They had even worked some calls together where he had to remind himself that she was not his wife in that moment, and it was her *job* to go back inside the burning building. To get down in the blood, glass, and alcohol in order to shimmy into an overturned, collapsed car. Or to calm a drunk belligerent biker and gain his compliance. Just as she had to wait outside on a possible suicide scene until Jacob and the other cops went in and made sure there were no weapons involved. EMTs could not enter a scene before they were cleared by law enforcement.

She remembered one day when she and her partner anxiously watched a house that deputies were in the process of clearing, and strained to hear what was going on. To her utter dismay, two deputies came running out as if fleeing for their very lives. Jake was not with them. Then, she saw him appear and motion Jill and her partner onto the scene while the two other cops laughed at her and how big her eyes had been.

She said, "Very funny, assholes, I'll remind you of that next time you roll a patrol car!"

"Aw, Jill! C'mon!"

They helped each other by being the soft place to fall when needed. Jill knew one thing she could absolutely never do in her career was to cry on the job. Crying was the kiss of death in such occupations. So she learned to suck it up. And then here came Jake. A man who understood the rules of engagement. She could tell him anything. Cry in front of him and know she was safe. After a particularly brutal call, she remembered how she'd snuck into the station's office cubicle, away from the bunks where the rest of her shift members slept. It was about three in the morning when she called, and Jake had answered the phone by simply saying, "Tell me." And she did. She needed it all out of her then and there.

And slowly he came to trust that she could harbor his deepest secrets and fears as well. Through it all she had never doubted Jake's devotion to her as she was sure he never doubted her devotion to him. Oh sure, there were always the cop groupies to deal with. Women in love with the uniform, hitting on cops to get out of a ticket or for their own sexual kicks. The groupies just came with the outfit. Accessories. She could handle them with ease. There were other kinds of females she could not abide, though. Like the ones who falsely cried rape after being arrested. It had seemed like something the guys just rolled their eyes at, so Jill never paid much attention to it. Until the day Jake came home and told her a woman he had transported to the county jail was accusing him of raping her in the patrol car. Suddenly it was real and horrific. How dare this woman lie like that? About *her* husband? An accusation like that could result in "unpaid time off pending an Internal Affairs Investigation."

These women rarely won their cases because they didn't realize that everything was recorded. Cameron County was just now catching up to technology's pace by placing cameras in each unit. But radio traffic had always been recorded. Without the benefit of cameras, officers gave a code over the air while transporting a female and read off their starting mileage on the odometer. When they arrived at the jail they would give their ending odometer readings. These transmissions were time-stamped as well, so no false claim ever really went very far. In some cases, the accusation didn't even clear the Watch Commander's desk that day because it was so outrageous.

Jake had once been accused of raping a woman forty-two times on a thirty-minute ride to jail—absurd on many levels, but such was the life of a cop. The guys on SWAT were giddy in anticipation of Jill's reaction. She and Jake were newly married then, and she had been more jealous in those days. That weekend, she saw the team on a training day where she was playing the part of a hostage. When she got out of her car the hoots and hollers began immediately.

"Hey, Jill? How'd you like that? He's a persistent little fella it sounds like!"

And then she heard, "Lucy! He's got some 'splainin' to do!"

And finally, "Not satisfying his needs on the home front?"

She shut them all up when she said, "Hey, as long as he didn't break his old record I'm fine with it." And walked away. Jake's laughter was full, loud, and long. She cherished it.

She had felt powerful then. Proud she'd gone toe-to-toe with them. And she realized it was the feeling of powerlessness that was eating her from the inside out now. This was her life and she wasn't used to being an idle observer. She was feeling the way she felt in the aftermath of her injury. When they told her she'd never work another day on her torn-up leg. At least not in her dream job. Jill had no backup plan in place. It never occurred to her she could lose her job to an injury. Hell, they all got nicked up and bruised, sprained and dehydrated. It all just came with the territory. They worked through the pain and always came back, sometimes working right through an injury. Until that day. That god-awful, irreversible day. And yet, it had happened. In memory, Jill reached down and rubbed her right lower leg, where the pain was most persistent and constant. A bone-deep ache that would never go away.

Jake had a mandated appointment with a psychiatrist coming up, which she knew concerned him. Hell, it concerned her, but they had talked about that and how it was always the unknown that scared people.

People almost always imagine scarier monsters, worse scenarios, and bloodier bodies than the truth bore out. It was usually much less intense or dramatic. There was even a reality show on television predicated around this phenomenon, where people were put in pitch-black darkness and then simple things were done to them or near them. Performers with night vision goggles would touch the contestants, then quickly move around and touch them again. A feather might be rubbed across their face. There were epic freakouts because of the total darkness. The not knowing what was there. Suddenly, a household broom was some horrific instrument of torture and all because someone had turned out the lights. The human brain's reaction to the unknown could be spectacular. Some contestants looked like they might spontaneously combust if the lights weren't turned on immediately.

The human brain and the unknown were a powerful combination.

And here she sat with a big-ass load of "unknown." She just couldn't shake the feeling that Jake was hiding something from her. She didn't want to believe that it had anything to do with his new female partner. But he *was* hiding something.

Of course, she was hiding something, too. But she didn't want to tell Jake about it. Not yet. It would be wrong to place a burden of worry and concern on his shoulders. Not until she knew for sure.

CHAPTER 17

The next morning, Jill was folding clothes in the bedroom. She and Jacob had made love in the night. It was good. Not coming-down-off-an-adrenaline-high good, but not bad for a couple of middle-aged married people.

She had a busy day lined up, and thinking about it made her stomach hurt. She had a class to teach at eleven, then one of her students who was struggling with writing believable dialogue was coming over for one-on-one tutoring, and after that she would be seeing both her sister and her mother. Seeing either one of them alone was bad enough, but together there was a tag-team effect that was enough to give a person gastrointestinal distress.

Out in the living room, the television was turned up too loud. Jake was out there flipping through the channels like a five-year-old with ADHD. And dry firing his weapon. His .45. Shooting at images on the screen. There was a certain rhythm to what he was doing. The SHHH STTKK of the sliding of the gun's action. Followed by flickering silence as the channel changed. Then the metal click of the pistol hammer. SHHH STTKK, channel change, click. An endless cycle. Jill laid a t-shirt on the bed. SHHH STTKK: left sleeve fold over. Channel change: right sleeve fold over. click: shirt folded in half. She folded another shirt to the same cadence, SHHH STTKK, channel change, click. She finally realized what she was doing and went to the living room where Jake held his .45 in one hand and the TV remote in the other. He put the remote down to work the action on his weapon, SHHH STTKK . . . Picked the remote back up to change the channel . . . then took aim at the TV and pulled the trigger, click. SHHH STTKK, channel change, click.

She watched as he continued, oblivious to her presence. She stared at the screen. He was murdering indiscriminately. Jerry Springer was the first to go, followed by Dr. Oz. Then Jane Fonda. Twice. Traitorous bitch. Jill's father had served in the Air Force in Vietnam. And now she was being honored as one of the hundred greatest females or something? It was disgusting. Jill shook it off and refocused on Jake. Apparently Jake wasn't feeling the same morning-after glow as Jill. It looked like maybe he was back in his bad place. He didn't even look up when she stood right next to him.

"Hey, where are you?"

"I'm right here."

"No. No you're not."

"Where am I, then?"

"I don't know. You're not here, though. You've gone away from me again. Are you back on your daddy's ranch? Is that where you are?"

"No."

"I think you are. I think you're back in Montana. With the snow and the sheep and the wolves."

"No."

"You're not here. And you're not there. Where are you?"

"Jill, I don't know. I guess I'm in the middleground."

"The middleground?"

"Yeah, I guess so."

"Well, you need to decide which way you're going to go. Back to the sheep and wolves, or forward to California. This is the Golden State, you know."

"I've heard."

In her soothing tourist-commercial tone of voice, Jill said, "Come to California . . ." which didn't get a smile from Jake. That line usually did. Instead he'd kept up the monotonous dry firing at the TV people.

Suddenly the Energizer Bunny appeared on-screen, and Jill threw herself in front of the TV.

"No! Not him! Not the bunny."

Jill grabbed the remote out of Jake's hand and quickly found Martha Stewart.

"You want to save the world? Shoot her."

Jacob smiled, worked the action again, though he kept the weapon pointed at the ceiling.

"Honey, you're downrange."

"What?"

"You're downrange."

She stared at him. Hands on hips.

"I am not downrange, Jake. I'm in our living room. And

aren't you working later today? Isn't that why you can't make Brodie's birthday party?"

"Yep. Afternoon and evening."

"Look at you! You're off duty and doing this! You've got me folding laundry in cadence. Stop it! Enjoy your morning off!"

He sighed and lowered his weapon.

"There's no such thing as an off-duty cop. I'm just trying to stay sharp."

"I know you are, but Jesus! Does it have to consume your every waking moment? When do you relax?"

"This is relaxing for me."

"No, honey. It's training. I know it for what it is. I just don't want you obsessing, unable to enjoy free time."

"I'm fine."

"Please, please take some time off. Read a book, actually *watch* the TV, go visit Oz, look at this."

Jill raised her t-shirt over her head and flashed him. Jake laughed. Neither of them wanted things to get tense.

"See? You need me to help get you out of that head of yours."

She walked toward him at the couch.

"It's just not safe to stay in there too long without a break, okay?"

He grabbed her waist and hugged her as she tapped him on the head.

"Okay?"

"Okay. I get it. I think I'll go visit Oz."

"Good idea. Does he know about Bryant?"

"Yeah, I think maybe he does."

.   .   .

Jacob found a grocery store in Hangtown and loaded up on goodies. He walked out with two bags full and a copy of the *Sacramento Bee* tucked under his arm. He put the bags on the passenger seat of his pickup truck, then sat behind the wheel and opened the paper to the classifieds. It took him a while, but he found a listing that looked perfect and circled it. He took out his cell phone and called the number in the ad. Once he was finished talking, Jacob started up his truck and drove away.

He had to walk up several flights of stairs to get to Oz's apartment. The elevator was out.

Outside the door, Jacob could hear Bob Dylan's forlorn voice pleading with his mother to take his guns away, because he just didn't have the heart to shoot them anymore. He stood there and listened to the song. He was afraid to knock. Afraid of what he might find on the other side. He hated to watch Oz's decline into a full-blown blue recluse, so he saw him less and less these days. It hurt too much. It hurt to see his mentor debase himself. But it also hurt to know that he could be looking at his own future. He'd thought the other day that the only way for Sesak to ever take his job was to outshoot him or kill him. But there was a third way. It was the way Jake himself had become primary sniper. His partner had gone 51–50. Lost his mind. If Jake went down the rabbit hole and never came back, then Sesak would become primary sniper. That was the third option.

Cowell had said, "We've gotta see how these hits are affecting you," and maybe the man was right. The psych appointment was just a week away, looming over him like test results at a cancer clinic. What would they find? What would they see when they examined his brain?

Jacob knocked, but got no response. The Dylan record ended. There was a pause as the tone arm lifted, and a light crackle as the needle sat back down into the opening grooves. Then Mr. Robert Allen Zimmerman was asking his mama to take his badge away, that he just had no use for it anymore.

This was bad. A Dylan 45 on repeat was a bad omen. Jake kept knocking. A long, authoritative cop knock. The kind of knock many of this building's occupants would be familiar with. He could just imagine some of them flushing their drugs down the toilet right about now.

Dylan was talking about a long, black cloud coming down when the needle was unceremoniously dragged across the record and the music stopped.

Jacob saw a shadowy flicker behind the peephole. The door opened.

Oswald didn't say anything. He made bleary, brief eye contact, then turned and made room for Jacob to enter. Piss, B.O., Old Crow, and Hoppe's. The usual odors.

"Bob Dylan. Has it come to that?"

"I'm afraid it has, Jake. I'm afraid it has. Nah, I just left it on in case Montezuma and Hay Seed showed back up. I'm fucking with their heads."

"Detectives Alejandro Cortez and Sayeed Hasan? They're okay."

"Yeah, they are. But I gotta give 'em hell. That's what crazy old fucks like me do. Give people hell."

"What else you got cued up? A little Johnny Cash? 'Don't Take Your Guns to Town'?"

Oz smiled. "You know it. And then 'Bang Bang,' Sonny & Cher. 'I Didn't Know the Gun Was Loaded,' the Andrews Sisters."

"The Andrews Sisters? And they call me old school. 'I Shot the Sheriff'?"

" 'I Don't Like Mondays,' Boomtown Rats."

"I don't get that one."

"Sometimes you gotta dig deeper. That song was about Brenda Ann Spencer."

"The, uh, San Diego elementary school shootings? She was the shooter."

"Right. Reporter asked her why she did it, she said, 'I don't like Mondays.' "

"In that case, good one. 'Saturday Night Special,' Lynyrd Skynyrd."

"A bit obvious after mine, but okay. 'Bang Bang (My Baby Shot Me Down),' Nancy Sinatra."

" 'Hey Man, Nice Shot,' Filter."

" 'Jeremy,' Pearl Jam."

"Yep. Jeremy spoke in class today. What about you, Oz? Did you speak in class? Did you speak to Bryant?"

"I'm saddened that you would ask me that. Truly, Jake. These days I'm less Pearl Jam and more Kiss. To wit: 'Love Gun.' "

" 'Love Gun'? Really?"

"Really."

"You got a girl?" Jake smiled, delighted by the idea that Oswald was seeing someone.

Oswald shrugged and said, "A companion, yes."

"Who's the lucky recipient of your high-caliber lust?"

"Why use names? A rose is a rose is a rose."

"You never were one to kiss and tell."

"My gun is quick, and my lips are sealed."

"I brought you some stuff," Jake said and sat the grocery sacks on the kitchen counter.

Oswald yawned and peeked into one of the bags. He dug to the bottom and pulled out a fifth of Johnnie Walker Red Label. He held it up and admired it.

"I guess I've been on your mind. This is a step up from the usual rotgut you bring me."

"If you look closely, I think there's some food in there, too."

Oz made a show of looking deeper and said, "Well, sure as shit."

He broke the seal on the whiskey and poured himself a quick shot into a jelly-jar glass. Downed it. Then poured another and offered it to Jacob.

"Waker-upper?"

"I generally try to wait till after 1700 hours."

Oswald shrugged and downed the shot himself.

"Mama's boy."

Jacob handed Oswald the newspaper folded open to the circled want ad. Oswald pretended to give it great attention, his mouth circled in an "O" of mock amazement.

"'Must have law enforcement experience.'"

He handed the paper back to Jacob.

"Well, I've certainly got that. Does it say 'burnt-out border-line alcoholic psychos need not apply?' It didn't, did it? Well, shit, I might have a chance. In fact, I recently interviewed with law enforcement. Aren't you proud? They showed a lot of interest in me."

"I just happened to see it, that's all. Jill and I have banked at the Morgan City branch for years. I, uh, well, I went ahead and gave the manager a call. Talked to him about you. He's interested. Call him."

"Maybe I will."

"You can use me as a reference. Cowell, too."

"Jesus. I really have been on your mind."

"Look, I'm not here because I think you shot Bryant. But I don't think you're the same man you used to be, either. And I think you know that. Do I think you're off your rocker, scary, dangerous? No, I don't. The reason I'm here is because I was on scene when Bryant took the hits. And I was shot at later the same day—"

"Someone took a shot at you?"

"Yeah. And I want your opinion. That's all. I want to know what you think."

"I'd love to sit down and palaver with you, Jake. Thing is, I'm not alone here."

Jake glanced at the closed bedroom door.

"She's still here? That is serious."

Oswald shrugged. "Not serious. You know me, Jake. I

subscribe to the four F's school of dating. Find 'em, feed 'em, fuck 'em, and forget 'em. Though I don't bother feeding 'em anymore."

Jacob crossed to the living room, to the television and the VCR that sat atop it and punched the eject button. VHS and 45s. Oz was definitely an analog guy. The machine made a good bit of mechanical noise before spitting out the tape. Jake looked at it.

"*Shane*? You showed her *Shane* and played her your Dylan records? I'd call that serious."

Oswald hung his head.

"What about the Kavanaugh poetry?" Jacob scanned the room and saw the book spread open facedown on the coffee table. "Yep, there—"

That's when Jake saw the brass shells set up like chess pieces on the coffee table.

"You showed her your collection? I've been married twenty some odd years and I've never—"

"How many is it for you now, Jake? Last I knew it was fourteen."

"I don't drink myself into oblivion every night looking at them."

Oswald walked over and picked up one of the empty shells. Studied it.

"And what will your last one be? *Who* will it be? This was my eighteenth, remember? My last."

Oswald moved the casing around in his hand, like a cardsharp manipulating a poker chip.

"Guy had beaten his wife over and over again. And that one night it went too far. We were on the neighbor's roof. Remember?"

Jacob swept the shells off the table, scattering them.

"It's bullshit! Holding on to the past."

"Oh yeah, you remember all right."

Oswald went calmly about collecting the shells, bent over, his back to Jacob.

Jacob headed for the door. He paused with his hand on the knob, his back to Oswald's back.

"It was nobody's fault. You know that."

"Do I?"

"You can't blame Bryant. And you can't blame me as your spotter. Once you've got the green, it's on you. And you can't blame yourself, either."

"Really? Bryant had no responsibility to know all the dynamics involved before giving a green?"

"You could have spoken up."

"She was my goddamn neighbor! I wanted to save her."

"Oz—"

"It's different when it's someone you know."

"It was still a good shot. No way to know the perp would squeeze the trigger when his brain short-circuited."

"No. The hostage died. That's the definition of it not being a good shot."

"Take the security job, Oz. It's time to put the past away."

Jacob closed the door on his way out.

amily is so special.

Jill thought this as she stacked birthday presents on the counter in the large eat-in kitchen. She was at her mom's house for her nephew Brodie's sixth birthday party.

It had been only one day since Jake had come home hiding a secret, and while things were okay between them, the idea that he was holding something back remained in the margins of her mind. It was like waiting for the results of a blood test. You tried not to think about it too much, but the news was coming. She just didn't know if it would be no-big-deal news or actual bad news. Life-altering, or just a bump in the road.

Jill watched her mother rinse lettuce (for a salad the kids would never eat) in the kitchen sink. Kate Brenner was, at sixty-two, a tall, stately woman. Elegant, even. The way she was holding up boded well for Jill and her sister, Megan.

Megan walked into the kitchen balancing two more presents wrapped in SpongeBob paper with a decorated birthday cake perched on top of the presents, and towing her eighteen-month-old toddler, Caitlyn. Miss Caitlyn had a blue pacifier parked securely between her lips, and cruised on in right behind her mom. Megan was also eight months pregnant and looked like she was about to tip over. Jill had to acknowledge that her sister was juggling all of this with grace. She had everything under control.

Seeing what Megan had, the life she'd built, made Jill feel jealous. And Jill didn't want to feel jealous. She hated herself for having that feeling and tore it down before it could get bigger. The closest she and Jake had gotten to having children was their two Saint Bernards, a male named Wyatt Morgan, and a female, Maggie Mae. They felt like real children to her and Jake. She remembered taking them out to parks and showing them off like a proud parent. *Look what my kid can do.* How people would come up to her and ask to pet them. They were big, imposing dogs, but kindness shone from their dark eyes. Jill could always tell how other people felt about Saint Bernards. If they called them "Beethoven dogs" they liked them. If she heard "Cujo," then she knew to hold the dogs' leashes tight.

Maggie Mae and Wyatt Morgan were both dead now. Maggie died of a bone cancer that was hereditary in Saint Bernards. Wyatt went not long after, mourning for his companion. And Jill was still too brokenhearted to replace them.

Caitlyn pulled at her mom's hem, and when Megan turned to see what her daughter wanted, the birthday cake slid from the top of the boxes in her grasp. In turning back to right the cake before it crashed to the floor, she knocked Caitlyn off-balance. And then somehow managed to save the cake and the presents and swoop down to catch Caitlyn before she fell down and went boom. It was quite a feat.

"I swear Jill, I don't know how I'm going to manage a third one. It's just not possible. We're going to have to give one to you and Jacob. Seriously. Pick one. Any one."

It was a joke. But it hurt. And Jill wondered if Megan knew it hurt. Of course she knew.

Family is so special.

Jill followed her mom out to the dining room to help set the table. Kate Brenner dealt out the party plates, and Jill added spoons and forks.

In a tone of voice that gave nothing away, Kate said, "So do we put out a plate for him or leave it blank as usual?"

"Mom, I told you. He's got a new partner and he has to spend extra time training her."

"A her? I didn't know that. Well, Roger is an actual new partner. Lawyers have complex responsibilities, too. And he's here."

"Brodie is Roger's son. That's different."

"That's fine, but family is family."

"Whatevs, Mom."

"Don't use that hippie talk with me."

"Mom, that is not hippie—"

"Your father had an affair. I think. I'm pretty sure. An office girl at the lumberyard."

"Oh for God's sake, he did not."

"I think he did. When men and women work that close and spend so much time together. Things happen. It's human nature. They start leaving for work early and getting home late. They stop going to family functions. There's special events at work. Daylong training sessions."

"That's not Jake. We're different. What we have is different."

"Whatevs, Jill. Whatevs."

"This is just absurd. Am I being filmed? This can't be real."

"And what it comes down to is they just act different. A woman can always tell when her man is different. You can tell. You can tell when they start hiding things. Secrets."

"Jake and I are different," Jill said, and was surprised at how quiet her voice had become. It no longer had conviction.

"Still, family is family. He should be here with you. It's suspicious."

"I'm not stupid. You know that, right? I'm not a stupid woman. I'm a published novelist. Reviewed in the *Washington Post*."

"Maybe *The Bee* will review the next one. Then I can show my friends."

Jill scanned the room one final time for hidden cameras, but accepted that this in fact was not a put-on. It was real. This was her reality.

Family is so special.

"All I'm saying is that he should be here with you. That's all."

Megan caught the tail end of the conversation as she brought in a stack of yellow Solo cups and a pitcher of lethal-looking red punch. She wasted no time getting in on the jump-on-Jill action. Tag team.

"That's right. And wasn't he an only child? He doesn't understand probably."

"She thinks he's cheating on her, too."

"No, I do not think that. And 'only child' has nothing to do with him not being here. What he does is life or death. Lives depend on it. You know that." Jill was glad to hear that conviction had returned to her voice.

Brodie came running into the dining room with a squirt gun in each hand.

"Auntie Jill! Did you bring me money?"

"Brodester! Hey birthday boy! You'll see later."

Jill scooped him up and covered his face with kisses.

"Is Uncle Jake out chasing bad guys?"

"He is indeed!"

Not quite under her breath, Megan muttered, "He's out chasing something."

Brodie showed Jill his squirt guns.

"I hope he catches 'em."

Jill adjusted his baseball cap and sat the boy back down.

"So do I."

Brodie ran out of the dining room, guns blazing.

"Bang! Bang! No more bad guys!"

The women watched him go. Megan frowned.

"If you had kids, maybe he'd get it."

Jill fussed with the helium-filled party balloons tied to each chair, trying to ignore her sister. She asked, "What else needs to be done?"

Megan's answer to this was, "I guess God knew what he was doing, not bringing children into that kind of life."

Kate looked up sharply and said, "Megan!" Even she thought that was too harsh.

"What? I didn't mean it the way it sounded. But, am I wrong? He has no concept of the importance of family."

Jill sighed, ashamed to find herself near tears. And there was no way on this earth that she would shed a tear in front of her sister or her mother. She scooped up Caitlyn, nuzzling her neck and giving her butterfly kisses. "Let's catch Brodie."

On her way out, she could hear Megan stage whisper to their mother, "What? So now it's my fault she can't get pregnant?"

Family is so fucking special.

Loaded down with gear, and sticky with a long day's worth of sweat and belly-crawling dirt, Jacob and Kathryn entered through the rear of the main building of the Sheriff's complex. They looked exhausted. Kathryn headed for the door to the women's locker room/shower. Jacob headed to the men's section directly opposite, then stopped abruptly.

"Hey!"

"What's up?"

"Good job training today. You've almost completed Phase One."

"Almost, huh? Thank you. I appreciate it. How many phases are there? You know, out of idle curiosity."

"Only a few. Depends on the trainee. But, I was wondering. After we get cleaned up, us *and* our weapons, that is."

Kathryn rolled her eyes. *Of course* the weapons, too.

"Would you like to go out for a drink?"

Kathryn stared at him. She had steeled herself for some new level of training hell to be proposed. Shooting while hanging upside down from a tree. Smearing fecal matter into open wounds before plugging a dime at a hundred yards. But not this.

"Uhm. Well."

"Unless you had other plans?"

"No, no. Yeah, okay. Sure."

"Great. Meet in the parking lot around 1800 hours."

"That's fine. I'll be there."

"Okay, then. It's a date."

Jacob turned and disappeared through the men's locker room door.

Dressed in worn jeans and a plain white t-shirt, freshly scrubbed and with still-damp hair, Kathryn stood beside her Ford pickup in the gated employee section of the Sheriff's complex parking lot. Waiting on Jacob. Men typically got themselves ready faster than women. She wondered if he was gussying himself up, getting ready for their "date." If he smelled like anything other than soap, she was going to make an excuse and bow out. If he was wearing cologne, she was hightailing it. God forbid, Polo. Fuckin' Denton.

But why was she so anxious? If a female deputy had wanted to meet up and have a beer after work, she wouldn't have thought anything of it. She would have appreciated the friendship. But there was a power discrepancy between Kathryn and Jacob. While he couldn't technically fire her, he was her trainer and her future within the S.O. in general, and within the SWAT team in particular, hinged on his approval. Jake Denton, the very married Jake Denton, held her future in his hands. And now he wanted to meet for drinks after work. This was bad. Fuckin'Denton. What exactly had earned him that nickname?

When he'd said "it's a date," she figured he was being cute. Ironic. But now she wondered. She could tell him that she was gay. That typically worked. Except for the ones who were into that, and it ended up enflaming their desire. She'd seen it before. What the hell was wrong with men?

She heard the back door creak open, and saw Jacob emerge. The evening breeze brought the smell of his cologne to her long before he made it down to her truck. Polo. He smelled like a teenager headed out for his senior prom. Fuck.

"I know a place just down the road. I think it's closer to your house, so if we drive our own cars we can leave from there."

"Sure, okay."

Jacob unlocked his vehicle.

"So just follow me."

The Sidewinder was a cozy bar with just a few tables and booths. The redwood bar was long and beautifully preserved, as were the vintage pool tables in the back. There was a small dance floor off to one side for live music. But tonight, the jukebox played.

Jacob and Kathryn found a booth in the back.

"I'm having a Corona. What can I get for you?"

"Corona is fine, thank you."

Jacob went to the bar, paid and returned with the two Coronas.

He sat and slid one across to her.

"Thank you."

Jacob held his bottle up.

"Here's to a long, dedicated partnership."

"Here's to an end to Phase One."

Jacob laughed. It was happy and unexpected. It caught Kathryn off guard. He seemed to light up from the inside. She clinked bottles with him. They each took a pull and then sat in awkward silence.

Jacob said, "So. I know you're not married, or I think I know."

"Nope. Not married."

She studied him. Wary.

"But you are, right? Jill?"

"Jill, yeah."

Another sip.

Jacob asked, "Any kids?"

"No. No kids. You?"

"Nope."

They both took another pull. Only dentistry could be more uncomfortable.

"Plan to have any?" he asked.

"Uhm, I don't know." Kathryn looked back at the pool tables, hoping to intimate to Jacob that this particular line of conversation was not one that engaged her.

"You don't?"

She faced him once again. "I don't? What? If I plan . . . ?"

"Yeah. You don't know if you plan."

"To have kids?"

"Right."

"No . . . I've never had to think about it. I mean, maybe, well sure, if I met the right person."

"Have you?"

"What?"

"Met the right guy?"

A long pause.

Kathryn finally said, "I'm not sure. Why are you asking me these questions? It feels uncomfortable."

"Just small talk."

"I didn't think you did small talk."

Jacob chuckled, and they both took another drink. Jacob got up.

"Just some things to think about. That's all. Men's room, be right back."

Kathryn watched him walk away. Nice ass. But not for her.

The birthday party was over. Jill and Brodie sat in the porch swing staring up at the moon. Jill had her arm around him.

"Auntie Jill?"

"Hmm?"

"Can I ask you somethin'?"

"Sure, little man. What's up?"

"Do you ever get scared for Uncle Jacob?"

"Do you?"

Brodie snuggled in closer and said, "Sometimes. I get scared he's gonna get hurt."

"Well, I guess I get scared, too, sometimes. But you know what? Uncle Jake works really, really hard at his job and he practices all the time to be very safe. So I've learned to trust what I know he can do." Jill wriggled a finger into the boy's ticklish side. "Like you on the basketball court . . . from the three-point line."

"I rock from the three-point line!"

"I know you do, I've seen it!"

The two were quiet for a while, listening to the insects chirping in the night.

Brodie said, "If Uncle Jacob dies can we split his stuff?"

Jill looked at the boy in mock shock, then exploded in laughter. Megan appeared behind them and cleared her throat.

"Brodie, time to say good night to Aunt Jill so we can head home and get ready for bed."

Brodie kissed Jill and she kissed and hugged him back.

"Happy birthday, sport."

Brodie scurried off the swing.

"And tell her thank you for your present."

"Thank you for my present."

"You're welcome."

"Okay Brodie, go give Grandma a kiss, she's inside."

Brodie ran to the sliding door and went in. Jill stayed seated in the swing as her sister loomed behind her.

"You know, I'm not sure I want you teaching my son that stuff."

Jill turned and looked her sister square in the eye.

"And what stuff would that be?"

"This whole 'superhero' thing like Jake's got some higher calling from God. He can take a day off anytime he wants to. He just doesn't. Like we're not important enough for him to even—"

"Oh, I see. So he should come here to Brodie's birthday party, and if someone takes hostages on the other side of town, who handles it? Well?"

"Well, how should I know, but certainly there are plenty of other officers."

Jill stood and faced her sister.

"Well, therein lies the distinction. There are other officers, but there is only one sniper. He can take time off and he does. But he's on call twenty-four-seven, 365 days a year. He can't control or predict when something happens and when it does he has to go. That's why you've never seen him drunk and never will. He lives his life in a constant state of readiness. If he isn't ready, there just isn't anyone else who can do it."

"Well, obviously an emergency is an emergency but—"

"The sooner he gets someone trained the sooner he gets to have someone else who can do it, then he can be here for things like this, don't you see that?"

Jill also believed, but would never in a million years tell Megan, that Jake felt a need to get his partner trained as much and as quickly as possible *before* his appointment with the psychiatrist. Just in case.

"All I see is all this extra 'training time' with a female partner."

"Please don't do this to me, Megan."

"Can't handle the hard questions?"

"You know what? Talk to your son. He's got the guts to ask the really hard questions and to face the answers. But since you are clearly clueless, next time, try thinking it through, you know? Before you open your fucking mouth."

Megan's jaw dropped open. Jill stormed by her and through the sliding glass door.

At the Sidewinder, Jacob returned to the table where Kathryn had nearly finished her beer. He looked at his watch.

"Do you need to go?" She sounded hopeful.

"Just checking the time."

He nodded at her beer. "You see an end to that?"

She stared at him, then grabbed the bottle and downed the last few sips. His beer was still half full.

"Okay then. Let's go," he said and stood up.

"What?"

"Let's go. We've got stuff to do."

Kathryn slid from the booth and followed Jacob outside.

In the parking lot, Jacob marched headlong for his truck. He called over his shoulder to Kathryn, "You okay to drive?"

"Of course I am."

"Great. Follow me."

Jacob got into his truck. Kathryn ran for her Ford to keep up.

Out on the road, Kathryn struggled to keep up with Jacob who made abrupt turns in front of her until she was hopelessly lost.

They emerged on a dirt road, and she had to slow down because the dust thrown up by Jacob's truck obliterated visibility. Her Ford bounced and swayed on the rugged road. She hunched over the steering wheel, trying to see. The dust cleared all at once and Jacob was stopped directly in front of her. She hit her brakes and came close to rear-ending him. A small gate was stretched between two creosote-laden poles and blocked access to the road ahead.

Jacob walked back to Kathryn's truck. She rolled down her window.

"I've got a key. I'll swing it open and you drive around me and through, then I'll follow. Just keep going about seventy-five yards and you'll see a little turnout area for parking. Anywhere is fine."

"Okay." She rolled up her window and did as he asked. The idea of being raped, beaten, and left for dead entered her mind. After driving through the gate she watched in her rearview mirror as Jacob pulled through, then exited his car and locked the gate behind them.

Raped. Beaten. Left for dead. And all the surveillance footage from both the office and the bar parking lots (if they even had any) would show, was that she arrived in her own vehicle and drove off in her own vehicle. If anything, it looked like she was chasing him.

She kept rolling forward and found the turnout Jacob described. She parked and turned off her car. And waited for her violent sexual assault. She was joking with herself, playing mind games. Kathryn could take care of herself. Even against a man as physically imposing as Jacob Denton. She wondered just what the hell he was up to, but she didn't feel like she was in danger. Yet.

There was a small weathered shed off to the right and beyond that, a large football field–size area, seemingly clear, though there were hulking shadows in the moonlight. The area was filled with something, but just what that something was, Kathryn couldn't tell. Jacob pulled up next to her and cut his engine. He exited his vehicle, and Kathryn followed suit.

Jacob pulled something from the toolbox mounted to the truck bed and put it in his pocket. Kathryn stood waiting. Jacob walked over to her.

"Are you drunk?"

"Drunk? No."

"At least a little buzzed?"

"Well, yeah, I can feel something. It was just one beer, though."

"Perfect. Get your rifle."

"What?"

"Get your rifle out."

Jacob marched toward the shed, unlocked a padlock, and disappeared inside. Kathryn retrieved her Remington from the truck. She heard a switch being thrown, releasing electricity, and suddenly there was light at the far end of the field. A small row of lights illuminated targets at the hundred-yard mark.

Jacob emerged from the shack and said, "Let's go. Bring everything you'd need for a call-out. Let's move."

Kathryn grabbed a large camo bag holding the rest of her gear and joined Jacob. There was a worn area in the grass and weeds just beyond the shed where people obviously laid to shoot. It was some other type of range, but a range nonetheless.

"Okay, fire it up. I need you to shoot a cold barrel shot at target one on the left and a three-round group at target two on the right. Clear?"

"No, not clear. You want me to shoot after I've been drinking? Isn't there a policy about—"

"Fuck policy. You say you're okay to drive and only feel a little buzzed. You need to shoot."

Kathryn, thinking she had latched on to the point of all of this, said, "No. I've had a beer. I won't do it."

She sat her bag and her rifle case down on the ground and folded her arms.

"Oh, I see."

"What? You're trying to check my ethics or something? I'm not shooting. I've had a beer. That's all there is to it."

"You're sure?"

"Yes. I'm sure."

Jacob leaned back into the shed and the lights went out at the other end. He locked the padlock on the shed.

"I'll tell Cowell tomorrow, and you'll go back to entry team or off SWAT completely based on his decision." He walked by her. "We're done here, you can go."

"Whoa, whoa! What the fuck? I'm out? Just like that? You fucking asshole. You set me up. You are not going to bully me into doing something I know isn't right."

"No bullying here. I can't use you."

"Why not?! 'Cause I'm not willing to risk my career on your bullshit?"

"It's not bullshit, and frankly, I'm disappointed. I actually thought you were coming right along, but you clearly have no idea what you're getting yourself into. So I need to move on to a new trainee."

She darted around him and stood in front of him. He just stared at her. She snatched his truck keys from his hand, then pitched them into the darkened field.

"You will talk to me. What is going on here? You're married and invite me out for a drink? On a date? And you question my ethics?"

"Jesus. I didn't mean it was a 'date' date. It's just a phrase. I'm sorry you thought otherwise."

Now she was infuriated and embarrassed, blushing wildly.

"Now, if you wouldn't mind retrieving my keys."

"I do mind. What is this? What is going on here?"

Jacob sighed.

"When you drink, how much do you drink? A beer a night? Two?"

"You asshole. I hardly drink at all and usually it's only one beer or one glass of wine. Okay?"

"Okay. You feel buzzed now from the beer?"

"I told you, just a little. But it's mostly eclipsed by anger."

"So, if we had a call-out right now, this second, would you respond to the alert?"

"Of course I would."

"Then don't you think you ought to at least see how well you shoot when you've had some alcohol? Or were you planning on never drinking again?"

She just stared at him, uncertain. It took a minute, but the shoe finally dropped. Kathryn realized what he was teaching her. The "date." Him making sure she had alcohol in her system.

"I get it."

"If you do this, you have to commit to it as a lifestyle. You have to learn your limits with alcohol, sleep deprivation, freezing temperatures, being sick, all of it. And you have to live within those limits every moment of every day. Otherwise, you might as well go back to patrol where you clock in and clock out and your free time is yours to do with whatever you want."

Kathryn's shoulders sagged under the weight of this unforeseen commitment. She looked away as she absorbed what he was saying.

"It's twenty-four-seven, three-sixty-five on my side of the fence. There is no 'off' time. You have to learn your limits and behave accordingly. I wanted you just a little buzzed. Most cops will admit to at least one beer at the end of their shift. So you need to see if you can still perform and how well you perform under those circumstances."

Kathryn looked at him. Her eyes weary.

"Holy shit. I get it."

"Yeah. Holy shit is right."

Kathryn turned to the darkened field, her back to Jacob. They stood in silence for a moment. Then she straightened up, lifted her shoulders. She pulled out a Mini Maglite flashlight and turned it on. She walked into the field, found Jacob's keys, and tossed them to him.

"Fire it back up, I'm in."

She turned and headed for her rifle.

Jacob moved to the shed, unlocked it, and fired up the lights again. Kathryn got her rifle out and dropped into position.

She said, "Cold barrel, left target, three-round group, right target?"

"Yes, ma'am."

She put ear plugs in and sank down into her rifle. Jacob put plugs in as well.

She fired. A crack in the darkness. Then slowly, methodically, three more shots crack, crack, crack.

She stared through her scope for a moment and assessed her performance. She seemed pleased. Jacob crossed to her.

"Let me see."

She stood up and handed him her rifle. He brought it up and quickly checked her shots through the scope.

"Look again," he said, and handed the rifle back to her. "And yes, I see you got two in the same hole."

She smiled.

"You smile when all three are in the same hole."

"Understood."

"You've had some alcohol, so I've no doubt you are on your way to all three in the same hole all right. Look how close your group is to your cold barrel shot."

Kathryn looked and was pleased but wasn't sure if she should show it.

"Go ahead and smile. Excellent job tonight."

And nothing followed. No rebuke, just the compliment.

"Just one last thing." He reached into his pocket and pulled out a portable Breathalyzer unit. She gave him a *you're kidding* look but quickly shook it off. Jacob Denton was not one to kid. She took in a breath and blew into the unit. It beeped after several seconds.

Jacob stared at the digital readout, then looked at his watch.

"It's been forty-five minutes since your last drink. The legal limit for driving is .08. You blew a .02."

She smiled broadly. As much in relief as anything else.

"So I'd say one is your max. What do you say?"

"I say, yes, sir."

Jacob smiled. Just a little. "Don't call me sir."

He put the Breathalyzer back in his pocket and went back into the shed. Suddenly the entire field lit up. To Kathryn, it looked like a junkyard at first. An abandoned car. Seemingly random construction debris. Castoffs.

"Welcome to Phase Two."

Kathryn smiled widely as she started to make sense out of the menagerie before her. She saw an old car, but with all its glass in place. The construction materials in another spot actually formed a small office cubicle. Farther down were walls with doorways and windows to practice breaching.

Simulations of situations they might encounter, right down to racks of shelves piled with rocks, though they could easily be the stocked shelves of a convenience store.

Suddenly it all went dark again. Jacob exited the shed and locked up.

"I think that's enough for one day. What do you think?"

"I think I want to kick your ass."

"Perfect. Pack up. We're done for tonight."

Kathryn stared back at the field of fun she had glimpsed so briefly and then whimpered like a pup denied a toy.

"I know, I know. We'll come back, I promise."

Kathryn laughed for the first time that night. Fuckin' Denton was finally starting to make sense.

Jill arrived home to a dark house. Even though she knew Jacob's schedule and that tonight was the night of the fabled alcohol test, she frowned at the digital clock on the cable box. She frowned at the emptiness and darkness. It was times like these that she missed Wyatt Morgan and Maggie most of all. When you have dogs, you never come home to an empty house. It was enough to make her think it was time to get a couple of Saint Bernard puppies. This home needed life in it.

She looked at the clock again. And frowned. Again. She thought, *Where's my code four?* Even though she knew where he was and what he was doing, they had a system, and tonight, for whatever reason, he wasn't following it. If he was going to be late, for whatever reason, he was supposed to call in code four to Jill. Code four, meaning safe. He never had to say why he was late. He could go grab a coffee with someone, go shooting, or just be writing reports. Because when you are married to a cop, you discover that you're also married to a clock. Your eyes watch and wait. And the later it gets, the tighter the knot in your stomach becomes. So that was the deal they'd made. He didn't have to answer to her, but he did have to let her know he was safe.

It wasn't a huge oversight, because he'd already told her where he'd be and why. But still. A female partner. And he seemed to be hiding a secret. Or maybe he was just worried about seeing the shrink. The man was hard to read.

She moved through the house, turning on lights. She turned on the lamp by the sofa, and put her keys and purse down with too much force. She stomped into the kitchen turning on more lights. She slammed cabinet doors, looking for something, but not sure what. All she could think about was the fact that her husband was out working late tonight. And that work consisted of having drinks—private drinks—with his female partner. And she hated herself for feeling jealous. She hated herself for letting her mother and sister get under her skin.

She pulled open a drawer, still looking for nothing in particular. There was a .38 in there. Most people kept pens and paper clips and bits of string and rubber bands and old twist ties and assorted crap in their junk drawer. Jill had a .38. There was one in the cabinet over the stove, too. And a .45 under the coffee table in the living room. And a Glock mounted behind the headboard of their bed. For emergencies. There had been death threats aimed at Jake over the years. It was part of the life. And she knew how to shoot, too. She enjoyed it. She was her husband's wife after all.

Jill also carried a 9mm on her hip around the house. Even if she had company or a student over for tutoring. It was concealed, so they never saw it. If she ran out to the store to get a jug of milk, the gun came with her. Tucked inside her jeans with a light clip holster in a natural spot against her hip. It was essentially invisible. She had a concealed carry permit, and she understood that a gun was for personal protection only. To protect your life.

Not to protect your car, your purse, or your wallet. It was to protect your life.

As one of her uptight writer friends once observed, Jake and Jill were "steeped in guns and gun culture."

True. But right now, she was just pissed.

She slammed the drawer shut. And went on to the next one.

Finally, she grabbed a coffee mug down from the cabinet, filled it with water and put it in the microwave. She turned the microwave on and opened another cabinet, pulled out a tea bag. She slammed this door, too. She opened the tea packet but managed to tear the tab right off the string.

"Fuck, fuck, fuck! God!"

The back door opened and Jacob walked in. He smiled broadly.

"Were you calling me? I thought I heard my name."

Jill turned her back to him and took the mug out of the microwave. She didn't want him to see her eyes. The anger, jealousy, and suspicion.

"You wish," she said. Easy breezy. Not quite.

Jacob entered with caution, setting his gear down quietly. Even if she was busy putting out a fire, Jill wouldn't keep her back to him when he walked in.

"Is everything okay?"

"Everything's fine. Fixing some tea."

She opened the cabinet to retrieve a new tea bag and slammed the door shut. He watched as she tore off the wrapping and threw the bag into the mug of hot water. She still hadn't turned to look at him.

Jacob walked up behind her and gave her a hug, but she stiffened at his touch. He backed away.

"How was Brodie's party?"

"Fine. Good. I didn't get a code four."

"I know, I'm sorry. I was so close to home I thought I might actually beat you here."

She pulled on the tea bag string, bobbing the bag up and down in the water.

"Problems with your sister?"

"No more than usual."

Jacob shrugged out of his jacket and continued to move softly around Jill.

"So you were training?" she asked.

"Just finished."

She turned around to face him. "I can smell the alcohol, for Christ's sake."

"Well, yeah, we did the alcohol test. I only had half a beer."

"Why didn't you just bring her here like you have every other partner you've had?"

"I don't know. I guess I didn't want to disrespect you by bringing her here."

"If she's just another teammate, why would I be disrespected?"

"Well, maybe you wouldn't be. I don't know. It just didn't seem right somehow. I'm sorry, I've just never had a female partner before. I didn't know it bothered you."

"Yeah, well neither did I. Welcome to the club."

"If it's any consolation, I'm pretty sure she's gay."

"Why? Because she didn't come on to you? Because she didn't soak her panties just being in the presence of the Great God Denton?"

"I do tend to have that effect on the ladies."

Jake had been aiming for a little humor to ease the tension between them, but he'd miscalculated. It was too early. He'd missed his mark.

"You are so fucking arrogant. Lots of people thought I was a lesbian. And look at us now. You know, a woman can be in this field and still be straight. And you know what else? It genuinely, truly doesn't matter. Your partner can sleep with whoever she chooses and it's really none of your business, is it?"

Jacob held his hands up. *I surrender.*

"Fuck. I'm sorry. My sister started in on the 'family' thing and here I am without you—again—at another family function, and you're out with this female. Having drinks."

She turned her back to him again. Ashamed of herself.

"Every single time you've trained a partner, they've either crapped out or left to become primary snipers somewhere else. Will you ever have a true partner who can step in as primary? Will *we* ever have any time off?"

"Cowell and I had her commit to three years, and she's a natural. It'll come."

He approached again and hugged Jill as before. This time she leaned back into him. She closed her eyes and let out a long breath as she relaxed into his body. Home.

"Would it help if I told you she called me an asshole and wanted to kick my ass?"

Jill laughed at this. She turned to face him.

"I guess she and I have more in common than I thought."

"Thought you'd like that."

They kissed and hugged each other tight.

"Well, she won't be kicking your ass on my watch, I can tell you that much."

"That's my girl."

The Sheriff's office took Lee Staley up on his ultimatum. They got a warrant for his rifle. It was a close call on the legal end. Probable cause was a subjective area of law. Oswald had the sniper skills, a possible ax to grind, owned the type of weapon used in the commission of the crime, and he lived in the area with an unsubstantiated alibi. But there was no concrete motive (he'd never made an actual threat) or even a witness who saw someone matching Oz's description in the area. Nothing actually tied him to the crime, but for probable cause, circumstantial evidence could be enough. In the end, Oswald was their only suspect, and he had pointedly refused to give up his weapon voluntarily when there was no logical reason for the refusal. The judge agreed with the S.O. and signed the warrant. The Winchester was sent to a lab for ballistic fingerprinting that would take a minimum of a week to complete.

During that time, there were no more rogue sniper shots directed at Jacob. No death threats against anyone at the S.O. It was an uneventful week all around. No SWAT activations. Kathryn started Phase Two of her training. Things were good between Jacob and Jill, and he started to feel less guilty for not telling her about the potshot someone had taken at him. He was hoping it was an isolated incident and not connected to Captain Bryant's murder. Or, at the most, a warning to keep his nose out of it. If the shooter had wanted him dead, Jacob knew that his body would be in a metal drawer at the morgue. A part of him also realized that once Oswald's weapon had been taken away from him, the shootings had stopped. If Oswald really had been behind it, it would also make sense that he had fired those warning shots at Jacob: *Stay away.* And according to the interrogation room sign-out log, Oz had departed the S.O. with enough time to track Jacob to the shooting range and set up a shot.

Detectives Cortez and Hasan otherwise made no progress in their ongoing investigation. No additional physical evidence was found. They had the one shell casing, and the bullets recovered from the scene, but until the ballistic fingerprint results came back (or another suspect was identified), they were useless. Everything was pinned on Oz's rifle. Still, they knocked on doors in Vista Canyon, questioned neighbors, made the rounds of local gun clubs and shooting ranges, interviewed people involved in gun culture. They pulled old case files and cross-matched with recent parolees who might hold a grudge against the captain (from any point in his career), or simply had the expertise to pull off such a shooting. Just trying to come up with another viable lead. Meanwhile, Lee Staley remained their only person of interest.

The bullet that was shot at Jake had gone through the Expedition's back window, hit the rearview mirror, exited through the windshield, and was stopped by a half-buried rock in the embankment. It was the same .308, 168g Sierra Hollow Point

Boat Tail bullet (preferred by snipers far and wide) as used in Bryant's murder, but the bullet was too damaged to determine if it had been fired by the same rifle.

And during all of this, Jacob had Friday's psychiatric evaluation to consider. He'd been evaluated when he first signed on with the S.O., but that was a long time ago, and consisted of just a few standard questions from a bored M.D., which, as he recalled, focused mainly on how easily he might get angry or frustrated.

The psychiatrist Cowell had set him up with was the real deal, though. This doctor would hold Jacob's career in his hands. If he didn't like what he saw when he peered inside Jake's mind, he could pull the plug on everything. The problem, the real worry, was that Jacob wasn't sure if he himself liked what he saw when he looked within himself. It was an odd career choice. Maybe the people who refused to shake his hand were the sane ones.

He just didn't know.

And if they took his rifle away, what would he do then? And what would Jill think of that? Maybe she wouldn't feel safe around him anymore. Maybe she would always be wondering what was broken inside her man.

So he worked hard and trained Kathryn hard. She would either be his "next man up," or his replacement.

He came home Thursday night and peeked to see what Jill had on the stove while she sat at the counter and reviewed his stack of targets.

She flipped through them and said, "Oz called this afternoon. He started the security job. Likes it. Said to tell you thank you. He said it was time to put the past away."

"Good. He needs to get out of his head."

"Look who's talking. Since we're going to be in the Canyon tomorrow anyway, I told him we'd stop by and say hello."

"Why tomorrow?"

"Tomorrow is your appointment with the psychiatrist. The fancy Vista Canyon shrink. You've hit the big time."

"Yep. Swimming pools. Movie stars."

"Well, it's tomorrow. Must have slipped your mind."

"Must have. I clean forgot."

They both laughed at the lie.

CHAPTER 19

Here they were. In Vista Canyon. Jill normally would have saluted her tree (or the absence thereof) in her usual way as they were forced to pass the area on the way to the psychiatrist's office, but knowing what had happened there to Captain Bryant made her somber.

As a deputy, Jacob had never liked patrolling the Canyon because of the condescending attitudes of the people in the ritzy neighborhoods—the sense of entitlement—which included some of the S.O. brass who located here. It was a desirable address, but not for Jill and Jacob.

The office was located in one of the newer buildings in the ever-expanding Canyon, part of a complex of medical facilities with several doctors in private practice covering a wide array of specialties including psychiatry, orthopedic surgery, pain management, neurology, an outpatient surgery center, and a state-of-the-art diagnostic/imaging center.

After checking the lobby directory, Jill and Jacob made their way through the massive building, holding hands like children lost in a dark forest. Once they made it to their destination (without the help of bread crumbs), they both scrutinized the psychiatrist's office lobby, looking for clues, trying to draw out information from what was present in the immediate environment. The walls were painted a muted green that was oddly calming. Light and dark blues and greens on accent pieces like picture frames, tables, and blinds provided a nice contrast in color. No chattering television mounted overhead. The framed paintings on the walls weren't corporate art, but well-executed originals that leaned toward the abstract.

And then there was the door. Two doors, actually. The exit door was just off to their right. And to the left was another door. It looked innocent enough, but that door led *back there* somewhere, and it was closed. A half wall with a countertop and a sliding, opaque glass window served as the receptionist's access to contact with patients. So far, so good.

Well, that wasn't exactly true. When they'd first checked in with the receptionist, Jill introduced herself and asked to confirm her husband Jake's appointment. The woman confirmed the time and said, "Oh! Jake and Jill!" Then in a singsongy voice she started, "Jake and Jill went up the—"

Jill cut her off, "Hill, yep, Jake was never seen again and Jill was arrested for loitering with intent." Jake almost cracked a smile, especially when he saw the receptionist hadn't the vaguest clue what to do next.

They had long grown accustomed to and become a bit weary of this reaction each time they met new people, but he'd have to say this was one of Jill's better retorts. He knew her quick wit was an anxiety response on her part. He pulled the girl safely out of Jill's crosshairs by saying, "We're a little early." And she plunged right back into Jill's scope when she said, "Oh, great, he's running ahead of schedule today, anyway." She flashed an *everybody wins* smile.

"Suicide cancellation?" Jill blurted.

The girl's eyes went big and she looked horrified, but since Jill had asked it in the form of a question, her face indicated she and her brain were struggling for an answer. "No, not that I'm aware of," she squeaked.

Jake smiled and said, "We're just joking."

The girl looked somewhat relieved and said, "It shouldn't be much longer."

Jake grabbed Jill's arm gently before anything else escaped her mouth.

They sat down in side-by-side chairs. Jill leaned over and whispered, "Sorry."

He said, "I know. I think she'll live."

As they settled into comfortable wood and padded leather chairs, they continued to scrutinize the office. The magazine selection was a bit bigger than most and covered a broader span of subjects. There was Muzak on the overhead, but not at an annoying volume. All in all, it was comfortable. Jill finally selected a magazine and Jake followed suit. *The New Yorker* for her, *Field & Stream* for him.

They sat in silence for a few minutes perusing their pages. The silence grated on Jill. She finally said, "Good magazine?"

"Yeah it's great. How's yours?"

"I don't know. I'm not reading, either."

They abandoned their magazines and both began scanning the office again. Their heads scanned left to right, in synchronized viewing mode. Suddenly Jake's head stopped moving. A split second later, Jill's stopped, too. How had they missed it during the first inspection? They both stared at the requisite framed medical license on the wall. Jill saw Jake's jaw tighten just a little, which usually made his ears jump in a cute way.

"If he's wearing Birkenstocks, I'm outta here."

Jill scoffed. "You cops. What is it about Birkenstocks and a Berkeley certificate that makes your brain shut down?"

"How much time do we have?"

Jill just shook her head and said, "Never mind."

Jake leaned further back in his chair and Jill joined him. This felt safer somehow, as if they'd found a secret hideaway in plain sight. They spoke quietly.

"Thanks for coming," he said.

"Are you kidding? I wouldn't miss this for anything. I've been trying to tell people you're crazy for years."

"Are you nervous?" he asked.

She made a dismissive shrug and with great confidence replied, "Nope."

"Why not?" he asked, like she had a secret that could save him.

She did. "If there was something wrong with you, well, I mean not counting the usual stuff, don't you think I'd be the first to know?"

Jake raised an eyebrow. "Oh, look who's talkin'. Didn't you have your shirt over your head the other day?"

Jill raised her head in a haughty posture and sniffed, "That was therapy."

"Ah!" Jake proclaimed as if he'd finally grasped some complex theory.

Then the receptionist opened the door. Not the exit door. The one that led *back there.* Where Jake's future hung in the balance.

Jill's eyes narrowed and she stared *back there,* where they played for keeps. Where a stranger would judge her husband and proclaim him fit or unfit to perform his duties. She could feel tension in Jake's body. Heat and raw fear were suddenly palpable and they scared her. Jake's right forefinger started tapping on the arm of his chair. His trigger finger. Tap, tappety tap, tap. She knew he wasn't consciously aware that he did this. Twitching that finger. She had told him a few times before when he'd done it that it was a tell. "If we were playing poker, you just told me you have no idea how to play this hand." And then, of course, the times they'd argued and she'd said, "Don't you dare twitch that finger at *me,* mister!"

With Jake's anxiety showing, at least to Jill, she knew it was all hands on deck time. So she did what she always did. She sat up straight, turned toward him and ran her hand through his hair and down to his shoulder. He turned toward her in this comfortable dance that brought peace and balance. They were eye to eye, foreheads touching.

She gave him a reassuring smile and said, "Easy, big boy. In just a few minutes we'll be walking out of here and you won't ever have to have that conversation with Cowell again."

Jake's eyes darted to the exit door and then back to Jill. She radiated absolute rock solid confidence. They both knew what was at stake here.

The receptionist who had been standing there in silence half coughed and said, "Officer Denton?" She said this as if calling him Jake would spark another outburst of God only knew what from Jill's mouth. Jake stood up.

"Right this way, please," she said and glanced at Jill.

As Jake reached the threshold to *back there,* he looked back at Jill. She winked at him and mouthed, "You'll be fine," as she flashed two thumbs up. Then the door closed behind him and he was gone.

Jill sat there utterly alone. Free to fall apart but not willing. It just wasn't an option. *Be good to him. Don't make me come back there.*

The receptionist opened the office door for him, and time seemed to slow down as Jake stepped across the threshold and absorbed his new surroundings. Jake thought he could feel Dr. Emmitt studying him. The doctor rose to greet him, but watched as Jake took in the environment. It was a nice, comfortable office with dark blue carpet, wood paneling around the room, several bookshelves with plenty of space to grow, and incredibly, a skylight just above the desk. It was actually between his desk and the two chairs facing the desk. It gave Jake the impression that the good doctor here had God on speed dial.

There were huge windows behind him that looked out onto

a small blot of the original landscape—a piece of land the developers had left undisturbed when they put up this complex. A view that reminded these interlopers what this had once been. What was still there and had been for centuries. There were live oak and pine trees, manzanita, other shrubs, and in the distance, the other side of the canyon. Jake took comfort in the view and mourned for the greater wilderness that had been lost.

Jake had yet to make eye contact with the doctor. It was because he knew he had the eyes of a predator. Sharp, intense, and wary eyes. He knew he could scare this man just by looking at him. He had perfected something Jill called his "sniper glare" and it was the closest thing to rattles on a rattlesnake when it came to letting someone know they were perilously close to a point of no return. *"Danger, Will Robinson! Danger!"* No place for that here, though.

Jake let out a sigh. He was putting off the inevitable. The horrible reality was he was going to have to sit down and answer this man's questions. And if he gave the wrong answers, his life would be forever changed. The thought that his future was in someone else's control was nothing short of terrifying. He had always been the master of his own destiny. Relied on no one but himself. And to know his professional future was, in this man's hands, torture.

The receptionist said, "Dr. Emmitt, this is Officer Denton," and closed the door on her way out.

Finally, Jake's eyes met Dr. Emmitt's (who looked barely old enough to shave), and time resumed its normal pace. Jake smiled sheepishly and said, "I'm sorry."

"Not at all. Welcome," Dr. Emmitt said and offered his hand. Jake looked down and was delighted to see the good doctor sported sensible loafers, not sandals. At least that's what he wore here in his office. Jake saw no point in thinking beyond that. What he had in the closet at home was his business.

The two men shook hands. The handshake was quick and firm. Jake noted the man's comfortable and confident grip. Jake often tested the handshake waters, applying pressure as necessary. A politician or a door-to-door marketer was likely to feel the bones shift in his hand. He had a special handshake for guys who were shaking his hand but eyeballing Jill at the same time. He'd studied faces, gauged reactions, and perfected techniques. When he rolled their knuckles there was no doubt of the message conveyed. His politician handshake said, *I'm on to you, Skippy, don't blow smoke up my ass.* He'd yet to find a Hallmark card that conveyed that message quite as well.

In the presence of Dr. Emmitt, however, he was professional and respectful. No need to tweak this man's knuckles, not with his future hanging in the balance. Besides, the guy had a very open and friendly face. Normally this sort of boyish face would put Jacob on edge immediately. Boys were not meant to hold authority. Since suspicion usually rose in him immediately, Jake was surprised to discover he believed this man. That he was exactly what his face and handshake said he was. Young, but sincere. He hoped to God his instinct was right. He needed it to be right. For everything to be all right.

Dr. Emmitt said, "It's a pleasure to meet you, Officer Denton. Or is it Deputy? Do you have a preference?" He motioned to the chairs across from his desk and Jake moved to the first chair.

"Either's fine, but please call me Jake."

"Okay Jake, please feel free to call me Sam."

Dr. Emmitt walked back behind his desk and sat down. He had a file there, and he flipped it open. He looked down briefly, then leaned back, pressed his fingertips together, and studied Jake for a moment. Then he started a slow side-to-side swivel in his chair. Jake could feel himself tensing up. All the good feelings were gone now. He just wanted to choke this prick out. Jake now realized what it felt like when he gave people the sniper glare. It was this same sort of studied silence that put people on edge. Made them nervous. Only this time Jake was the one under the microscope. The predator was prey. This guy was giving him the shrink stare. And he fucking well hated it. Perhaps that was the point. Just when he felt he couldn't stand it another second the doctor spoke.

"So, Jake, why are you here today?" He asked this as though Jake had just shown up unannounced. Like maybe he thought Jake was gonna hit him up for an investment in a time-share opportunity, or to buy a box of Girl Scout cookies or something.

"My lieutenant? He set this up."

Still swaying side to side Dr. Emmitt said, "Yes I know, but why do you feel you've been sent here today?"

Head games. He'd read the guy wrong. Jake was losing patience, and he knew he couldn't afford to. So he did a seat adjustment of his own and said, "My lieutenant thinks I need to talk about my shootings."

Side-to-side, slow, hypnotic swaying. "But you don't think it's necessary?"

"No, I don't," Jake said. Crisp. Now the asshole was bobbing his head in a slow nod as if in deep, contemplative thought. Swaying and nodding. Like it was a fucking parlor trick. *Who the hell does this guy think he is?* Jake sat straight up in his chair and favored the good doctor with one of his sniper glares. And damned if the guy didn't react at all. The ballsy prick was playing with Jake's career, and Jake was about to get up, break some bones in his Berkeley hand and tell him he'd had enough. Thanks, but no thanks. Let Cowell do whatever he thought he had to do.

But then the doctor said, "You've never been evaluated for this before?"

Jake just shrugged and raised his eyebrows in response. *Your move, Brain Boy.*

In the lobby the receptionist was staring at Jill, who held a magazine in her lap. It was open, as if she were reading it, but Jill stared off at some distant thing. Slowly, as if she could sense the girl's gaze, Jill looked toward the little sliding window and saw that the girl was indeed staring at her. Jill forced a quick smile and picked up her magazine, only then noticing it was upside down. *Great.* The receptionist was probably buzzing the doctor right this second to explain that the live one was still in the lobby.

Jill raised the magazine up until it covered her face and said softly, "Good, Denton. Very cool."

．　　　・　　　・

In Dr. Emmitt's office, Jake and the doctor were just looking at each other. At least the prick had stopped swaying, nodding, sashaying, whatever he was doing.

He finally looked down at the file and said, "So you are a patrol deputy, twenty years with the Sheriff's Office, and you also serve as primary sniper on the SWAT team. Is that correct?"

Jake nodded once.

"Okay, thank you," he said, still looking down. "And according to what I have here, you've had, uhm, seventeen confirmed, ahh, well it says here 'kills' in your fourteen years serving as a sniper?"

Another nod.

The good doctor sighed. "I feel we've gotten off on the wrong foot here, Jake. And I'm sorry about that. The truth is I don't see many people like you."

Jake said, "Well, that makes two of us."

This made Dr. Emmitt smile, but Jake would not allow himself to smile.

"No, I guess you wouldn't be anxious to run to someone for support." The doctor chuckled. "Okay. Fair enough. We're even. Let's start anew and see if we can't get this done and you'll be on your way. I imagine this is the last place you want to be."

"Short of a dentist's chair, that's about right."

"Well, I'm above dentistry. Thank God." And this time they didn't have to pretend they weren't smiling, they just let the smiles come and wore them well.

The doctor sat upright in his chair and looked at the file

again. He said, "Well, let me back up from the number of, uhm, encounters."

Jake was amused that the man had trouble saying the word *kills*.

He said, "Can you tell me about your first experience?"

"My first kill?"

"Yes."

Without hesitation Jake said, "Daylight, multiple obstacles, seventy-eight yards, no wind, head shot through a glass window." He had rattled it off so quickly and succinctly he even surprised himself. He wondered what the doctor would make of him having such knowledge at the forefront of his brain, readily available. Would he find it ghoulish or morbid?

Dr. Emmitt said, "How about, say," as he looked at the file, "your ninth? Do you recall that?"

Again, as if by rote it spilled out of Jake's mouth. "Night shot, one obstacle, fifty yards, fifteen-mile-per-hour breeze coming from the west, open head shot."

Now they were both into it. How well could Jake recall them all? Dr. Emmitt pressed on, "Your fourteenth?"

"Thirteen and fourteen went together. Early evening, cop killers, multiple obstacles, one hundred five yards, stiff twenty-mile-per-hour wind from the north, head shots through two separate windows."

Dr. Emmitt forged on as if Jake were some sort of autistic savant. "What's an obstacle?" he asked.

"A hostage," Jake answered.

This put a pause on the rapid-fire exchange.

Dr. Emmitt sat back again. "Really?" he asked. "They're not people? Human beings? They're objects?"

Jake said, "The second you make them people, you lose your edge."

Dr. Emmitt picked up a pen and started writing in the file, which made Jake worry. He looked up and said, "Do you always remove yourself from the emotional aspects in this manner? Dissociate? Compartmentalize?"

Jake paused to see how this definition fit in his ear and was surprised to see that was exactly what he did. He finally shrugged and said, "It's the only way. Hostages are obstacles to shoot around and bad guys are nothing more than moving bull's-eyes on a target."

Dr. Emmitt said, "I see." Then wrote in the file again.

Jake hoped he wasn't being too honest. He didn't really know any other way to be, but he wasn't sure if his answers would save him or condemn him. He was completely out of his element here.

The doctor finished writing, sat back, and said, "Well, no matter how you rationalize it, you really are killing one or more other human beings. How do you feel about that?"

"I don't get off on it if that's what you mean," Jake growled.

Dr. Emmitt raised one hand and said, "No, no, of course not."

Jake felt he had to explain to this educated man what the streets were really all about. "Look," he said, "most of these people forfeited their rights to be 'human beings' a long time ago. They don't play by the rules of humanity and they don't care."

"So they deserve it?"

"When they harm other innocent, law-abiding people, you bet they deserve it." The second it came out of his mouth Jake wanted to snatch it back, but he couldn't unring that bell. At some point, this guy might go completely Berkeley on him and ask him to turn over his weapon. He could do that. He held that power.

They sat in an uncomfortable silence for a moment. Finally, Dr. Emmitt said, "How have you been able to do this job for so long without it affecting your emotions?"

Jake leaned forward. "The bottom line?"

"Please," said Dr. Emmitt, "that's why we're here."

"I don't know them," he said.

"Excuse me?"

Jake rushed into the void, anxious to clear this up. "The people I've shot. I don't know any of them. I've never even known a hostage. I've just been lucky, I guess."

Dr. Emmitt nodded and he weighed Jake's statement. "If, by chance, you knew any of the people involved, could you still take the shot?"

Jake took a moment to look out the window and ponder this very point. The precise point Oz tried to drive home to him. Jake looked back at the doctor and said, "I'd like to think I could still do my job, but I won't know the answer to that until it happens."

Dr. Emmitt nodded. "Have you ever shot a hostage by mistake?"

"Never."

"Well, if you killed or wounded a hostage by mistake, how would you deal with it?"

Jake sat back in his chair. His right trigger finger started in as he thought. Tap, tappety, tap tap. He suddenly realized he was doing it and stopped. As far as he knew, the doctor hadn't caught that. He'd have to thank Jill for pointing that out to him for sure now.

He said, "Well, I'd feel awful about it. But I can't control every situation. The hostage could move, the ammunition could be bad, there are any number of variables that wouldn't necessarily mean I made a bad shot. Jill would remind me of that."

"And who is Jill? Your wife?"

Jake smiled. "Yes, Jill is my wife."

"You seem very pleased about that."

"I am."

"So am I correct in assuming you have a solid support system at home?"

"I do."

"Good for you, Jake, that's a rare commodity." Dr. Emmitt wrote in the file for a moment and then set the pen down with an air of finality.

This was it. A decision had been made. Jake could feel it coming. It was all going to come down to what came out of this man's mouth. Jake thought how strange it was in that moment to know that a whole set of other lives would be impacted based on the mere utterances of this man's next sentence.

Dr. Emmitt said, "Well Jake, I think you're dealing with your situation in a realistic manner considering the nature of your work. I don't see any reason for concern. I'll fax a report to that effect to your lieutenant today."

Jake nearly fell out of the chair. Even he had underestimated how important this moment was to him, and here it was behind him now and in his favor. He couldn't wait to tell Jill.

The doctor stood up, and Jake pulled himself up, too. They met near the door and Jake shook his hand again. "Thank you, Doctor."

Dr. Emmitt said, "I'd like you to take one of my cards and if you ever need to talk about a particular scenario or you start having difficulties, I hope you'll give me a call."

"Thank you," Jake said, still shaking his hand. He realized the appropriate point of release had long passed and said, "Sorry!" and released Dr. Emmitt's hand.

The doctor shook it as if to restore blood flow and said, "That's quite a death grip you've got there."

Jake laughed out loud. The doctor reached for his office door. He opened it and they stepped into the small corridor. Dr. Emmitt patted Jake on the shoulder and said, "Keep up the good work, Jake. I admire what you do."

"Thank you."

And just like that, Jake opened the door from *back there* and he was free.

When the *back there* door finally opened, Jill looked up. Her eyes met Jake's and she exhaled a long breath she hadn't known she'd been holding. She saw it in his eyes. They were fine.

Officially.

Jill stood as Jake introduced her to Dr. Emmitt.

"So, this is the ship's captain, eh?" Dr. Emmitt extended his hand.

Jill narrowed her eyes but shook the doctor's proffered hand. What was up with that little remark? Oh yeah, she was steering Jake's vessel. Had it been true, she would have laughed out loud. At this point she didn't know what to think. Just what had gone on in there? Dr. Emmitt met her gaze with a kind smile.

"He gave up the goods in there." When her eyes narrowed further, he quickly said, "He says you take wonderful care of him."

Jake couldn't possibly have discussed their personal life with this stranger. "I do my best," she stammered. The doctor didn't know how literal she was being. She was doing her best and floundering. At least that's how it felt. It was as if the good news had drained her, not energized her. What the hell was wrong with her? They were fine! Jake had just said so with those eyes. Those piercing blue eyes. She could lose herself there, and often did. Another peek at Jake's eyes confirmed his previous message and she wondered why she still felt edgy. She realized she was still holding the doctor's hand. Tightly. Way too tightly. She saw the whiteness from lack of blood flow to both of their hands. She immediately wondered why he hadn't let go.

"It was so nice to meet you."

Past tense. We're outta here!

"Thank you for your help," she said and released his hand and stepped back. Jake moved toward the exit and Jill followed. She was three steps from freedom when she heard it.

"Mrs. Denton?" Damnit! So close. And why did she feel the need to run anyway? What the fuck!? Swirling hormones, lack of sugar? What was triggering this fight-or-flight response in her? And why had she chosen flight? She'd never chosen flight in her life. She was a fighter. Jake finally noticed she was not her-self, moved closer and put his arm around her. She leaned into his embrace.

The doctor still stood in his doorway watching. Jill could feel it. His eyes were trying to bore through her skull to get at the gray matter inside. Furrowing ever deeper into her head. And now he'd spoken her name. *Mrs. Denton.*

"Do you have a minute?" Dr. Emmitt said, motioning to-ward his office.

"Uhm, sure," she said, as though she were fine with it. She reminded herself they were there for Jake, not her. And Jake's eyes said they were fine, so why worry? Jill stepped over the threshold of the door to *back there* and into the doctor's office where he closed the door behind them.

Jacob sat down where Jill had been sitting. He could feel her in the residual heat in the chair. He picked up a magazine and held it in front of his face. The receptionist at the window, who'd been mute throughout it all, remained mute. But her eyes went wide and her eyebrows skyward when she heard Jacob mumble, "Don't make me come back there."

Jill sat in the chair Jake had just occupied. She could feel it. He lingered somehow. It had always been that way for them. They were always connected in ways neither of them understood. It just was what it was, whatever the hell it was, and they accepted it. Safe in his lingering warmth she relaxed into the chair then looked up at Dr. Emmitt.

He'd been watching her every move. Cheeky bastard. More

words popped into her head; pervert, peeping tom, nosey parker, Berkeley graduate. He'd been relishing her discomfort, she was sure of it. Like a predator circling wounded prey. Well, that was a bit harsh. She just couldn't work up any real righteous indignation or anger toward this man. Not now. Not after he'd said they were officially fine.

"You look comfortable there, almost cozy," he said.

She added "delusional" to his list of crimes, still trying to find fault. "So how can I help you?" she blurted.

He chuckled and said, "That's usually my line."

She was distressed to see he had a great smile. And indeed he had a warm, trusting face, with big puppy dog eyes.

"I'm sorry. I've been a bit of a flake."

He smiled. "I don't know if I agree with that assessment. You've got quite a grip, I'll give you that. I imagine this visit has been weighing on your mind for a while. Can we agree on 'cautious'?"

She smiled. "We can."

"How are you feeling now?"

"Good . . . relieved." His brow furrowed a bit.

"But I've not said anything. How do you—"

Jill cut him off. "Jake told me." A long pause. She hated getting personal but he clearly needed an answer. "He told me with his eyes," she finally said, then added, "I'm curious to know what this is about."

"This?"

"This. Me. In here. I wasn't prepared for that. And I can guarantee you Jake wasn't, either." Maybe she could dislike this guy if she gave him enough time. But what he said next removed all hope in that regard.

"That sounds rather ominous. Should I lock my door? Put a chair under the knob?"

She stared at him, saw the twinkle in his eye, and couldn't help but laugh out loud. "That would only slow him down and simultaneously piss him off," she said through laughter. "And don't ask me how I know."

And that made him laugh.

In the lobby Jake had flat given up on the magazines and was pacing the floor like a caged animal. What the hell were they talking about in there? The doctor had said he was fine and now this? Would she come out with a tear-streaked face to break the news to him? That things *weren't* fine after all? That he couldn't work anymore? He quickly dismissed those thoughts. He'd looked Dr. Emmitt—*Sam*—square in the eye. He trusted what he saw there.

He was more worried about Jill than anything else. She had enough on her plate living with him. He knew she could feel the changes in him. Changes he didn't understand himself. Like, what was this need to pass his knowledge on to Kathryn? Was it more than just wanting a partner who could relieve him sometimes? Why was he treating her differently from his other spotters? Taking special interest in her. Nothing sexual about it. The fear that he was one bad shot away from ending up like Lee Staley, broken down, unable to escape the past. Taking risky shots, like when he shot through the girl's earring. Was he tempting fate? Or did he simply believe in his own capabilities? You had to believe, or you would never be able to pull the trigger. That was the job. When Cowell had asked him, "What if you had missed?" Jacob had wanted to say, "What if I had missed? I have to ask myself that question every time I perform my job. What if I had missed? And the answer is always the same. I didn't."

But what if you do, Denton? What if you kill a hostage? What then?

"I'd feel awful about it," is what he'd told Dr. Emmitt. But would it consume him? He just didn't know. And if it did consume him, it would consume Jill, too.

Maybe he should have shared some of this with Dr. Emmitt.

He wasn't happy about Jill's sudden "interview" with the doctor, either. He hadn't planned on that. He wasn't prepared. He'd exposed her to this and chastised himself for it. He should have left her at home and immediately realized the chances of her staying there were slim to none. She would have simply driven to the appointment in her own car. She was at his side, good or bad, always.

And then he heard it. It came from the office, he was sure of it. It was the unmistakable sound of laughter. Holy Mary, Mother of God. They really were fine. Officially.

CHAPTER 20

Jake and Jill stood in the good strong late morning sunshine outside the medical building.

"Looks like you fooled another one, Denton."

Jacob said, "I reckon I did. Why did he want to talk to you?"

"No reason. Said he just wanted to acknowledge that my role as your wife could be just as stressful. That if I ever wanted to talk—" She held up one of Dr. Emmitt's business cards.

Jake held up an identical card.

"It's like we both got golden tickets to the Wonka Factory."

"I guess I'm Charlie Bucket. And that would make you, what, Veruca Salt?"

"You can kiss my Veruca ass, Fuckin'Denton," Jill said. "I guess this means we're both more or less sane. So, should we grab some lunch or do you just want to go out and shoot somebody?"

"Let's do the lunch thing. We can always shoot somebody later."

"And I told Oz we'd stop by the bank and say hello."

"Let's go."

"You got it. Hey—" Jill glanced at her watch. "We're earlier than I thought we'd be. Wanna invite Oz along for lunch? Be able to talk longer. Celebrate a little."

"Sounds good."

It was Friday, lunchtime, so Golden State Savings & Loan was busy with fast-food workers, painters, drywallers, groundskeepers, and assorted day laborers cashing their paychecks or withdrawing funds for weekend adventures.

Jill scanned the lobby looking for Oswald, but Jacob spotted him first, stationed below a street-facing window, keeping an eye on the customers in line as well as the tellers handling their transactions. Theft in a bank was far more likely to be an inside job than a gunman walking in off the streets, but embezzling clerks didn't make good lead stories.

Jacob touched Jill's elbow and nodded in the direction of the man who had taught him so much. Lee "Harvey Oswald" Staley, sharpshooter, poet, and adherent to the four F's school of dating.

Oz held a special place in Jill's heart, too. She knew he and Jake had been through the fire together. She knew that Oswald trusted Jacob Denton with his life. And vice versa. And when Oz fell, it had affected Jill as much as Jake. Because when she looked at Oz, she knew she was looking at a possible future for her own husband. A nervous breakdown. Alcoholism. Insanity. A blue recluse in training.

But it looked like Oz was pulling himself out of the tailspin.

With his salt-and-pepper crew cut and crisp guard's uniform, he looked reborn. Jill crossed the lobby to him, and he smiled broadly when he saw her. In the end, they both loved Jake, and that was enough of a common bond to make them love one another as well.

"Congratulations on the job. You look great, Oz." She leaned forward and kissed him on the cheek.

"It's the monkey suit. And you don't look so bad yourself. Wish I could say the same for your husband."

Oz nodded to Jacob across the lobby. The two men exchanged a look of understanding.

"Well, we're all getting older, aren't we?"

"Speak for yourself, sister."

"You wanna grab some lunch with us?"

"There's nothing I'd love more, but my girl is taking me out for lunch."

"Are you sure? She can come with us. I'd love to meet her."

"Nah. She's shy. You two go ahead. Jake's probably broke out in a rash being this deep in the Canyon."

"Well, it was good to see you, friend. We'll have you and your girl over for dinner. Sound good?"

"You bet."

Overcome with emotion, perhaps because seeing Oz like this today was proof that a bad future could become a good future, Jill reached forward and hugged Oz with all her might. She spoke warm words into his ear.

"I mean it, Oz. It's wonderful to—"

A muted crack echoed through the bank. Jill looked above

and to her left and saw the plate glass window at the front shatter and the treated glass turn opaque.

"What?" was all she could say, and really, it was all any human being would ever be able to say when life as they knew it suddenly and inexplicably shifted into a new, far less pleasant reality. It was what the observers of the Hindenburg disaster said, it was what villagers said when napalm bloomed across their jungle home, it was what office workers said when they looked from their Twin Towers windows on the morning of September 11th.

Jill's head turned, looking back, back toward her husband who might be able to make some sense out of what was happening. *Jacob would know.* And as she turned, observers could see brown speckles of blood across the left side of her face and forehead. A man screamed, but Jill did not hear it. She saw Jake, already in motion, coming to save her. She reached up to touch the wetness on her face. Her fingers came away bloody.

Oswald?

She turned back to look at Oz. His mouth was moving, like a ventriloquist's puppet, but no words were coming out.

She saw that the bullet had entered just above his left eye and took out the back of his head. Oswald's body slumped to the floor at Jill's feet. And now Jill was the one who was screaming, but she didn't hear that, either.

The inside of Golden State Savings & Loan was controlled chaos. Cops, paramedics, detectives, civilian authorities, and customers were everywhere. No one else appeared to have been wounded.

Physically, anyway, save one older man who had fallen during the initial moments and had injured a hip. He was loaded onto a gurney and then into a waiting ambulance.

An empty blue-and-white Cameron County Transit Bus was parked just outside the main door. A deputy ushered the customers and employees, who had formed a long line, onto it and spoke loudly.

"We are transferring you to a safe location. Please do not make or take any calls, texts, or any other forms of communication at this time. Please do not discuss what you may have seen or heard with anyone else. At the secure location, detectives will take your statements individually. You will be able to contact your families from there. Safety first."

The majority of people in line were in shocked silence. They boarded the bus as directed, like zombies, the walking dead. EMS lingered with a few who were more deeply in shock.

Detectives talked to key bank employees and took notes. One, the bank manager, pointed out surveillance camera locations. Officers were already taking measurements and drawing preliminary sketches. Oz lay where he'd fallen. This was where the measuring and triangulation of key markers would point back, like an accusatory finger, to the direction from whence something wicked had this way come.

The medical examiner was already on scene and would oversee the process of removing Oz's body once all the measurements and processing were completed. He had already confirmed to Cowell that it appeared to have been a single, long gun bullet that had dislodged half of Oswald's brain. As gruesome as it was, they could not rush. He had to lay there in front of God and everybody until all the details had been assimilated.

Jacob and Lieutenant Cowell were huddled off to one side. Jill sat, wiping blood off her face. Kathryn stood, feeling awkward, beside her.

A paramedic rolled an empty gurney by with a portable oxygen tank and a blanket on it.

"She's in shock," Kathryn told the medic and grabbed the blanket from the gurney.

Jill stared off into space. Kathryn put the blanket around Jill's shoulders. Jill realized what Kathryn was doing and turned abruptly.

"No, I'm not in shock, and I don't need this." She shrugged the blanket off her shoulders. Kathryn grabbed it off the floor.

Jill looked up and saw the deputy's gold name tag, *Sesak,* and realized she and Kathryn were face to face for the first time. *The two women in Jacob's life,* Jill thought, and realized what a Danielle Steel kind of thought that was.

Jill said, "I'm sorry. Please forgive me. I understand what you're trying to do and I appreciate it." She reached out and touched Kathryn's arm. "I really do, but I'm fine."

Kathryn refolded the blanket and handed it back to the EMT. The medic moved away to see if anybody else required aid. Jill and Kathryn shared a small smile.

"I'm Kathryn Sesak. It's a pleasure to meet you, Mrs. Denton. I'm only sorry it's under the current circumstances."

The two women shook hands, and Jill said, "Don't call me

Mrs. Denton. Call me Jill. I'm glad to finally meet you, too. I hear you like to go out drinking with my husband."

Kathryn gave a little eye roll and shook her head in resignation.

"He says you're a natural, and Jacob Denton does not say such things lightly."

Kathryn said, "I'm learning from him. Jake almost seems like a father to me, but you could be my sister."

"Heh. You should see my sister."

Lieutenant Cowell moved away from Jake and squatted near Oswald's body. He peered up to where the bullet had pierced the front window. Cowell went to the window, where a few bits of cracked safety glass lay on the floor, blown inward. He looked back at Oz and then through the bullet hole at the rooftop of a low building across the street.

"Take a look."

Jacob stepped up and peered through the window with Cowell.

"The shooter was following you. Or more likely waiting for you. How long were you in here before the shot?"

"Two, maybe three minutes at the absolute most. It wouldn't have been possible to follow us here and then have time to set up that kind of shot through glass. The shooter was lying in wait."

"Who knew you'd be here today?"

"I guess any number of people within the S.O. could have

known I had the appointment with the shrink, but nobody knew I'd be stopping at this bank."

"Nobody knew you'd be here today?"

"Just Oz. Jill told him we'd stop by and say hello."

"What about your partner?"

Jacob thought carefully before he answered.

"Yeah. I told her what my day looked like, but—"

"I'm just keeping my mind open. The list of people who knew you would be here today is yourself, Jill, Kathryn, and Oz. Jill or Kathryn could have mentioned it to others. And we'll never know if Oz mentioned it to others."

"Wait. Jill said Oz said something about a lunch date. And he had a woman in his bedroom the other day."

"Name?"

"He was coy about it."

"We've got detectives at his apartment now. I'll let them know we want info on a female visitor. And we'll have prints by this afternoon. I doubt she wore gloves."

"I can't believe he's gone."

"Look, Jacob, you're in danger, you know that, but honestly, I'm more afraid for Jill. We've got to get her far away from here. Out of state would be ideal."

"What?"

"This shooter is killing the people around you. Fuck, Jacob, he's killing them in front of you. You said yourself he could have killed you last week if he'd wanted to."

"You're right."

An overwhelming guilt settled on Jacob's chest. By hiding

what had happened at the shooting range, he'd potentially put Jill in harm's way. He should have told her.

Cowell said to Jacob, "I just need you a little while longer, then I want you to be with your wife. Away from here. Let's get Jill home for now. We'll send a unit with her."

Jacob walked across the lobby to Jill and Kathryn. Kathryn walked away to give them some privacy.

Jill looked up at her husband and read his face.

"We need to be worried now, don't we?"

Jacob crouched down and met her gaze. He stroked her arm.

"Who would be hunting you?" she asked. "Or are they hunting us?"

"That's what we're going to figure out." Jacob cleared his throat. "I have to tell you something." And he told her about someone taking a shot at him at the range. He told her he was sorry for hiding it from her.

"I should have told you."

She nodded. *Yes, you should have.* But he saw in her eyes that she wasn't going to hold on to this. She had already forgiven him. She didn't have to say the words.

"We have to go away, don't we?"

Jacob nodded. "There's a unit here to take you home."

"I'll pack light."

"I'll catch up with you soon."

Jill stood and Jacob kissed her forehead.

He watched her walk out the front entrance, but then she turned around and came back in. He thought his wife was coming back to him, but instead she walked up to Kathryn. She put her hand on Kathryn's arm and spoke. Jacob wasn't a lip reader, but he knew what Jill was saying to his partner. *I trust you. Watch over him.*

Jacob watched Jill leave the bank and get into the patrol cruiser waiting for her outside.

Jacob went back to Cowell and looked to his lieutenant for direction. *What next?*

"You and Sesak are coming with me. We're pulling all your case files until we can come up with at least one suspect."

"But all of my cases are dead."

CHAPTER 21

Jill packed clothes into an overnight bag. She was crying freely now. She was indulging herself. She saw a shadow flicker outside her bedroom door. It was the deputy assigned to her. She went to the bathroom to wipe the tears from her face. She didn't want him to see Fuckin'Denton's wife in a moment of weakness.

The EMTs had cleaned her up when they checked her for injury, but there were still little clots of blood in her hair. And little lighter bits of dried matter that she didn't want to think about. There wasn't time for a shower, so she ran a brush through her hair, but the clots wouldn't break. *Screw it,* she thought, *I'll make time,* and jumped in the shower.

Once she was clean, dried, and dressed in a t-shirt and jeans, she felt at least a little better. But then she threw up in the toilet. No warning, no preliminary nausea. Just enough time to pivot to the porcelain bowl and hurl. The same thing had happened yesterday. And the day before that, too. And her period was almost two weeks late. She hadn't mentioned it to Jake. There had been false alarms in the past, and her periods grew more and more irregular the older she got. She saw no point in getting Jacob worked up and worried over it, so she just kept it to herself. Well, almost kept it to herself. She'd thrown up when Susan was here for tutoring, and confessed that she "wouldn't mind" being pregnant. Other than that she kept it to herself. And hoped it might be true this time. That maybe Megan wouldn't have to give her one of her babies after all.

She felt cold and knew it was the shock and stress and the after-effect of the vomiting. She had dressed and was trying to get a sweater down from the closet shelf when she heard someone call out, "Mrs. Denton?"

She walked out of the closet and was irritated to find that the uniformed deputy had opened the closed door and walked into the room. He'd entered her bedroom without her permission. He hadn't even knocked. Unless she hadn't heard him because she was vomiting.

She knew who he was. Billy Simon. Simple Simon. Jake didn't like him. He'd applied for SWAT as a spotter on the sniper team, but had been rejected three times. Simon had held a grudge, but petty jealousies and grievances were as common in police work as they were in any other field. It meant nothing. When a cop or a cop's family was in danger, they were brothers and sisters. They took care of their own.

Still, he shouldn't have just walked into her bedroom.

He had two bottled waters in his hand.

"Just wanted to check on you, Mrs. Denton. Make sure you're okay."

"I'm fine."

"I hope you don't mind," he said and indicated the waters. He held one out to her, but she shook her head no. So he'd taken a peek inside her refrigerator? The guy was kind of a creep. Not professional.

And then she suddenly felt like she was going to cry again. Why was she being such a bitch? He'd come into the bedroom to ensure her safety. With the shower, she'd been in here far longer than she'd intended. He walked in unannounced in case something bad was going down. He was putting his life on the line to ensure her safety. And she was going to begrudge him a bottle of water?

And the tears came, and she hated herself for being so emotional. She actually started choking and sobbing. Racked with grief for Oz and fear for her husband's life.

Simon put down his water bottle and put a hand around her shoulder. Rubbing her back. The other hand running up and down her arm. And she was repulsed by the feel of him. He felt like a reptile. His hands felt sweaty and awkward like a boy who had never touched a girl before. Or a lizard who had never touched a girl before. But what was he supposed to do when confronted by a wailing woman? What choice had she given him? She tried to get herself under control just so he could stop touching her. God, she wished Jake was here.

Then he was stroking her hair. And that was just too much. Lizard claws in her hair. She pulled away. It was a rude rebuke— *I don't want you to touch me*—and they both knew it.

"Thank you. I'm fine now. I—"

There was a knock at the front door, and Jill thought, *Thank God*. Saved by the bell.

Simon unholstered his weapon. Jill was startled. No wonder they called him Simple Simon. He was like a kid playing dress-up, pretending to be a cop.

Alone in her bedroom, Simon and Jill stared at each other, the drawn weapon between them. This felt weird to Jill on so many levels. Like there was some kind of unwelcome sexual tension, but also like there was a threat. With the shock and stress of the day, she couldn't tell if it was just because her perceptions were off, skewed.

The knock came again. More insistent this time. But it wasn't a cop knock. It lacked authority. But it was enough to break the weird tension between them. Jill followed Simon into the hall, through the living room, and he motioned her to the door. He positioned himself so that he would be behind the door and nodded at Jill to open it.

Jill had time to wonder why Simon didn't simply answer the door himself. Wouldn't it make more sense for the armed deputy to open the door than the unarmed woman who might have a killer after her? Especially with a marked unit out front? Either way, Jill never opened her door until she knew who was on the other side.

She had a .45 in a holster fixed under the coffee table. In fact, she had weapons in strategic locations throughout the house. But her hand instinctively moved to her right hip. Her personal weapon, a model 26 Glock 9mm that she normally wore when she was home alone, was in her overnight bag. She hadn't wanted Simon to see it on her—it was concealed, but most cops could spot the telltale bulge—so she'd put it in the bag. She would put it on her hip when they got to their destination. She had a concealed carry permit but thought Simon might be uncomfortable knowing she was armed. Still, her fingers itched to grab the gun hidden under the table, but she let that idea go and called out, "Who is it?"

"Jill? It's Susan. I took your advice about the father in my novel. I've got the revised manuscript. All printed up. Is everything okay?"

Thank God, Susan. Little, rodent-like Susan. Her own personal hamster. Jill did not want to be alone with Creepy Simon a second longer. *Not a hamster. A possum. Could possums fight?*

Jill moved to unlock the door, but Simon motioned with his gun and stopped her.

He shook his head: *Not a good idea.*

At a scarred old conference table at the Sheriff's Office, Jacob, Cowell, and Kathryn were gathered. They each had a laptop in front of them, and stacks of old folders—case files—were piled high around them. They were poring through Jacob's old cases and reports. Just looking. For anything. They had crime scene investigators on-site at the bank and the secondary scene of the rooftop across the street where the shooter likely took the shot. The bullet had been located, and preliminary results (simple visual inspection) indicated that the bullet that had taken Lee Staley's life was most likely a Sierra HPBT, as had been used in the other shootings. Science felt that the bullet was in good enough shape for ballistic fingerprinting, but that would take time. So far, no additional evidence had been found.

Detectives and technicians had collected evidence from

Oswald's apartment with no immediately useful information having been discovered. There was no sign of anybody living at the apartment other than Oz. They had found only books and bottles and bullets, the expected detritus of a lonely, old, alcoholic gun nut. Prints had been lifted from doorknobs, glassware, tabletops, dirty dishes, the bathroom, and all the other usual surfaces, and were currently on priority processing at the lab in Sacramento. As far as anyone knew, Oz had been a shut-in, so the prints would most likely belong to Oz himself, Jacob, Deputy Palucci, Detective Cortez, and Detective Hasan. Some of the prints, they were hoping, would belong to the girlfriend who was supposed to have met Oz for lunch that day. Although, if she and Oswald had just started seeing each other, you could hardly blame her for turning around and scramming from a bank surrounded by police cars and emergency response vehicles. But it was essential that they talk to her. She was really the only lead, the only human avenue of investigation they had.

A secretary brought in more folders. These were older case files that had yet to be scanned and digitized. Included were cases that were part of Jacob's day-to-day activities as a patrolling deputy.

"Got something here," Kathryn said. "Domestic disturbance. Jake's report notes that the husband had a 'large' gun collection. All legal."

"I remember," Jacob said. "Hell of a nice collection."

"Rifles?"

"No. All handguns. Revolvers mostly."

"Put it aside for now," Cowell said.

Kathryn asked, "What were the flags you mentioned before, Lieutenant?"

Cowell said, "Where there were close relatives left behind. If a family member made a threat. Or tried to sue the county. Or if the perpetrator might have had ties to organized crime. Drug families. Christ. I don't fucking know. Anything. Even if you just have a feeling."

Jill stared at Simon's drawn weapon. She wondered what he was going to do with it. From the other side of the door, Susan's furry little nocturnal voice said, "Jill?"

Jill motioned for Simon to lower his gun and said, "She's a student of mine."

Jill unlocked the door and swung it open. Susan scurried through, wearing an oversized gray cardigan, tan corduroy slacks, and black boots. Her little paw hands were clutching her marsupial handbag. She saw Jill's pale color, felt the weird vibe, and said, "My God! Jill! What's going on? There's a patrol car—"

The door shut, and Susan saw Simon standing there, weapon drawn but barrel down at his side.

"Jill! Are you okay? My God! Is it your husband?"

Jill took Susan's face in her hands, trying to calm the woman. Bring her down a notch.

"No, it's not Jake. A friend of ours was murdered today. Nobody knows what's happening. I may be in danger. You need to leave." Even though she wanted Susan here with her, Jill knew she couldn't put her student's life in danger just because she wanted a chaperone.

"Leave? You're in danger?"

"Yes. Leave now, Susan. Please."

Susan turned to Simon and nodded at the gun in his hand.

"Let me get this straight. Someone got murdered, Jill might be next, and your job is to protect this silly bitch?"

A deer-in-headlights glaze clouded Simon's eyes. With those few words, everything had just shifted, but his mind refused to latch onto what exactly it meant. Nonetheless, cop instinct kicked in, and his gun hand twitched and began to rise. Too late, though.

In one fluid motion, Susan pulled a handgun from her bag and shot Simon squarely between the eyes. The report was deafening inside the house. Susan showed no emotion whatsoever.

"Well, you are piss poor at your job, son," she said to Simon's body. She grabbed Jill by the hair and slung her to the floor. Then she started kicking her.

"Wouldn't you agree with that, Jill? Wouldn't you agree Deputy Hole-In-The-Head is piss poor at his job? He's pretty good at bleeding, though, look at him."

Jill did as instructed and looked at Simon. The bullet had gone in more or less between the eyes, but the blood wasn't coming from the entry wound. Or even from the gaping exit wound. Blood chugged out of Simon's nose in great dark hiccups like black milk from a jug.

Jill felt Susan's boot connect with her side two more times in quick succession. The second blow felt like it broke at least one rib. She heard it crack. Then the boot toe smashed into her temple and everything went dark. Jill's last thought was that she reckoned possums could fight after all.

. . .

Kathryn, Cowell, and Jacob studied the files in silence. Jacob had just pulled out his phone to call Jill when Kathryn mumbled something.

"Huh?"

"I said, I don't know."

"Don't know what?"

"I don't know. Maybe I'm just being a daddy's girl."

Jacob said, "Jesus. Anything, Kathryn. Anything."

Kathryn held Jacob's gaze, then scanned the open folder again.

"Fourteen years ago. A bank robbery. Apparently he wasn't a career criminal. Other than petty theft, no previous record of any kind. Never anything violent. Just some desperate guy who held up a bank. One of your 'average Joes having a shitty day.' When the cops showed up, he went nuts. Just lost it. He shot a customer who ran for the door. Shot her in the back. Then barricaded himself in the bank. It became a hostage situation."

Kathryn turned the page and looked directly at Jacob. Cowell watched and listened.

"After a three-hour standoff, he refused further negotiation, threatened to shoot more hostages. Then cut off all communication completely. Jacob got the green light and neutralized him."

Cowell said, "So?"

"So, two hours after that, officers on the perimeter located the suspect's vehicle outside the bank parked in an alley. His six-year-old daughter was locked inside."

Jacob said, "I remember. Of course I remember. Captain Bryant was heading the team at the time. He gave the green light. I was in the final phase of training. It was my first time as primary. Oswald was my spotter, he cleared the shot. And I pulled the trigger."

"Name of the daughter?"

Kathryn flipped through the file. "They didn't know it was his daughter at first. She wouldn't speak." She found the right page. "Rose. Rose Kaufman."

Cowell opened up a searchable database on his computer.

"That name mean anything to anybody?"

None of them recognized the name, but Jacob spoke up and said that when he'd asked Oz about his new girl, he'd just said, "A ROSE IS A ROSE IS A ROSE," which was just the kind of oblique shit old Lee Harvey loved to throw around.

"I got a hit at *The Sacramento Bee*. They carried the story," Cowell said and swiveled his laptop around for them to see a black-and-white photo of a little girl. The caption read BANK ROBBER LEAVES DAUGHTER WAITING IN GET-AWAY CAR. "They only ran the photo because she was a Jane Doe at that point. They were fishing for leads." Cowell turned the laptop back around and started clicking the keys. "I wonder what Rose Kaufman is up to these days. Let's try Department of Social Services, Child Protective Services."

But before he could finish entering the name, his phone chirped at him. He picked it up and read the message. "From Hasan. Fingerprints were rushed through the lab. Results were as we suspected—Jake, Cortez, Hasan, Palucci, and Oz. One last distinct print is unknown. But get this: there was a hit on it. A match. But the record is sealed."

Jake and Kathryn both said, "Minor."

•   •   •

"So, you see, your husband's not really a guardian angel, he's the angel of death. That's the book I've been working on. And it's almost finished. What do you think about twist endings as a literary device?"

Jill was sitting at the kitchen table, her hands cuffed in front. Susan sat on the other side of the table and had a gun trained on her. Her head and side throbbed from the kicks Susan had rained down on her. She was a vicious little bitch. Through the fog of pain, Jill was still trying to wrap her mind around the fact that Susan Weaver, the little timid possum, had tricked her so thoroughly. She would refuse to believe any of it if she hadn't actually seen her murder Deputy Simon. There was no doubt.

"There's a certain school of thought that a twist ending is the hallmark of commercial fiction and cable television. The literati find it beneath them. What do you think?"

"I think you should go fuck yourself."

"I thought you might feel that way, what with the critical notice your novels received. You're firmly planted in the tradition of literary fiction. But I don't mind slumming."

Susan rooted around in her voluminous handbag and pulled out a small purple-and-white cardboard box.

"What do you think about this as a plot device? A way to up the stakes?"

Jill recognized it immediately. She had an identical one hidden away in the back of her bathroom cabinet. It was an EPT pregnancy test. Jill wasn't sure why Susan would want to know for sure whether Jill was pregnant or not. What the reason would be. But the threat of whatever was coming was enough to chill her bones. She felt an immediate maternal reaction, an instinct to protect the life that might or might not be growing inside her.

Jill wedged her cuffed hands under the kitchen table and used all of her might to try and flip it. The table was heavy oak, but Jill found the strength to turn it over. Susan was caught off guard, and the table knocked her and her chair over. She was caught under the overturned table, but not pinned. The chair held the table up at an angle. Plenty of space for Susan to scurry out.

The .38 in the kitchen drawer was closest, but it was really too close. As far as Jill knew, Susan still had the gun in her hand and could put a bullet in her back before Jill even had time to wrap her fingers around the one in the drawer. So she propelled herself through the kitchen door and on into the living room. The .45 strapped under the coffee table was her best bet. She dove to the floor and buckled her hips and shoulders to get under the table. She reached her cuffed hands up to draw the weapon. But it was gone. Just disappeared.

From above, she heard Susan say, "Yeah. I took that gun last time I was here, on the floor with my laptop. Cops and cop wives are pretty predictable."

Susan reached under the table and pulled Jill out by the hair. She cracked her revolver across the bridge of Jill's nose, breaking it. Blood and pain blossomed in equal amounts.

Through the blood, Jill said, "You can beat the living shit out of me, but I guarantee you that you will never get me to pee on that stick."

"Well, you know, I love a challenge. I really do. I've been preparing for this for years now. Paramilitary training camps alongside skinheads and would-be mercenaries. Some very bad people. People driven by hate. So believe me, Jill, if I wanted you to pee on a stick, pee in a cup, or pee on a high voltage wire— you would do it. Believe me, you would do it. But I don't need you to. I've already peed on this one."

Susan held out the plastic test stick. There was a positive result in the round display window.

"I'm pregnant, Jill. And if you're pregnant too, then that means we're both carrying a sniper's child."

At first, Jill thought Susan was telling her that they were both pregnant by Jacob. But she just couldn't process that idea. Her mind wasn't working right. Too much had happened too fast. Not to mention she'd taken some fairly brutal blows that resulted in a broken nose and at least one broken rib. But it dawned on her what Susan was saying. Susan was pregnant by Lee Staley. She carried a sniper's child.

Susan pulled Jill to her feet and pushed her back into the kitchen. Jill complied. She pulled Jill's cell phone from where she kept it in the back pocket of her jeans, then sat her down. She started opening cabinet drawers, rummaging, looking. From the back, she still looked like nothing more than a mousy girl lost in an oversized cardigan.

"Holy shit, how many guns do you two have?" she said and went on to another drawer. "Okay, good," she said and turned to show Jill the pair of Craftsman pliers she'd found. She went back to her purse and rummaged there until she found a bank deposit slip. She held up the pliers and the deposit slip and said, "Now guess what I'm going to do with these? First though, we need to text your hubby. Let him know you've been hurt. Probably gonna need medical attention."

Jacob had tried to call Jill twice in the last five minutes, but her phone just rang and went to voice mail. He knew that in all likelihood, it meant nothing more than that she was in the shower or something. But nothing about today was normal, so he'd asked Cowell to have Sergeant Heidler contact Simon to make sure everything was okay.

Cowell had obtained an emergency injunction to unseal the closed case files. The name of the minor child whose prints matched the print found in Oswald's apartment was indeed Rose Kaufman. He had a secretary reading and summarizing Kaufman's DHR case file aloud over the phone on speaker.

". . . Family Protective Services. Prone to violence. Placement after placement ended in some type of violent dispute. She disappeared at age seventeen. I've got a picture here."

Cowell, Sesak, and Denton all said, "Fax it. Now!"

They got up and stood at the fax machine. Waiting. It only took thirty seconds, but it felt like a year. It was just a headshot of the type used for an ID card. It was a fax of a photocopy, so it was blurry. But Jacob recognized Susan Weaver immediately. Jill's timid little writing student. He was about to speak up when his phone vibrated and relief washed over him when he saw that he had a message from Jill. He opened the message to read it.

The desk phone beeped. Cowell crossed to the phone, punched a button, and Ray Heidler's voice came over the intercom.

"Simon's not responding by radio or cell. Should I send units?"

Cowell looked up at Jacob, but Jacob was already gone. All he saw was the man's thick shoulders clearing the door.

"Well, fuck! Shit! All right, Sesak—"

But Kathryn bolted from her chair and out the door, too. After her partner.

Kathryn emerged onto the S.O. fleet parking deck. A cruiser screeched around a corner, clipping the bumpers of two parked units as it came. Kathryn ran out from a stairwell door and jumped in front of the out-of-control car. She held her hands out and squeezed her eyes shut.

The car stopped. She opened her eyes to see the chrome bumper rocking to and fro against her knee caps. Kathryn scrambled into the passenger seat next to Jacob.

"Like I said, partner . . . I'm in."

Jacob stared straight ahead, then punched the accelerator. He tossed his cell phone into Kathryn's lap, and she read the open message from Jill. *I'm hurt. Come home now.*

The car screamed out of the parking deck.

Once on the road, Jacob hit the light bar and siren.

As they neared his home, Jake killed the siren and lights, cut the engine, and allowed the cruiser to coast silently into his driveway, stopping behind Simon's patrol car.

Jacob and Kathryn approached the house with their weapons drawn. Jacob listened at the door but heard nothing. He turned the knob and found it unlocked. He shook his head. Bad sign.

Jacob breached the doorway first, followed by Kathryn. They each took in the bloody, utter surprise of Billy Simon's dead eyes. This was real.

Jacob moved through the rooms with his weapon held at shoulder level. He was quick but cautious. Kathryn covered him every step of the way. They cleared the entire house to ensure no other victims or perpetrators lay in wait.

Jacob stood in the living room and yelled, "Jill!"

Kathryn holstered her weapon. She put her hand on Jacob's shoulder.

"She's not here, Jacob, but you need to go back to the kitchen."

Jacob walked into the kitchen. He saw the overturned table. There was a pair of pliers and a balled-up piece of paper on the counter. And blood. A good bit of it. Someone had been hurt. He secured his weapon and picked up the pliers. He studied them for a moment then put them back down.

He picked up the balled-up paper. Looked at it a moment, then unwrapped it. As the paper opened, he saw it was a bank deposit slip. As he unfurled the paper completely, something fell from it and hit the table.

A finger nail, French manicured, torn from its nail bed, encrusted with blood. Jacob's jaw tightened. He grabbed the pliers and hurled them across the room where they imbedded in the Sheetrock wall.

There was something else on the counter. Kathryn knew right away what it was. A pregnancy test stick. She put on gloves and carefully picked it up. She read the result window, then held it out for Jacob to see.

"Oh, Christ. Oh, Jesus. Jacob?"

Jacob looked. He knew not to touch it since he wasn't wearing gloves. He shouldn't have touched the pliers.

Jacob collapsed into a chair. He covered his mouth with his hand.

Kathryn's radio squawked, and she stepped away and spoke into it.

Jacob could vaguely hear the conversation in the next room, but not what was being said. It was just noise. He was lost, trying to decide what to do next.

". . . Jacob . . . Jacob . . . Jake!"

He looked up at his partner.

"We're hot. Bank robbery. Takeover. Multiple hostages."

"Cameron Citizens Bank?"

"How could you know that?"

"Promise me."

"Promise you what?"

"Don't tell. It's my shot. Nobody else. Me. My shot."

Jacob held the deposit slip out to Kathryn. Cameron Citizens Bank.

He knew what it was now. It was an invitation.

And Kathryn understood what her partner was asking of her. *Don't tell.* Otherwise, Cowell would never allow Jacob anywhere near that bank with a rifle in his hand. Not if he knew Jill Denton was a hostage.

And Jacob wanted to save her.

Nobody else. Me. My shot.

CHAPTER 22

Eddie Palmer looked up at the two women who had just entered the vestibule of the Cameron Citizens Bank in downtown Morgan City. They appeared to be in distress. The closed circuit security cameras clearly captured the faces of Susan Weaver and Jill Denton, although that footage would never be needed for proof in the events that were about to unfold.

Eddie almost always used the ATM or the drive-thru teller, but today he had come inside the bank because he wanted a crisp new fifty-dollar bill to put inside his niece's birthday card. You could never tell the quality of the bill the automated teller might spit out, and he didn't want it to get crinkled in the pneumatic tube of the drive-thru.

He stood at the courtesy counter, his bald head shiny from the overhead fluorescent lights. Eddie was using a ballpoint pen attached to the counter with a ball chain cord, filling out a withdrawal slip when he heard the women entering.

His niece, Ashley, was fifteen now. Something of a troubled

child. Tattoos, body piercings, pink hair. She would probably use the money to buy designer drugs—bath salts or something. Frankly, right now, Eddie wished he'd never set foot in this bank, because something was very, very wrong with those two women. One of them had twin trails of black dried blood scabbed from her nostrils to her chin. And both her eyes were deeply bruised. One was swollen shut. She still had both her ears, but otherwise the little lady looked like she'd gone ten rounds with Mike Tyson.

Ashley had always been a troubled child. Even as a toddler, bad things seemed to happen around her. Over the years, he had given quarters, pocket change, then dollar bills, fins, saw-bucks, on up to twenties, and now, at age fifteen, the fifty-dollar bill was apparently the new norm. Eddie had been saving for hair plugs, and throwing fifties around like he was J. D. Rockefeller wasn't going to get him a headful of flowing locks.

His sister always took Ashley's side if anybody dared say giving a troubled teenager all this cash might not be in the girl's best interest. Or suggested the child might need guidance. Or therapy. Perhaps a father in her life. No, his sister just said kids'll be kids, and why don't you just relax, Eddie? Just relax. Well, he didn't understand why he should have to give the little thug fifty bucks, but his mother had chimed in too. She said, "Just do it, Eddie. Family is important."

The dark-haired mousy-looking woman pushed the beat-up woman through the vestibule. The woman went sprawling into the lobby, facedown, probably worsening her injuries. Everybody in the bank looked up to see what was going on. Eddie wondered where the guard was. Surely the bank had on-site security. The dark woman stayed in the vestibule. She was doing something to the outside doors. Eddie decided that she probably wasn't cleaning them. That probably wasn't Windex and paper towels she had pulled out of the gear bag she had brought in. No, it looked to be some kind of locking device.

The bloodied woman had gotten back up to her knees. It was a struggle. The woman had clearly had the hell beat out of her. Plus her hands were cuffed in front. The woman managed to get herself upright. She turned and addressed the entire bank.

"She has a gun! Behind me! She has a gun!"

The patrons, the tellers, everyone including Eddie Palmer (*but not the guard, where was the guard?*) looked at Jill as though she were a lunatic. Nobody wanted to believe this could be real. Especially Eddie, but he knew it was. Because of Ashley. Because Ashley had brought him in here today, and anything even remotely tied to his niece Ashley invariably turned to shit. His quick little dash into the bank to get a crisp U.S. Grant had certainly turned into a big steaming pile of doo-doo. Maybe if Eddie himself weren't so anal-retentive. Wouldn't two battered twenties and a dog-eared ten-spot have done the job just as well? It was only going to end up crumpled in some dealer's greasy front pocket anyway. Why did Eddie have to be like this? And why did Ashley have to poison everything around her?

Finished securing the outer double doors, the mousy woman (whom Eddie no longer thought of as *mousy,* but *bad*) turned around. She kicked open the vestibule door, her oversized gray cardigan lapping open behind her, and she stormed into the lobby. The open sweater exposed the sawed-off shotgun broken across her waist and the rest of the arsenal secured to her body. It reminded Eddie of that high school massacre in Colorado. Instead of the Trenchcoat Mafia, this lady was part of the Cardigan Mafia. Dylan Klebold by way of Mister Rogers' Neighborhood.

Everything was unfolding in slow motion now, and Eddie had time to reflect that Ashley probably would have made a good girlfriend for Dylan Klebold. Ashley would screw pretty much anything, and getting laid probably would have adjusted that troubled boy's attitude quite a bit.

The guard finally showed up. He was an older man with a snow-white handlebar mustache. Eddie saw that he was pulling up the zipper on his uniform trousers as he emerged from the back. He turned to the bloody woman with a look of perplexity. She screamed at the guard.

"Shoot her! She's got a gun!"

The bloody woman motioned over the guard's shoulder, where behind him the bad woman whip-locked the double barrel shotgun into one piece. She did this action one-handed and raised it into firing position.

The bloody woman saw that the guard just wasn't going to react in time. She dove for his holstered weapon. Her cuffed hands fumbled with the restraint strap.

But it was too late. Far too late. The bad woman was on them. She fired the shotgun point-blank into the guard's back. The man's body lurched forward and collapsed in a bloody heap, taking the beaten woman down with him. The bad woman stepped over both of them and retrieved the guard's gun. She waved it at the beaten woman.

"What? Is this what you wanted?"

The woman turned and fired the guard's gun at a bank employee, killing her. Eddie thought the murdered woman might have been the manager.

"Did anybody else want to see this?" the woman said, bringing the gun around in a deadly arc. Nobody wanted to see it. In fact, pretty much everybody in the bank was on the floor, huddled into corners, under desks, bodies wrapped around chair legs. Eddie Palmer was one of the very few still standing. Frozen into place.

Eddie—quite calmly—turned the withdrawal slip over and wrote on the back of it. He wrote: *Dear Ashley, fuck you, Uncle Eddie.* And then he folded it into a neat square and tucked it into his front pants pocket. He was sure the CSI people or maybe the Coroner's office would find it and make sure it got to the proper recipient. Then he dropped to the floor and curled up into a tight ball.

CHAPTER 23

O utside, on the streets of Morgan City, a Sheriff's office cruiser squealed onto the main street of the business district. Another cruiser, lights and siren blaring, turned in from a side street. Another cruiser, riding full-out code three, joined the first two.

These units caught up to more responders up ahead. More joined these. Fire trucks. Ambulances. A police helicopter loomed over this incredible fleet of emergency vehicles. The news vans and choppers were en route.

And out in the glaring hot California day, an anonymous black van carrying the Cameron County Sheriff Department's Special Weapons and Tactics team rolled through the city streets. Fast. Insistent.

Inside, the eleven team members (ten men and one woman) were dressed in varying shades of white, gray, and black—their daytime urban BDUs that would look more natural on a business rooftop than greens or tans. They held on to overhead straps as the vehicle swayed and sped forward.

Fast. Insistent.

The team faced forward in the van, where a dry-erase board was mounted. Lieutenant Joe Cowell faced his team, gesturing to the whiteboard.

The board showed a diagram of the Cameron Citizens Bank, surrounding structures, and landscape. Several areas were marked in red, including an exterior spot marked SNIPERS DENTON/SESAK.

Jacob Denton studied the diagram. The area inside the drawing of the bank was filled with black dots, and the words *hostages, number unknown*. In Jake's mind, these black dots were obstacles to his target. It was a mind game. It had always been a mind game. Like Oswald had taught him. They weren't people, they were obstacles. And the objective wasn't a human being, it was a target.

Except that wasn't true today. The target would be a woman who had been a guest in his home. The obstacle would be his wife, Jill. His wife who was apparently pregnant, but had not told him so herself. But everything had been staged for him. He had been summoned here. Drawn here. He was being manipulated. So he did not know for sure.

His eyes moved from the bank and the obstacles. He stared at the red dot on the whiteboard that marked the sniper's position on a rooftop across the street from the bank. And for a second the red on white blurred. It became fresh red blood spilt on crisp white snow. Jacob remembered how that snow had once been clean, unspoiled. And he could hear the jagged heavy breathing of a boy struggling to break through the ice-crusted snow to keep up with his father. And he could hear the man say to the boy,

"You have to do it, son. She's suffering."

The boy and the man had come to the end of the blood trail. The vast plane of snow behind them was broken and spoiled from their long trek.

The trail ended just outside a small enclosure in the foothill rocks obscured by the limbs of a spruce tree.

The boy pulled back the spruce limb to see the she-wolf resting in blood-soaked snow. Around her, three wolf pups suckled from their dying mother. The boy backed up, horrified. He backed into his father.

"You have to do it, son. Killing's hard sometimes."

The boy nodded, his chin quivered a bit, then steadied. Richard Denton held back the spruce branch for Jacob.

"It's time."

A tear fell down the boy's cheek. He brushed it away, raised the rifle and took aim.

The shot echoed through the foothills and across the broken field. And then another. And another. And another.

The boy would grow into a man. And the man would realize that he had been branded that day. There was no going back from a killing. And there was no living with it.

CHAPTER 24

The bank was eerily quiet. All of the customers and staff were gathered inside the tellers' cage. All of these hostages lay side by side, facedown on the floor. Susan paced back and forth through them, shotgun at her side. It was a Stevens model 311 .410 break-action double barrel shotgun with the stock cut off and formed into a hand grip. It was easily concealable under the armpit. Not necessarily the weapon of choice when robbing a bank, but Susan had her reasons.

One reason was the psychology of it. The shotgun, especially with the sawed-off side-by-side barrels and the modified quasi-pistol grip, was intimidating. It encouraged compliance. People know it spreads. They know the risk of death or traumatic, disfiguring injury is significant. It was a bad-ass-looking weapon, relatively light to carry with the shortened stock and barrels; but ultimately, with those modifications, it was really useful for only one thing, and that was blowing people's heads off.

The other reason was psychological as well. Her father had

carried a weapon just like this. She had seen it. Held it once. The Stevens was no longer in production, but easily obtainable on the secondary market. She modded this one herself. She had been studying rifles and marksmanship for quite some time now, but she had also become a scholar of pain, a student of brutality. That's where the Stevens came in. A rifle was an elegant, precise instrument, but a shotgun was a blunt, brutal weapon. Perfect for this moment of retribution. Her daddy was carrying this weapon the day they shot him.

Susan executed the break-action of the shotgun to expose the loading breech. She ejected the spent shell she had discharged into the guard's back and replaced it with a fresh .410 gauge round so that both barrels remained lethal.

And so she paced, fully loaded shotgun at her side. She was waiting for the forces outside to take their places.

She stopped and stood over Jill. Planted her foot squarely in Jill's back. Jill turned her head to look up at Susan. *What?*

"Close your eyes."

Jill stared up at her.

"Just do this for me, Jill. Close your eyes."

"I'm not going—"

"Please. Author to author. Friend to friend. Captor to hostage. Close your eyes."

Jill kept her eyes open, and Susan pushed the muzzle of the shotgun against the back of her skull, forcing her head back down.

"Close enough. Okay, you're in the bank one day. You need to make a withdrawal because you left your ATM card at home.

A lunatic comes in, bolts the doors, weapons drawn. You're a smart girl. You know what this means. You and everyone in there are hostages. Do you remember seeing something like that on the news, Jill?"

Susan waited for a response. When she got none, she pushed the muzzle of the shotgun even harder against Jill's head, prodding her.

"That was in Sacramento, wasn't it?" Jill said, paraphrasing the script from the day she spun a similar scenario for Susan.

"Atta girl," Susan said, and gave the back of Jill's head a teeth-rattling love tap with the gun barrel. "Some poor security guard tries to save the day and gets a shotgun blast for his trouble. It happens everywhere, Jill. All over the country, all the time. Only this time, it's *your* bank, and *you're* in there with the lunatic. She's just killed two people in front of thirty witnesses. You're all side by side, facedown on the floor."

"She won't kill us, will she?" Jill asked.

Far off, Jill could hear sirens, the throb of helicopter blades. Men's voices shouting outside. Somewhere inside the bank, a phone was ringing. Over and over. Ringing. An amplified voice outside, saying pick up the phone.

"Jill, to be honest, I have no idea. Either way, you've seen her face. You know who she is. It doesn't look good for you."

Jill squirmed under the muzzle of the shotgun, trying to turn her head, to see Susan's face. To get a read on her.

"And then you hear it. Sirens, in the distance, growing louder. A silent alarm, perhaps, or someone heard the shots. Help is on the way. You allow yourself a glimmer of hope. The police have arrived. But your gunman friend grabs the man next to you, hoists him to his feet and drags him to the door."

Jill sobbed, knowing what was coming next.

Susan grabbed the meek little bald man curled up in a tight ball on the floor and dragged him to his feet.

"No, Susan, please, no. Don't take him. Take me. Please, we're the ones you're mad at."

"A police negotiator tries to initiate conversation, but your friend isn't listening. Instead, she shoots the man in the head and pitches him out into the street."

Tears were streaming down Eddie Palmer's face as Susan forced him toward the door at gunpoint. In a way, he'd seen this coming his way from the moment he looked up and saw the two women come into the vestibule.

Jill, like Eddie, had resigned herself to a dark fate to be met on this day, but she just couldn't abide the thought of her doom affecting any more people. She just couldn't stand it.

With Susan's attention focused on getting the man to the door, Jill struggled to her feet, fighting the pain from her splintered rib. Her cuffed hands clawed for purchase as she pulled herself up on top of the tellers' cage barrier. She struggled to her feet once more, reawakening dormant pain from the old injury to her leg. She ignored her leg's protest, and leapt from the counter, her body on fire with pain. She landed on Susan's back. Jill got her cuffed hands over Susan's head and around her throat. She rode that bitch like a bucking bronco. Susan angled the shotgun back and fired, trying to shoot Jill off her back, but the explosion only put a hole in the ceiling and deafened them both. Jill worked her cuffs into Susan's neck, throttling her and yanking her from side to side.

Eddie watched the show, a possible reprieve from the blast that had been promised for his head. Her air supply cut off, the bad woman was losing steam, winding down. She collapsed. The shotgun clattered across the tile floor. Jill remained on Susan's back, straddling her, and with the handcuffs still under Susan's throat, she yanked back viciously.

Some of the hostages were standing up now and looking over the barrier of the tellers' cage. One or two cheered Jill on. Eddie spotted the shotgun and inched toward it, thinking he just might escape Ashley's poisonous influence yet. Some of the hostages watched him.

One girl urged him on, "Get it! Pick it up!"

Susan was coughing, choking. Drawing on the last reserves of energy left inside her oxygen-starved body, she placed her hands against the floor and pushed herself up and onto her knees. Jill held on, using her cuffed hands as a garrote. Susan grabbed Jill's forearms and heaved forward, propelling Jill over her head and onto the floor. Jill landed on her back with a solid thud, in front of Susan.

Eddie picked up the shotgun. He had never touched a gun in his life, and really, he didn't even like violent movies. But he found the trigger easily enough. His finger just went there naturally. And he swung the Stevens in the direction of his captor. But Susan, her breathing harsh and ragged, was already on him. Her chest was against the twin bores of the weapon. He was not one for violence, but Eddie Palmer did something that neither his sister, his mother, nor his niece Ashley would have ever thought him capable. He squeezed the trigger. But the firing pin struck only an empty chamber. The Stevens double barrel had double triggers. The forward trigger, the one Eddie's finger just naturally found, had already discharged the right barrel. If there had been time, Eddie probably would have figured out that the rearward trigger would unleash holy hell from the left barrel. But Eddie wasn't a sportsman. And time was too short. Susan grabbed the Stevens by the muzzle and forestock and shoved the weapon into Eddie's chest. She held on, and Eddie went down on his ass, his visions of heroism dissipating.

All of this in a matter of seconds. Jill was already coming back for more. She was at Susan's back just as she was taking the Stevens away from Eddie. Susan knew Jill was there behind her, to take advantage of the skirmish. And as she shoved the shotgun forward to knock Eddie down, she yanked back viciously to keep the gun in her possession, and with that same backward pulling motion, she slammed the cut-off stock into Jill's face with a loud crack of the already-broken bone and cartilage in her nose. Jill collapsed. It was over for her. She had no fight left.

Susan swung the shotgun around and ordered the hostages in the tellers' cage back down on the floor. She took a minute to catch her breath, then dragged Jill, who was only barely conscious, over to a desk. She used her key to refasten Jill's cuffs around the desk leg. Susan grabbed the bothersome little bald man whose name she would never know and headed for the door. He was a weak man. Compliant. A little streak of bravery for a second there. Too bad for him he was too stupid to work the offset double triggers.

She unlocked the doors and threw them open. Outside was bright and she squinted against the setting sun. Officers had set up barriers to control the growing crowd and media presence, so Susan and Eddie had the sidewalk and street right outside the bank to themselves. Like a little stage.

She kept Eddie close in front of her. A human shield. She had studied hostage situations and police response. She didn't believe that enough time had elapsed for the authorities to have a plan in place. Certainly the FBI wouldn't be on scene yet. There was no shoot-on-sight authorization. All they knew at this point was that there had been a silent alarm at the bank, communication could not be established, and the doors were locked. They didn't know who had taken the bank or why. She assumed Denton had found the deposit slip and the fingernail. So they knew what was likely going on inside, they could guess, but didn't actually know. They had no proof. She was ready to show her hand.

Susan brought the sawed-off shotgun out from behind her back.

From the street, beyond the perimeter, she heard an officer yell, "Gun!"

But before that single syllable had escaped the deputy's mouth, Susan had pulled the rearward trigger on the Stevens, and Eddie Palmer's head vaporized.

She pitched the body in the street and ducked back in the bank before anybody could quite comprehend what had just happened.

Susan Weaver had played her hand.

Back inside the bank, Susan unlocked Jill from the desk

and rclocked the cuffs around her wrists. She yanked Jill to her feet.

"The lunatic returns. Only this time she pulls *you* up, holds *you* in front of her and presses the gun to *your* temple."

Susan tossed the shotgun aside. The Stevens had been for crowd control. And to show the police she meant business. It would be too unwieldy for the close-up work she had planned next. She drew a snub nose .38 from her side and put the revolver to Jill's head.

Jill closed her eyes, waiting for the bullet.

"You won't be seeing it on the news this time around, because this time, you are the news. You're a human shield for a subhuman animal. You're completely unaware that somewhere out there, out in the quiet and the dark, in a place you'll never see, a man waits. All he does is handle situations like this. In all this hell you've been through, only he can make it right."

Susan cocked the gun. Jill winced in anticipation.

"You think he's out there, Jill? I bet he is. Your guardian angel. And he can save you. With one shot. With one perfectly placed shot. Think he can do it now, with his precious pregnant wife in the way?"

"You're already dead, you just don't know it."

"I've been dead since I was six years old," she said and shoved Jill forward, toward the door, her fate.

CHAPTER 25

t's time.

Denton and Sesak were in place on the roof of an accounting office across the street from the bank.

Just moments before, upon their arrival, they had been on the street below. They were taking last-minute instruction from Cowell as the perimeter was being established. Jake had already told Cowell that Jill and Simon were gone when they'd gotten to the house. He felt bad about the lie, but Simon was beyond help, and Jill was still alive. Jacob would lie, cheat, and steal if he had to. To make sure he was on that roof. Because there was no way he'd be permitted on scene if Cowell knew Jill was a hostage—much less be allowed to take the shot.

Everybody was caught off guard when the female suspect emerged, holding on to a male hostage, shot the man in the head, and retreated back into the bank before anyone could even comprehend what had just happened. It was lightning fast.

And now, belly-down on the rooftop, Jacob thought back on

his father's words to him thirty-five years ago when he presented Jacob with his first rifle, the .22 Revelation. He could still hear his father's deep, even voice.

"It's time," was what his father had said to him.

Kathryn looked through the binoculars and keyed her mic.

"Team Two in position."

Only Jacob and Kathryn knew that Jill was one of the hostages. If and when it became known, Jacob was counting on it being too late for Cowell to do anything about it. Because Jacob would surely be barred from the scene. But he knew in his heart that he was here today to save Jill's life. He had trained his whole life to remove the human aspect of what he was doing. The shot would be his alone.

Bank robberies fell under federal jurisdiction, so there was the additional possibility that he and Sesak could be replaced or augmented by an FBI sharpshooting team. The feds usually didn't arrive to a bank robbery until well after the festivities were finished. But this was a takeover, a siege, with multiple hostages involved. They weren't here yet, but he knew the FBI would be mobilizing.

But he also felt in his heart that this was going to be over in a matter of minutes. He wasn't worried about the feds. He believed that Susan had killed that first hostage for a reason, because even when a suspect is holding a gun to someone's head, protocol requires some attempt at negotiation before the use of deadly force is authorized. But if the suspect has already killed, the green light is essentially automatic. She wanted this thing to move fast. She wanted, quite literally, to force Jacob's hand.

From the roof, he saw SWAT team members move into view. Two-man teams covered the door and crouched below the windows.

In a great circle around the entire scene, the media and public watched.

It's time.

There was a flash of light as the front door opened, reflecting the setting sun. A figure emerged. It was Jill and Susan, so close together they formed one silhouette. Jacob already had his rifle positioned on bipods, his body settled into position.

Through his scope he saw Jill and Susan. So cleanly magnified, it was as though he could touch them. Susan held a gun to Jill's head. Jill's face was so bruised and swollen that she was nearly unrecognizable.

The two women were impossibly close. There was no shot.

Susan kept Jill near to the exterior bank wall—ensuring that no shot could come from behind them. She knew what she was doing. A semicircle of hundreds of people watched.

Cowell yelled to Susan, "What do you want?"

"It's very simple. I want Deputy Jacob Denton to shoot me. Somebody is going to die today. Me or her. You've seen me kill already. You have no other choice."

Cowell said, "Suicide by cop? All of this because you want us to shoot you?"

"No, I want Denton to *try* to shoot me. With his precious pregnant wife in the way. Get it?"

Cowell got it. His mouth hung open as he realized the bloody bruised beaten hostage was Jill Denton. He hadn't recognized her at first, but there was no doubt in his mind now.

"I don't think he can do it. Not with his bitch in the way, carrying his baby. I'll bet he misses and kills her. Let him live with that the rest of his fucking life!"

For perhaps the first time in his career, Cowell did not know how to proceed. His sniper's wife was the hostage. This shit was not in the procedural handbook. There was no protocol for this. Jacob Denton was compromised, but he was the only person on scene qualified to save the hostage.

He needed time to think, but Susan wasn't going to give it to him.

She said, "I'm pulling the trigger in five seconds. No time for reflection. No time for backup."

Above, Jacob looked through the rifle scope.

He saw that the revolver to his wife's head was cocked. It was pushed so hard into her temple that Jill had to hold her head at an unnatural angle. Susan's knuckles were white with tension. He could see that the pressure of her finger on the trigger had moved the trigger inward, to the first stop. He had never seen a hostage in such imminent danger. The suspect appeared to be putting three and a half pounds of pressure on a four-pound trigger.

Over Kathryn's earbud, Jacob heard the tinny crackle of Cowell's voice.

And Kathryn's response, "Copy. Suspect at street level. Obstacle. Team Two ready and in position."

More from Cowell.

Then Kathryn, "Team Two copies."

Then directly to Jacob, "Hostage in imminent mortal danger. Green light."

Jacob took careful aim. Variables were going through his mind. So many variables went into a shot. So many. They were endless. He just wanted to melt into his scope, but the variables were torturing him.

Below, Susan held on to Jill like a rag doll. Jacob tried not to see his wife's injured face, the blood, the dark bruising, one eye swollen completely shut. He tried not to see that, not to feel it.

Susan's body and head were behind Jill's. There was, at most, only a hairline of an opportunity for a shot.

Jacob's finger tightened on the trigger.

The shot was plainly impossible.

Jacob's finger tightened even more on the trigger. So close. So close to release.

It's time.

CHAPTER 26

Everything was in play.

The same sets of variables shuffled through Jake's mind with every shot he ever took—whether it was range practice or an actual hostage situation. His mind worked the same. He never took into consideration the humanness of either the target or the obstacles. Why would he? How would that improve his accuracy? It wouldn't, and he knew that.

He remembered that he had told Sesak, "You have to learn to look past them. Make them obstacles, block them mentally, do whatever you need to do in your head to negate that familiarity. If you can't do that, bad things happen."

He'd said, "Doubt. Hesitation. Guilt. These things can destroy you. After the shot is taken. Doubt. Hesitation. Guilt. These things can destroy the hostage. Before the shot is taken."

And now, on this rooftop today, he went through his familiar list of variables, so that he could tick off each one as he always did and then jump down the rabbit hole. Melt into his scope and find the perfect peace of the reticle.

Today was different, though. Today he was plagued by doubt, hesitation, and guilt.

He knew that the one thing he needed to do, the most essential thing, was to forget Jill. To be there for her, to save her, he needed to pretend that she didn't exist. He had to dehumanize her. To make Jill an obstacle.

You have to do it, son. Killing's hard sometimes.

What was the perfect path between the rifle and the target? The clicks on his scope were like the clicks of tumbler pins in a combination lock. Which path, no matter how miniscule, bypassed the obstacle? What was the combination that unlocked that path?

From the street, he heard Susan's voice. Her voice carried well.

She yelled, "Five!"

He blocked it out and focused on the combination. He ticked off the combination that would open the perfect path.

He thought about the wind. Always. Always there was the wind. What he felt on his face here on this rooftop was a steady, gentle four miles per hour breeze from the north, but that could be completely different at street level where Jill was—*Jill, that was Jill down there.*

On the street, particularly given the topographical breaks of the city buildings, there could be gusts, so he looked down—*Jill, that was Jill down there*—for dust, papers, leaves on ornamental trees, anything he could see to gauge the wind.

From the street, he heard, "Four!"

Distance. It looked to be 105 yards. Long range estimation was one of the hardest assessments to make, second only to judging the wind. The only concern was where the projectile would strike in the vertical plane. From 35 yards up to 110 yards, the amount of bullet drop was of no consequence. After 110 yards bullet drop became an important factor as the projectile slowed and you had to compensate. This was right at the tipping point. Maybe one click up? Maybe the New Guard of snipers had it right. Just push some buttons, then pull the trigger. No expertise. No dope book. No variables. Maybe Sesak had fresh batteries in her wazoo gadget. Then he would know for—

"Three!"

And there was the sun. It was going down—*Jill, that was Jill down there*—and he had to factor in the reflective surface of the glass of the bank windows around them. The glare could alter his vision—*was Jill really pregnant? Why didn't she tell him?*

Collateral. None in the foreground, the deputies had it cleared. But what was behind the glass windows? Collateral? No. Jake knew that with the suspect outside, SWAT team members would have already breached the rear of the bank, secured the inside, and escorted all the bank people out the back doors. Clearing the shot for the sniper. He'd heard no gunfire, no skirmish, so he assumed Susan was acting alone and the evacuation had been swift and efficient. No collateral concern.

Temperature. Metal expands as temperature—

"Two!"

Radiant heat waves coming from the tar roof could impact

his depth perception. Too many variables. A shot was impossible. But, goddamnit, that was Jill down there, and that crazy cunt had the gun pressed right up to her head. Punishing her with it. And that was Jill. And the margin, the path, the combination was measured in millimeters. There was no room for error. There was no peace in this reticle.

He could not trust himself. He couldn't take Jill out of the equation. He could not dehumanize her.

"One!"

But time was up. A shot had to be taken. Jill would die if he didn't take the shot he knew he could not take. He could not trust himself to make it.

You have to do it, son. Killing's hard sometimes.

"Zero!"

Jake stood up, revealing himself. "Susan!" he yelled. "Susan, I'm here!"

And he waved his arms in perfect silhouette to the lowering sun. A sniper giving away his location. The ultimate sin. Then he ducked down. Observers on the street could see his dark figure running away from the roof's edge.

As Jacob made it to the rooftop exit door, he paused just long enough to look back and make eye contact with his spotter. His trainee. He spoke two words to her. And then he was gone.

CHAPTER 27

The crowd grew quiet. Radio chatter stopped.

Jacob emerged from the crowd and onto the stage Susan had set. The arena.

He stood in front of Susan, hands open at his sides. No guns. No vest. He'd removed all of his tactical gear.

"No," Susan said. "Go hide like a coward. You shoot people from your hiding place."

"I'm here. In front of you."

"Then you better pull your sidearm and try to take a shot."

"I'm unarmed."

"I have nothing to lose. I will put a bullet in her head. You saw the pregnancy test, right?"

Jacob looked to Jill for confirmation. She was sweaty, in shock, her hair hanging in dirty clumps. Her face was bloody, one eye swollen shut and seeping dark fluid. He couldn't tell if it was true or not. It didn't matter. Not in this moment.

"You know what you're gambling here. I'm giving you a

chance. If you make me pull the trigger myself, then I guarantee you she will die. But if you take the shot, then she has a chance."

There was no way out of this. She was going to make him take the shot. He had no choice. Stand here and watch his wife and unborn child slaughtered, or retreat and fire the bullet himself. She was right. It was a chance. His mind was in turmoil, trying to come up with something. A solution. He *should* retreat. His natural position was belly-down on a rooftop. He wasn't a negotiator. His only concern was how to deliver the bullet. What could he say to this woman who held his world in her hands? Little mousy Susan Weaver. He had never suspected. She had seemed scared of him. Intimidated. Jill had called her a possum. And Oz had called her by her real name. Rose. *A rose is a rose is a rose*. The little girl found outside the bank. Rose Kaufman. He remembered Jill talking about Susan's novel. About a little girl whose father robs banks. Rose.

Jacob said, "You don't have to do this, Rose."

"No. No. Don't try to fuck with my head. I'm ready to pull the trigger."

"I'm sorry for your loss. I truly am. If I could go back in time—" But he stopped there. He wouldn't lie to her. If he could go back in time, he'd take the shot again. "I don't know. He had a gun. People's lives were at risk."

"He was desperate. He was just trying to take care of his family."

"I understand that now. But then, all I knew was that he was a man with a gun, holding people hostage. I had no choice."

"You had a choice today. And now you're trying to trick me.

I'm pulling the trigger. You could have saved her. I gave you the chance."

And he remembered seeing Jill reading Susan's book, engrossed in it, and he had asked her, *Is it good?* And she nodded and said, *Yes, except for one thing.*

"Your father was just a thug."

Jacob saw Susan's knuckles grow even whiter as she squeezed the revolver harder. The muzzle so cruelly forced to Jill's temple. Susan's finger applying even more pressure, the cocked hammer now mere ounces away from tripping and sending the firing pin to strike the primer.

"You're the thug," she said. "The murderer. He could have been talked down. You know that in your heart."

"He shot a woman in the back. Your father was trash. Human trash."

And he saw that he'd pushed it too far. He'd pushed her over the edge. And he was going to get what he had wanted all along. He was going to get the bullet. He was going to look down the bore of her weapon, maybe for just a millisecond, but he knew that in that wisp of time he would see down into it, and he would see snow and blood. He would see the dark path from which he'd emerged.

"You win," Rose said, and in one fluid movement, she shifted and brought the gun forward.

Jake got what he wanted.

He heard the sharp crack, the controlled explosion. Hell unleashed.

Jake's world went dark for a moment. He was in the middle-ground. Perfect peace. Jill's cry brought him back to the light.

He could see again. And what he saw was that the top right quadrant of Rose's head was gone. And as her body pitched forward, Jacob saw what was left of her brain, glistening wetly in her cranial cavity.

There was the soft sound of her body thudding against the concrete, then absolute quiet. No sound. Like a Montana field covered in snow. Just waiting to be broken.

Then there was a warm crackle of radio static as Kathryn keyed her mic from the rooftop above. Her voice, professional and assured, transmitted across the tuned-in radios of media observers, scanner junkies, and law enforcement personnel. It echoed through the streets.

"Target down."

The eerie quiet remained. It was shock. Jacob had seen it before. When the lightning came down from the sky like retribution from a vengeful god, it cowed the people into silence.

Then, clear as day, he heard Cowell speak. A tone of resigned awe in his voice, the lieutenant said, "Fuckin' Sesak."

Jacob's legs went weak on him. He thought he heard the crowd cheer. It was loud. The spell had been broken. The god had been named. They were happy. Relieved. Safe. The god was a just god.

Jacob and Jill crawled to each other. It was just a few feet, but it felt like miles. But they made it. And they held each other.

The only thing Jill could manage to say through her swollen face was, "Are we clear?"

Jake nodded and held her tight.

"Crystal."

CHAPTER 28

Tombstones stretched as far as the horizon, with a ribbon of pavement threading its way throughout. Amongst the granite markers, a long shadow touched and passed over the buried dead.

Jacob thought of what had gotten him here today. His life choices. The path that he had forged. The path that wound like the pavement through the graveyard. Here amongst the dead, he was thankful that the one closest to him was still alive. Jill's injuries were healing. The bruising around her eyes from the broken nose had been spectacular. Like a sunset after an atomic bomb. But now it was little more than orange-brown smudges.

She'd been hospitalized for a few days. To set her cracked ribs, observe her after the blows to the head, tape up her nose. Mainly for observation after the shock. The posttraumatic stress. For the pregnancy.

Jake had sat with Jill in the hospital each day. Kathryn came by a couple of times. She brought flowers. After some awkward small talk, the three of them just sat in an easy silence.

Once he was back out on patrol, and there was time to talk, Kathryn wanted to know why Jacob hadn't taken the shot himself. He was clearly a better shot. He had more experience. A dope book as thick as a Sunday newspaper. He knew the variables in play. Knew them cold. Was it because he couldn't completely block his emotions?

And he looked at her for a long time, as though mulling over just how much of the truth he should share with her, and he'd said, "Well, Sesak, it's like this. I had them both in my sights plain as day. And you're right, I had those variables down cold, and the environmental conditions were ideal. But I couldn't find the perfect peace of the reticle. I couldn't let myself disappear into the scope. And do you know why?"

She shook her head.

"Because it occurred to me, I hadn't paid the last installment on Jill's life insurance."

She smiled. *Fuckin'Denton.*

"Did you want to die? Was that your plan? Because, you know, you should be dead. The idea that Rose Kaufman missed the killshot while that close is preposterous."

"She didn't miss. She never got the chance. Thanks to you."

Kathryn nodded.

"And it's not preposterous. She'd been holding the gun against Jill's head for a good while. Pushing it hard, holding it tight. White knuckled. I saw that through the scope. It's hard for anybody to hold their hand in one position for too long, and when you add in the extreme tension and force she was exerting, I knew muscle fatigue had set in. As snipers, we train for it. We have exercises to relieve and prevent it. I knew the muscle fatigue would cause her round to go low. That's if she got off a shot at all. And I didn't figure you'd let her get one off. And I positioned myself so that there were no bystanders around me."

"In case she did get off a shot."

"Yeah. So I knew what was in play. I took a chance. I just had to get the bore of that gun off Jill's head. I knew you could make the shot."

"But how?"

"I trained you. You passed."

Kathryn nodded, thinking about Phase One, Phase Two, the alcohol test. All of it.

"And now I'll have a true partner. I can be with my family more. Just like I said to you. It's time."

Jacob's shadow continued on through the cemetery. There was a second shadow as well. Jill. The cracked ribs and deep tissue bruising still pained her if she moved too fast. But she was okay. She was alive. Her husband was alive. And a new life continued to grow inside her.

The two shadows stopped and fell over a tombstone. Newly engraved. Jacob squeezed Jill's hand. In her other hand she held several roses. Jill walked to the stone and placed half of the roses on top. She saved the rest of them, then stepped back to Jacob.

"I'm going to put these on Captain Bryant's grave."

Jill moved away, leaving Jacob alone with his old partner, with Oz.

Jacob approached the cold stone. He read the inscription.

LEE STALEY

1959–2015

THERE ARE MEN TOO GENTLE

TO LIVE AMONG WOLVES

Jacob reached into his pocket and retrieved the small cloth bag. He opened it and looked at the spent cartridge shells inside. Still just seventeen. He pulled the drawstring closed and kneaded the bag in his hand. And he thought of the last words he'd spoken to his friend.

It's time to put the past away.

It's time.

Jacob kneeled and placed the bag on Oz's grave.

ACKNOWLEDGMENTS

We would like to thank our extended families for their support, as well as Robert Guinsler, Stephen Torres, Ellen Schlossberg, Peter Farris, Becky Hann Kraegel, Robert Leland Taylor, Rita Kempley, and Charlie Bennett. We are indebted to our editor, Peter Joseph, for his inspired guidance. And a special thanks to Linda Andrews and the staff of the Hoover Public Library.